DON'T SWEAT THE SMALL STUFF

DON'T SWEAT THE SMALL STUFF

A NOVEL

DON BRUNS

Oceanview Publishing

LONGBOAT KEY, FLORIDA

ISBN-13: 978-1-60809-047-1

Published in the United States by Oceanview Publishing,
Longboat Key, Florida
www.oceanviewpub.com

2 4 6 8 10 9 7 5 3 1

PRINTED IN THE UNITED STATES OF AMERICA

To Tom and Dick Smothers. Your rapport, your sense of timing, your comedy, your entire story inspired me to create Skip and James. Thank you for all the enjoyment you've given millions of people over the years.

ACKNOWLEDGMENTS

Thank you to Linda Reilly, who gave us the genre "Dude Done It." She plays an interesting character in the book. And thanks to Angie Clark, Dr. Ken Clemens, Virginia Crouse, and Judy Schiller who lent their names to characters in this novel. The charities you donated to appreciate your effort. Please let it be known that I hijacked your identities and you are much nicer people than you appear in the book. Most of you. Margie Bush, thank you for finding the petting zoo in Indiana. Thanks to Maryglenn for the wonderful work on publicity, to Bob and Pat Gussin, my publishers, to Rachel, Susan, John, and Mary A. for all the hard work. To George for the wonderful covers, to Don Witter, Jay Waggoner, Bill Lodermeier, Mike Trump, and the entire crew from Ohio. To David and Marsha in Sarasota for their generosity; to my wife, Linda, who edits all my novels; and to Jody Stacy who introduces all the new spy gadgets. Thanks to Rich Theodore for his medical advice.

Don Bruns
Sarasota, Florida

DON'T SWEAT THE SMALL STUFF

CHAPTER ONE

I found the article again, the one about the dead body on the carnival ride, and I wished I'd mentioned it to James the first time I saw it. The story was online, on an archived page of the *Miami Herald*. It was one of those stories that tells you something happened, then leaves you up in the air. You never hear the end of the story. We've all seen those. For weeks you search the paper, the Web, and there's never an ending. Never a final summation that tells how it all came out. Well, I found the story after the fact, and in this case, I know exactly "what happened." I was there for the ending. So was James. And Em, Angie, Pugh, and a cast of characters too lengthy to mention here. We now know what happened, how it happened, and why. The story was written by Jonathan King.

RIDER DIES FROM AMUSEMENT RIDE INJURY.

Correspondent Jonathan King

A thirty-two-year-old woman was killed yesterday when her safety bar malfunctioned on a ride at a North Miami shopping center. The ride, operated by Moe Show Inc. had been inspected by local authorities upon installation Wednesday.

The Cat's Pajamas carnival ride spins at a high rate of speed, investigators said, and Ellen Bernstein of Palm Grove was thrown from her seat. Her body was found in the mechanism below the ride.

I cringed when I read that passage. Her body was found in the mechanism below the ride. I tried not to think about the gears probably chewing her up. I've seen some dead bodies, but that would be just too gruesome.

Spokesperson for the Palm Grove Plaza said that Moe Show Inc. was entirely responsible for the rides and safety of all riders.

Owner Moe Bradley stated that all rides were inspected on a regular basis and they were looking into the matter.

No other details are available at this time.

I'd seen the article, eight months ago, but hadn't paid much attention to it. Later, I remembered it, but didn't really think it could impact anything going on in my life. If I'd mentioned it to James, and if I'd said no to James, I could have saved my friend James and me a lot of trouble. But then again, trouble seems to find us no matter what.

CHAPTER TWO

The tartan skirt hit her mid-thigh, and I admired the tanned legs. She sat at the counter, staring straight ahead, a brown mug in front of her. We stood in the doorway surveying the small coffee shop, the counter, and ten tables.

James tapped me on the shoulder. "Got to be her, amigo."

I nodded. I couldn't take my eyes off the girl. A tall blonde with shoulder-length hair and a marvelous figure.

"Built like a brick shithouse, Skip."

Leave it to James to bring it down a notch.

"Was that the description?"

He rolled his eyes. "*Attractive young lady drinking coffee.*" His eyes drifted back to the blonde-haired beauty. "Hey, man, I don't see another single female in this room, do you?"

Two older gentlemen sat at the table directly inside the door, a chessboard on their table. I couldn't tell if they were playing chess or just staring at the board. It didn't seem to matter to either of them.

"I mean, there's two good-looking women over there," he pointed to a sofa in the corner, "and two couples in the back

3

there, but my contact is supposed to be by herself. I only see one lady sitting by herself. The lovely lady at the counter. Tell me I'm wrong, amigo."

"I don't like it, James. What if it's not her?" It wasn't unusual for James to make an honest mistake. It wasn't unusual for James to make a dishonest mistake. You could never tell with James.

"Come on pard, it's got to be her. So what do I have to lose? I've just got to figure out a unique approach." He stared at her, then turned to me. "I could say, 'You're the most ravishing creature that I've ever seen in my life.'"

I thought for a moment. Then it came to me. "But you'd be plagiarizing Jeff Goldblum in *Life Aquatic*." James knew thousands of movie quotes. But then, I usually figured them out so I guess both of us were full of useless trivial crap.

"Can't pull anything over on you, Skip."

I wasn't exactly proud of that.

James turned and walked to the counter, keeping his eyes on the attractive young lady. I stayed where I was, not knowing what to expect. He stepped up to the condiments basket and I watched him pull out a white sugar packet, look at it, then look down at the girl. She hand-brushed her hair back from her face and sipped coffee from her brown mug, never looking to her right or left. A consummate pro.

James walked back to the doorway. Smiling at me, he waved the sugar packet. "Got a pen, pardner?"

"What are you going to do?"

He shrugged his shoulders. "I've got an idea."

I don't think he had a clue what was going to work.

I fished in my shirt pocket. As a salesman, on the rare occasions I actually convinced a prospect to sign a contract for their home security system, my company required me to carry a pen.

This one had about twenty seconds on it. I'd actually signed one contract with this pen.

James took the cheap plastic ballpoint pen, studied the tiny white packet, and started crossing out printed words. He held the sugar packet in his hand, letting me watch the process. When he was finished he put *my* pen in *his* pocket and handed me the little sack of sugar.

"James?"

"Read it."

He'd crossed out almost everything on the packet. The name of the company, the copyright and patent information, the nutritional content, the slogan 'Make Life A Little Sweeter' and whatever else had been on the printed package. Two words remained. *Sweet. Sugar.*

I frowned, not having a clue where he was going.

"Hey, I've got to impress her. I've got a lot riding on this."

"And how is this going to impress her?"

"Watch and learn, grasshopper."

James shifted his shoulders, gave a tug to his khaki cargo shorts, pulled down his Banana Republic T-shirt, and strode to the counter. The well-dressed gentleman always gets the lady. But the girl never glanced his way.

I walked closer, not getting dangerously close, but close enough to watch the master at work. I was ready for his defeat and humiliation. After all, this was my best friend, and I wanted to be there for him when he succeeded and when he failed. And this time he was particularly vulnerable.

"Excuse me, miss?"

She deliberately took another sip of her drink, finally glancing at him with some disdain. It was obvious she'd been through this before. I could see the contempt that she had for him.

"You must have dropped your name tag. It has to be yours."

James handed her the packet. She refused it, looking at him with cold eyes cutting into his soul.

"This name tag, ma'am. It has to be yours. The name fits you perfectly. Am I right?"

Again he offered the small packet.

Finally she took it from his fingers. I could see the skepticism on her face, a frown and a curl on her upper lip. She glanced at the sugar packet. Looking up at him, she blinked. Then I could see her mouth the words. *Sweet Sugar.*

I had to give James credit. He stood his ground, smiling and watching her reaction.

The girl looked back at him, a smile turning up the corners of her mouth. Her eyes were bright, and I could see her pearly whites sparkling.

"You—" she took a deep breath. "You are good." She looked back at the packet, and I could see the twinkle in her eyes. "Oh, you're good." Then she laughed out loud. "Where did you get this idea to . . ." pausing, at for loss for words.

"You're Agent Hot Pants?"

"I am." I swear she blushed.

"Simply reporting as ordered ma'am."

"Yes you are. I swear—listen, I'm not supposed to say this, but you are the best one yet."

James turned and winked at me. I decided my consoling services were not required at this point.

"I don't want to blow this," my best friend said, "but would it be out of line for me to call you sometime?"

The drop-dead gorgeous female smiled even wider. "Out of line? Yes. Way out of line. In fact, that question should get you disqualified. You know that, right? You could be ruining your chance to get this job."

James didn't flinch.

"I think it might be worth it."

A coy look on her face. "Oh, do you?"

"I do."

"I'm serious. You understand this could cost you the job?"

My roommate nodded, his confidence never waning.

The smile remained on her face. "But," she hesitated, looking right into James's eyes, "if you'll give me your pen, I'll write down my number. That's what you want, right?"

He nodded.

"On the sugar packet." I saw her jot down the number.

That was the last I ever saw of my pen.

CHAPTER THREE

"I got the job, pard." He was sprawled out on our worn cloth couch, drinking one of my Yuengling beers. "She gave me the highest rating of anyone in the group."

"Heck of a way to interview for a job, James." I closed the door and threw the mail on the kitchen counter.

"Hey, they wanted creative, they got creative. I just try to give 'em what they want."

An *Ellen* rerun was on the tube and she was bopping up the steps to her audience. He was watching it without really paying attention.

"Got a date with her tonight. I'm not supposed to say anything. She's afraid they'd have grounds to fire her."

"And you might not even get a chance to start your new job." I walked ten steps to our refrigerator and grabbed the last beer.

Nodding, James sipped his beer. "Need the job, Skip. Got to buy us a new truck."

The last one had been blown up when I tossed a bomb meant for us into a parking lot. I'd saved both of our lives, but his beat-up, run-down box truck had been parked in that very same parking lot. It's a long story, but James's old box truck was history, and he was determined to replace it with another truck. Not a new truck. There was no way he could afford new, but a used truck that we could put a couple thousand miles on. James had decided that we would make our fortune in the spy business—private detectives—and part of the business had us driving the box truck around Miami soliciting private eye work, disguising the truck as a plumber's vehicle, a carpenter's transportation, a pool maintenance truck, or whatever struck his fancy.

Prying off the bottle top, I took a long pull. It had been a tough day, and I'd made four calls, none of them amounting to anything. You spend two hours in someone's home, explaining all of the details and benefits of your home security system, and at the end of the pitch, just as *you're* asking for the order, *they* ask for their free gift and open the door for you, suggesting that you leave. So I gave them the cheap wine glasses and left. I hoped the glasses broke the first time they washed them. There were days when the job just wasn't worth it. There were weeks—months—when it wasn't worth it.

"So I start next week."

"And you're still going to work at Cap'n Crab?" James was a line cook for the fast food restaurant in Carol City, and I didn't think they could exist without him.

"I am. For a while. Either this new job, or our P.I. firm will kick in soon, Skip, and I'll say adios to C.C."

I secretly wished him the best, but I was afraid it wasn't going to happen any time soon.

"Speaking of the P.I. business, what's in the mail?"

We'd filled out the forms: citizenship, education and all of that. Then, we'd lied. Well, Jody, our private eye connection in Delray Beach, Florida, lied for us. He had gone on record saying that we'd worked for two years as his apprentices. So we supposedly knew all the rules. Right. I'm not certain that Jody knew all the rules. We'd never worked for Jody in our lives, but we had purchased some surveillance stuff from him. It didn't matter. According to the rules regarding a P.I. license, we should have qualified. But so far, no confirmation.

I picked up the flyers, past-due notices, and bills, and sorted through them. "They're going to shut off the cable in a week if we don't pay."

"Yeah, yeah." James watched the TV and took another swallow of my beer.

"And what's this? I thought you paid the electric bill last month."

"I thought I did too. You gave me half?"

"I did." I gave him a stern look. "You know I did."

"Oh, we decided to use that to buy—"

"No, *you* decided to use that to buy an alternator for the truck." The truck that we no longer had. The truck that had been destroyed in the fire. In the explosion. "Why didn't you return it?"

"Got it on eBay, amigo. Saved some serious money. And you can't return eBay stuff. Can you?"

"You never told me *we* saved some money." I seemed to remember my share being full price.

"Oh. Well, it makes no diff. We're gonna be rollin' in the money soon, Skip. Trust me."

I didn't. I tossed the bartender school application to him, along with the going-out-of-business flyer from the adult novelty shop on Third Street. Ready Teddy's was closing. Even the adult entertainment business was having hard times. Where would you get your next vibrator, your blow-up doll, sex swing, or glide gel?

"Nothing again, right?"

And there it was. The letter we'd been waiting for. As crazy as the idea was, I got a jolt when I saw the return address: Florida Department of Agriculture. Don't ask why the Department of Agriculture. This is Florida. They just do things a little differently here. The D.O.A. is the one that licenses private investigators. So I was excited. But then, maybe it was a rejection. The way our lives were going, it had to be a rejection. Had to be.

Ignoring James, I tore open the envelope.

Dear Mr. Moore and Mr. Leser. The spelling of James's name had been massacred. It is our privilege to tell you that your application for a P.I. license for More or Less Investigations has been approved.

We had no business being approved. I knew it, but I'm not sure my roommate had a clue. "We're in business, James."

"No."

"Yes."

"Skip. We're official. Damn. Buddy, pal, you and me—the state of Florida recognizes us as crime fighters." He jumped off the couch, drained the bottle of beer, and took five giant steps to the refrigerator. Our apartment is very, very small. You can pretty much go anywhere in just a few steps.

I watched him, smiling, knowing what was coming next.

"Where the hell is the rest of the beer?"

"Well, it was your turn to buy." Two times ago.

"We need to celebrate." He grabbed my car keys from the counter. "Come on, Skip, let's go get a drink. We're P.I.s, right?"

I had to admit it. We were.

CHAPTER FOUR

I listened to James go on and on about his date with Agent Hot Pants, then dropped him off at this ten-story modern Miami office building on Biscayne Boulevard the next morning, ten a.m. sharp. He wanted to make a good first impression with the new boss. It was probably the last time he'd be on time. I drove back into Carol City and halfheartedly called on three leads. All of them lived in small rundown cement-block houses.

I knew they didn't need security systems. I'm sure they knew they didn't need security systems. Two of them weren't even home. They were the losers. No cheap wine glasses for them.

James was done at one p.m. Three hours for orientation, and I picked him up right outside the building.

"Gonna be a snap, Skip."

Everything with James was a snap. Seriously, things came easily to him. "Explain exactly what it is you're doing."

"Okay. This guy who set up the Agent Hot Pants interview. His name is Moe Bradley. Moe Bradley and his two sisters own four traveling carnivals. You know them. The kind that play county fairs, mall openings, that kind of stuff."

I nodded my head. The name Moe Bradley rang a bell, but I couldn't place it. "And what do you know about carnivals?"

"Stay with me, brother. Moe and the two ladies own these four carnivals, and they need someone to market them."

"Market them?" I hated carnivals. And I hated carnies. Carnies are the guys who run the rides, the ones who hand you the baseball and dare you to knock over the milk bottles. Carnies sell you the waffle cones that are fried in ten-day-old grease, and they're the ones who leave you hanging at the top of the Ferris wheel while they take a smoke break. That's what a carnie is. I suppose some of them were all right, but my father had always warned me about these traveling bums. They were gypsies who would just as soon shoot you as look at you. They'd steal a woman's purse and her baby and never think anything of it. That's what my alcoholic father said.

On second thought, maybe he didn't know so much.

"Let's say that one of the carnivals is playing in Jacksonville. I get on the Web and find a chain of grocery stores up there. Then I call those stores and offer them free kids' tickets for the rides on Tuesday. They're the good guys, giving away free tickets for all the kiddies."

"Okay." I pulled the ugly yellow Ford Taurus away from the curb and headed back toward the highway. "You give away free tickets. How does that make anyone any money?"

"Amigo," I could hear the change in his voice, "you're not going to do a drive-by at Em's place? This is more serious than I thought." Looking at me with squinted eyes, he motioned back over his shoulder toward Bayshore, where Emily's condo looked out over the water at South Beach.

I shook my head. "No."

Emily often played "She loves me, she loves me not." I'd saved her life and she pledged undying love. Then she had second thoughts. This time she was going through one of those phases where she thought I was too immature and she had to reevaluate our relationship. The trouble was, she was quite right. I was too immature. I was still hanging out with James, and that proved it. Anyway, it was better not to see her until she worked it out. So far, I always came out on top. I was praying.

James rolled his eyes and shook his head. "Your problem, amigo."

And it was. My problem.

"So anyway, they give away the kids' tickets, and we get a huge crowd of *paying* parents on Tuesday. You see? Kids get free admission, but the parents have to pay for all the extras. Cotton candy, slurpies, those big doughy elephant ears—you know. So we have a great Tuesday."

Keeping my eyes on the road, I nodded. "Paying parents. That doesn't sound like rocket science."

"Moe wants me to…"

"Moe? Already it's Moe?" What was it about that name? Something in the news recently?

"Down to earth guy, Skip. But very classy. I want to be him someday. Says 'call me Moe.' So I did. I do. Moe wants me to find new ways to promote the carnivals. I've got a list of all the rides, all the promotions they've done in the past, and I've just got to study them and find new ways for the man to get revenue."

Actually, it sounded right up James's alley. He was very creative and the little shtick with Agent Hot Pants proved it.

"Angie Clark, Skip. She is so hot. She's part of the carnival so I'll get a chance to see her on a regular basis."

"You've had one date. One."

"She wants to know all about me, man. Very interested. Very involved."

"So you'll see this Angie on a regular basis. And what's a regular basis?"

"Three days a week. And I get paid a percentage of any increase in revenue. Pretty cool, uh?"

"This guy Moe. He's going to show you the books?"

James studied me for a moment. "You think he'll try to cheat me?"

"He's a carnie, James."

He was quiet, thinking it through. "Nah. His two sisters. They wouldn't let it happen. I mean these ladies are all business. Tough. Shrewd. I met them up in the office, Judy Schiller and Virginia Crouse."

"Schiller and Crouse?"

"Yeah. You nailed 'em already. I got the impression there's no first names with these two. *Mrs.* Schiller and *Mrs.* Crouse. They're dead serious."

"Sounds like a legal firm. Schiller and Crouse."

"Or a comedy team. But there's nothing funny about them. I don't think they'd let Moe cheat anybody, but you never know. I'll deal with that later."

"So your job is just to sit in the office and think? Come up with ideas?" What kind of a job was that?

Out of the corner of my eye I could see his sly smile.

"James?"

"There's a little breaking-in time that I wanted to talk to you about. I think you're going to like it."

I knew I shouldn't listen. But he is my best friend, so I waded in. "Breaking-in? What kind of breaking-in?"

"Well, it involves getting to know a little more about the operation. You see, there's a Moe Show just about three miles from our apartment, and—"

"A what?" I took my eyes off the road for a minute, giving him a look of surprise. Then it hit me. Moe Show. The carnival had a string of accidents in just the past year, where rides jumped the tracks, and in two or three instances riders were thrown from their seats. And I was pretty sure there had been at least one death. At least one. I'd read about it or seen it on TV. A dangerous carnival to say the least.

"A Moe Show. Moe's carnival."

"Oh." I wasn't sure James remembered or even knew about the accidents. The death. Maybe if I'd said something then, but I didn't.

"We've been invited."

"To what?"

"To the carnival. It's in this lot beside a mall, and—"

"Why?"

"They want me to see it firsthand. Experience the rides, the concessions, and . . ." he hesitated. Whenever James hesitates, there's trouble.

"What, James?"

"They want me—us—to spend three nights in a trailer. You know, mingle with the rest of the guys, so I get the feel of what's going on."

"Oh, jeez." I almost stopped the car and threw him out. Sometimes I don't think James has a brain in his head. "You're going to camp out at a carnival? Do you think Angie Clark started that way? Do you think Agent Hot Pants had to spend three nights in a trailer to get her job?"

"Listen, Skip, I was hoping that you'd—"

"I'll bet she didn't."

"All I'm asking is—"

"No."

"It would mean a lot, man, and—"

"No." Apparently he'd forgotten about our last "camp-out" at Reverend Preston Cashdollar's revival meeting. Well, I hadn't forgotten. "Come on, James. You do remember that we camped out in the truck when we had the fast-food concession at

Reverend Cashdollar's revival tent meeting. You do remember that, don't you? Almost got us killed." That had been a surreal experience. "I'm not doing that again."

"Compadre—"

"Tell me that Schiller and Crouse are staying for the weekend. Tell me that Angie—Agent Hot Pants is going to stay for the weekend."

"I don't know if she—"

"Who is she, James? A carnie? Like the rest of them, a high school dropout? Someone who shills for suckers like you?"

"When did I ever shill for suckers?"

"That sounds like what you're doing to me."

"Dude—"

"Come on, James. This is a carnival. A bunch of misfits who can't do anything else. Run a ride, run a game, run a scam."

James took a deep breath. "Skip, I'm trying to earn money for a new truck." He closed his eyes and rubbed them with his thumbs. "A new truck to replace the truck that exploded when *you* threw that bomb into the parking lot."

"Don't you even start with that crap. I saved your life, James. If that bomb had gone off inside, we wouldn't even need a—" It hadn't been a pleasant evening.

"Skip. I *need* a truck. I need you to—"

"No."

James was quiet. I coasted through a yellow light, checking the rearview mirror for cops. The ancient Ford Taurus had a busted taillight and a back window that was cracked so bad I couldn't see through it. I'd already had two warnings to get the thing fixed or junk it. I glanced down at the dashboard and the oil light was flashing. Damn. I needed a new car—just to keep my job.

"Skip. I really need that truck. *We* need it for the P.I. business. And with our P.I. license, we're gonna make a boatload of money, amigo. A boatload. Listen, all we've got to do is run a couple of rides, maybe work in a concession stand and just get a feel for the whole thing. I need you pal, because—"

"James. You mean we actually have to operate the rides? We'd be carnies? How could you even think of asking me?" I was thinking about the liability too. Hopefully, the Moe Show had addressed the problem with their rides. I didn't want any deaths on my watch or James's watch.

"Compadre, it's important. I'm asking."

"What part does your girlfriend play in this scenario?" For some reason it was important to me.

"I don't know."

"James, you went out with her. She got you hired. Who is she?"

"She works for Moe. She's really into me. That's all I know. Come on, pard."

"I want to know who she is. I need to know the players."

"She does odd jobs, fills in where she's needed. I don't know. I think she keeps his books. This is a small business. Everybody wears a lot of hats, okay? But help me out here. Spend the weekend."

"What about the sisters? How do they figure in?"

"I told you. Schiller and Crouse, they're straight shooters."

"After one meeting, one date, you've got the entire operation figured out, is that right?"

"Dude, I'm pretty good at seeing the big picture."

He was so *not* good at seeing anything.

I took a deep breath. The truth was, I had no plans. My girlfriend, Emily, had taken a break, I didn't work Saturday and Sunday, and James tended to be my weekend entertainment. What was left?

"Okay. I'll go. But I won't like it. I swear to you, James, I will not like it."

And I didn't.

CHAPTER FIVE

To be fair it was an Airstream. Something with a little quality. Maybe ten years old and run-down, but an Airstream trailer nevertheless, a silver-blob-shaped trailer that generations of campers had grown to love, and it had a small (very small) kitchen, one bed, and a couch. James suggested since I was just along for the ride, I sleep on the couch. I suggested otherwise.

"That's my car outside, James. I drove the two of us here. I'm here because? What? I work for this fleabag carnival? No. I don't think so." I threw my hands up. "I'm here because I love the smell of sweat and popcorn?" Actually, the aroma from the carnival, the cotton candy, popcorn, and fried meat was not unpleasant. The food vendors had parked their trailers, and even though the rides had yet to be assembled, the food operators were preparing their cuisine for the carnies and the early visitors who like to watch a carnival set up. But I couldn't tell James that. "No. I'm here because I'm a friend. Actually, I'm the best friend you've got. Don't mess with me, James. I'm taking the bed. Got it?"

"Pard, it's my gig."

"Then you work it, *pard*, and I'll go back to my apartment and my own bed."

There was no more argument.

The Bayview Mall wasn't really a mall and had no bay. There was no view of the bay. I'm not sure that there was a bay anywhere nearby. The strip of stores consisted of typical Carol City low-end bargain-basement operations. Jenny's Slightly Used Furniture, The Bauble Brigade, a novelty jewelry store, and one of the more popular stores in Carol City, The Money Man, where you could cash your check or get an early tax refund for only 25 percent interest. James had used them once.

And then there was Harry's Hideaway, a cheap, sleazy bar with the door wide open, and a handful of local patrons drinking shots and beer at the bar. According to the sign, starting at six a.m. Baby Bonanza was a former clothing store for infants that was now for rent, and Fabulous Fabric appeared to be a store that sold cloth from bolts. I had a good feeling Fabulous Fabric would be the next retailer to go under. I'm not sure people in Carol City can afford a sewing machine.

James and I walked up the cracked, crumbling concrete sidewalk that fronted the shabby store facades. Flaking stucco in faded pink, blue, yellow, and green smears covered their walls, and as we peered through the dust-streaked windows, the insides appeared almost desolate and empty.

"The carnival will bring in the people."

"But who would shop in these stores, James? What are these people thinking?"

"I don't know, amigo. Pretty nasty place, I'll admit."

At the end of the strip was the 8/12, a carryout that supposedly carried their store hours in the name of the operation. It was ten a.m. and the paper sign in the window said "back in twenty minutes."

"Can't even get a Coke at the convenience store. We're going to be here how long?"

James took a deep breath. "Friday—today. Saturday—tomorrow. Sunday. We tear down on Monday morning and—"

"We what?"

"Tear down."

"*We* what?"

"Tear down." He looked at me like he thought I'd gone deaf. I hadn't. I'd heard him perfectly well.

"Oh, no. *You* tear down." Giving him a hard look, I said, "As you pointed out earlier, I'm just along for the ride."

We walked back to the dusty dirt plot of ground where our trailer stood. Four trucks had arrived, one pulling a brightly painted trailer, complete with a border of golden flames. The name "Freddy's Fun House" was splashed across the side. The golden painted flames burned through the letters and I couldn't help but wonder just how much fun you could have in a small trailer like this.

The second truck was a beat-up flatbed with a saucer-like ride on the back.

Two semis were parked by the side of the road, each carrying what appeared to be half of a full ride. Six empty round cages with roofs, long sections of a green and gold metal bar, and the huge head of an otherworld dinosaur creature were piled on the trucks.

"That's the Dragon Tail." The voice was deep and smooth.

I turned around and the big man with swept back gray hair was pointing at the two trailers.

"It's the ride that guarantees traffic."

"Traffic?"

"That's the signature ride of the Moe Show. The Dragon Tail."

James stepped up and placed his hand on my shoulder. "Moe, this is my best friend, Skip Moore."

The man reached out with a darkly tanned arm and grasped my hand. The grip was strong and firm, a guy who was used to physical work.

"Glad to meet you, Skip. I'm Moe Bradley. Welcome to the Moe Show."

Somehow, coming from him, the name was less embarrassing. After all, he was Moe. The Skip Show or the James Show wouldn't ever work.

"My trailer is right over there."

I glanced at the edge of a grove of trees. On a concrete slab, the sleek black and silver motor home shone brilliantly in the early morning Carol City sun.

"Forty-five-foot American Eagle. Almost like living at home, boys. Come on, I'll show it to you."

I looked back at our dinged up thirty-foot Airstream and thought about the different levels of luxury.

"We're going to have one of those, Skip. Someday." James whispered with that faraway look in his eyes.

We hiked the short distance to the motor home and stepped inside. I will go on record as saying this might have been the most impressive living area I'd ever seen. Remember, I come from humble beginnings, and James and I live in a dump. *But*, I have visited some pretty fancy places in my time, and as far as I was concerned, this was opulence at its finest.

A fifty-inch flat screen television was mounted on the wall in front of me, and marble tile graced the entranceway. Thick, luxurious, green carpet covered the floor, like walking through rich green moss, and a leather furniture grouping curved around the TV screen. The open area led to a kitchen, and as we continued into the dwelling I could see the countertops were granite, with swirls of browns and reds. Cherry hardwood cabinets filled the walls and the kitchen table was an intricate butcher-block design of hardwoods.

"If you're going to travel, and you can afford it, I believe in traveling with style."

It wasn't a brag. Just a statement of fact. Here was a man who'd worked for it and had something to show for it. I could see why James was impressed.

"There's a whole lot more to see, but for now, have a seat. I've got a rather involved question to ask you two."

James and I sat down on the butter-soft leather sofa. Moe stood in front of us, nodding his head and smiling.

"Anyone for a drink?"

It was ten fifteen in the morning. Not that James and I didn't sometimes have a drink at that time, but that was between the two of us. Right now we were with his employer. It didn't seem to be the appropriate thing to do.

"No. It's a little early in the morning." I was proud of my roommate. James was saving himself.

"Too bad." Moe walked to the kitchen and pulled out a bottle of orange juice from the refrigerator. I was somewhat embarrassed. He'd simply meant a little bit of healthy nourishment.

"Well, a taste would be good." I was up for some OJ.

"Great." Moe reached back into the refrigerator and pulled out a bottle of champagne. He pulled off the foil, twisted the metal cage from the plastic stopper and popped it out. The stopper shot to the ceiling and white bubbles foamed from the mouth of the bottle.

"I start most mornings with a mimosa," he said. He poured three healthy glasses of OJ and champagne and handed them to us. This would be a morning to remember. For a lot more than just the drinks.

CHAPTER SIX

The alcohol surged through my body, and the soft leather surrounded me like a glove. The three of us sat on the couch and toasted the success of another Moe Show. And I was just along for the ride.

"Gentlemen—" I always got nervous when someone called me Mr. Moore, or referred to me as a gentleman. For good reason.

"Gentlemen, I've asked you here for a very important reason."

James gave him a very hard look, eyes squinted and concerned. My roommate thought this visit was an affirmation of his employment. If there was another reason, he was clueless.

"First of all, James was our number one choice for marketing director."

I had no idea James had a title. I suppose in a small way I was upset about that. I always thought I'd be the first one of us to have an actual job title. Other than the title "gopher."

"We, my sisters and I, are looking forward to your ideas, your energy, and your unique perspectives on things. Angie— Agent Hot Pants—has assured me you are a very unique individual." He gave James a faint smile. I wondered if he knew they were already dating.

"Thank you." James nodded.

"But there's a second reason for me to talk to you." He stood up, swigging the rest of his mimosa in one gulp. "You boys have a private investigation company, am I right?"

"We do." James was on his feet. There was fire in his eyes, and he'd totally come alive. I have to admit, I was amazed. How did this guy Moe know we were private investigators?

"How did you know that?" This guy was amazing. The Private Investigator license was not even forty-eight hours old.

"James told Angie. Angie mentioned it to me."

Well, there you go. It's not private if you tell everyone.

"And I need a P.I. firm."

"For what?" I couldn't fathom what good we would be to a Moe Show.

"For a little undercover work. To find out who is trying to sabotage my company."

James sat back down and drained his mimosa. I can say with authority that we were both stunned.

"Moe, why would someone try to sabotage your carnivals?"

"That's your second assignment, James. To find out why."

I looked at my roommate, and he could see the concern on my face. I mean, it still was a concept that we were grappling with. The concept of being serious private investigators. Jody Stacy was a private investigator. We were amateurs. And here was someone actually trying to hire us.

"In the past year, four of my rides have had major accidents."

I knew I'd been right on that subject. I finally remembered I'd read about it in the *Miami Herald*, but too late to warn James. I should have told him then I had doubts about his new position, but now it might mean a job. I was secretly glad I'd kept the story quiet. This might be a new source of revenue.

"Four accidents, and one death."

Pretty serious stuff. "One death?"

"These were rides that were checked out, Skip. Rides that were almost foolproof. And yet, for a variety of reasons, people were thrown off of them. Little things, like a loose screw."

Not only thrown. An innocent had been killed. I'd read about the death but never got all of the brutal details.

"A seat belt broke loose. It's almost impossible for that to happen. Almost impossible. But, a customer was thrown to the blacktop pavement. Serious injuries. On another ride, a safety bar snapped. Now, unless someone sawed through those heavy metal bars, that just shouldn't happen. The rides today are foolproof. Really. Foolproof. But," he paused, taking a deep breath, "the bolts had come loose and she was thrown under the ride, into the mechanical gears and—"

I interrupted quickly for fear that Moe might actually describe the blood and the gore that surrounded the death.

"So you're saying it has to be sabotage."

"At first I thought it could be explained away. I thought to myself that accidents do happen. Even the big guys have accidents. Disney had two trains run head on into each other. The Eaton Brothers lost a car from the top of their Ferris wheel. Win's Spectacular had a plane from the kiddie ride fly off its moorings. Things happen, boys, but in this case I don't see any other explanation."

"Moe, there must be something else that could explain these accidents."

"No. Nothing else. A gear snapped on another ride we nicknamed The Ameba, and the entire operation came to a screeching halt. And this was one day after The Ameba had been thoroughly inspected by a Florida State licensing agent. Thoroughly inspected, guys. We should have been on solid ground."

"What happened?"

"Two riders slipped under the safety bars and were thrown from their pods. One of them walked away. The other was mangled by the remaining pods. She's confined to a wheelchair and takes nourishment from a bottle." Moe sipped his champagne and juice and swirled the liquid in his mouth.

We were all silent for a moment. It was a wonder that Moe Shows were still setting up shop. I was amazed. Being vaguely familiar with the situations and hearing them firsthand was a different situation all together.

Setting his drink down, he said "We're as thorough as we can possibly be. Our insurance rating," he spread his hands out palms up, "was very high. Now—now we're in a couple of nasty lawsuits and some people are reluctant to even visit our little show. This could kill us, guys. Kill us."

"So you want us to look into this matter?" James sat still as Moe stood up, walked to the kitchen, and brought out the carton and bottle. He poured us another orange juice and champagne.

"Not just look into the matter." He stood above James, looking down at him with a frown. "I want you to find out who is messing with me. I want to know who's trying to destroy this business, and I want to know why. The Dragon Tail will be set up this afternoon, and I'd like you guys to keep an eye on the ride. To operate it alongside our two young operators. Check out our staff. Do whatever you need to do. I need to stop these so-called accidents from happening. I can't afford to have anything else go wrong. Do you understand?"

This was a second job. And I was only along for the ride.

"And keep it quiet. If our employees think that you are investigating them, well, it could be dangerous for you."

That's what I needed. More danger in my life.

"Now I'm aware that Skip is only an observer, but I'm

willing to offer the two of you two thousand dollars for this weekend."

I was no longer an observer. Danger no longer bothered me.

"If you can find out why someone is trying to destroy my livelihood, I need to know why, and I need to know who."

A pretty big order. So if we were unsuccessful—

"Moe," James had downed his second drink and was feeling champagne courage. "If we use all of our resources and can't find any clues at all. I mean if nothing happens at this Moe Show, then we don't get compensated. Is that what you're saying?"

Moe Bradley pursed his lips. "I don't want to be unfair, but—"

"But we may put a lot of effort into this investigation and it may not pan out. Mr. Bradley, I heard you say that sabotage is the only explanation, but really, it's possible isn't it that these rides could have just broken? It's possible that there is no one trying to destroy your carnival." I wasn't about to commit myself for the fun of it. James and I had done that before and almost gotten killed.

"Please, call me Moe."

"Mr. . . . Moe, we will have expenses." I was remembering the equipment we bought from our mentor Jody Stacy on our last spy case. High-tech microphones and cameras were expensive. Very expensive. "And if we incur these expenses and there really isn't a saboteur, if we find nothing, then we've gone through a lot of time and money."

"All right." Bradley hesitated and I could hear the wheels turning inside his head. "If you find nothing, you still get a thousand dollars. Does that work?"

If someone was sabotaging the rides, they'd already killed a customer. If they found out that James and I were investigating them—

"One thousand dollars for the weekend."

It worked for me.

"Skip?" James gave me a questioning glance.

I nodded.

Moe had a slight grin on his face.

"We're on, Moe." My best friend beamed a smile of confidence. "If there *is* someone here who is trying to sabotage the carnival, we'll do everything in our power to figure it out."

Moe nodded. "There's no question about it, James. Someone is. I have the utmost faith that you two will find out who it is. But keep a low profile. Got it? You don't know the kind of people we're dealing with here."

I knew they were carnies. And you can't trust a carnie.

CHAPTER SEVEN

By afternoon the rides were up, rock music was blaring from cheap speakers, the colorful lights had been strung, and the whole place looked and smelled just like a carnival. James was escorting Angie to a meat-on-a-stick wagon, his arm around her waist, and I stopped and got a watered-down fresh lemonade. A handful of people wandered about, and the Ferris wheel was slowly spinning in the sky, a couple of kids and a young couple waving at us from above.

An anemic roller coaster ran up small inclines and down shallow valleys on a neon orange track with only three occupied cars, and as I watched an old man throw darts at the balloons in a nearby booth I felt something bump my butt. Hard.

Spinning around, I saw the culprit. A mangy goat with a brown goatee looked up at me with what looked like a frown. I stepped back and the goat stepped forward. No horns, but the animal gently butted my leg, then shook his head and gave me that nasty frown again.

"Sorry, there. She's just playin'."

He'd surprised me as much as the goat had. The little guy

stood about four feet tall and wore a pair of faded blue overalls. No shirt, just those overalls and a pair of black rubber rain boots.

"Esmerelda walked away from the petting zoo over there," he pointed to my right, "and Garcia didn't even notice."

"Garcia?"

"That old sheepdog. See? He's supposed to help round up the animals, but sometimes I think the job overwhelms him." The man was gently chewing. Food, gum, something. As he chewed, the goat chewed.

Rust-colored rails surrounded the small circle of dirt and sand where the man's petting zoo was located, and a lone trailer stood off to the side. I could see the big dog panting in the Carol City heat as he watched the little man, the goat, and me from inside the rails.

"I'm Winston." The short guy stuck his hands in his pockets, eyeing me. "That's my zoo."

I glanced back and saw a small donkey, what looked like a black pig, several ducks and chickens, and a deer.

"Winston Pugh. Actually, Winston Pugh Charlemagne, but I just use the first two." He frowned and spit tobacco from between his two front brown-stained teeth. I stepped back and the goat stepped forward.

"Esmerelda. Back off."

Two carnies pounded poles into the dirt in front of Winston's zoo with small sledgehammers. They lifted a wooden sign up and hung it from hooks on the poles.

Winney Pugh's Petting Zoo

"You're the new marketing director?"

I felt somewhat self-conscious looking down at the little guy. Even with his head tilted back I was staring at the top of his shiny scalp and two tufts of white hair that framed his ears.

"No. That's my roommate James. He's with Agent—" I caught myself. "Uh, Angie, over by that food wagon."

"Ah, Angie. She's a pistol, that one. You two be careful of her, you hear me?" Pugh kept on chewing. And frowning.

"Careful?"

"Trust no one, son. Best advice I can give you."

Two chubby children ran by, the girl with a cone of cotton candy and the boy holding a stick with a cellophane streamer that halfheartedly blew in the still air. Their overweight parents trailed behind, already appearing to be exhausted from the excitement.

I turned my attention back to Winston. "And you call your zoo Winney Pugh's Petting Zoo?"

He looked back at the sign, turning back with a gleam in his eye. "I do. And Disney hates it."

"Disney hates what?"

"Come on. You know."

I gave him my puzzled look.

"Walt Disney World. You know. They've been trying to close me down for years now."

"Why would Disney try to close down your petting zoo?" I stared over at the run-down trailer, the rusty rails that surrounded the ring, and the mangy animals that seemed subdued by the midday heat.

"Why? Because they are the mouse that roared. Because, young man, they can. Disney owns the copyright on Winnie the Pooh, and they claim I'm infringing. Imagine. Me?" He reached into a deep pocket of his overalls and pulled out a crumpled sheet of paper. "Here's the letter."

I shook my head.

"No, read it."

I unfolded the yellowed document and glanced at the print. I could tell right away that there were too many *herewiths* and *The party to whiches* and all the other legal verbiage that I would never understand. The letter was dated September 1, 2001, and signed by Don Witter, Esquire. Very official. I nodded, looked at the technical language for thirty seconds, and handed it back to Winston.

"It says they're gonna sue me, doesn't it? Doesn't it? But I ain't changin' the name." The little guy folded his arms across his chest and shook his head.

"Good for you."

He spit a stream of brown juice that almost hit my foot. "You stop by some time. I live in that little trailer over there, and we'll have a shot of tequila. We'll talk about this den of thieves and the stuff that goes on here. You wouldn't believe."

Grabbing the goat by the skin on her back, he trudged back to his small zoo, his oversized black rubber boots kicking up dust and the goat tripping over its feet as it struggled to keep up. The sheepdog gave him a sharp bark and frantically wagged his stub of a tail.

I watched him go, wondering what kind of a life he had. On the road with the Moe Show, traveling with a herd of small animals and the proudest moment in his life was showing off a letter from a Disney attorney threatening to close his little run-down animal parade. A letter from 2001. They'd probably forgotten all about Winston Pugh Charlemagne.

"Hey, pard. The chicken on a stick really—"

"Sucks." Angie Clark finished the sentence. "I think your roommate James believes I'm a cheap date." She gave me a great smile and I smiled back. "If this is the best he can do—"

I whiffed her perfume. Frangipani, sweet and sensual.

"James usually starts with cheap beer and peanuts. This is a step up, Angie."

"Oh. Then I'm flattered." She grabbed his hand and held on tight. If this was love at first sight, then maybe there was hope for all of us.

I wanted to tell James I'd already had a lead. Well, maybe it was a lead. Winston had suggested we have a drink and talk about 'the stuff that goes on here.' Sounded like a lead to me.

"Skip, have you seen the Dragon Tail in action?" He pointed over his shoulder and I realized I'd missed it altogether. Hard to imagine. The ride was as impressive in size as it was in motion.

"There's a family of four just got on."

The golden head of the fire-breathing dragon puffed billows of real smoke from its mouth, and the body shimmered green, like scales on a big fish.

"Thing's frightening, isn't it?" He and Angie watched as the tail slowly curled and twelve green and gold cages curled with it.

"So the tail is just that string of cages?"

Angie's eyes got wide and she looked at me. "Just a string of cages? Oh no. They're called cars, but there's more than that. You wait, Skip. This ride is crazy."

The tail straightened out from the curl, then, like the snap of a whip it shot into the air.

There was a crack and I heard shouts from the riders. It looked like the chubby family of four was in the end car, but I couldn't tell as the tail rose straight up, did a twirl at maybe forty feet and snapped to the left, hung there for several seconds, snapped to the right, and dropped like a stone.

"My God." My stomach flipped and I wasn't even on the Dragon.

"Want to ride it with me, James?" She squeezed his hand even tighter, and I could tell right then. Angie Clark was a thrill freak.

He looked back at me, rolled his eyes, then back at the Dragon Tail, the smokey, fire-eating dragon with a devil's tail that threatened to shake every bone in your body.

"Sure. I'll take you on the ride of your life."

"We're next." She looked longingly into his eyes.

"But not tonight."

"Not tonight?"

"No. Sorry. Skip and I have someplace we've got to be in about fifteen minutes and we can't be late."

She pouted and let go of his hand.

"Tomorrow, Angie, I promise."

James turned, grabbed me by the shoulder, and steered me toward the trailer. Looking over his shoulder he said, "See you later, babe."

"You coward." I looked him in the eye. "I can't believe you just pulled that. You're a coward."

"Coward? Coward?" He sounded somewhat proud of the accusation.

"You heard me."

"Cowards live to fight another day, pard."

He continued to push me along, and I searched my mind for the quote.

"I give up. Who in what movie said cowards live to fight another day?"

"It's not from a movie."

"Then where's it from?"

"Some Greek guy named Demosthenes. I read it somewhere in school. At least it was something similar to it, like the dude who runs away stays alive. But I made this one up. A coward lives to fight another day." He let go of my shoulder as we approached the silver Airstream. "It's kind of the way I live my life, Skip, in case you hadn't noticed."

CHAPTER EIGHT

"So you think this Winston guy knows something? Already you've reached that conclusion?"

I straddled the kitchen chair, taking a long pull of beer. "No. I don't think he knows anything. Well, maybe, but he did say this was a den of thieves and that I wouldn't believe what went on here. Who knows, James? I think it's worth talking to him."

"Let's have that cactus juice. Let's sit down with the little guy and see what he has to say." James sipped on his beer, sprawled on the couch, his foldaway bed.

"I can set it up. He's about one hundred feet away."

He stared at the window, holding the bottle with two hands. "Angie is staying over, Skip. Tonight."

"Here? In the trailer? It's a little small, James."

"No. Not *here*. She's in that trailer by Moe's. It's the yellow and white one. I should probably head over there and—" He hesitated.

So Angie Clark *did* overnight with the carnies.

"You're right, James. You go, man. Stay with the girl. I'll deal with this. After all, *I'm* the one who wanted to have a private detective agency. *I'm* the one who wants to buy a new truck. I'll just head on over to Winston's trailer, and if *I* solve the case, I'll be sure to share half the money with you."

My voice was about three times louder than when I started.

"Because you are my best friend, amigo. Why don't you just let me take care of everything?"

He stood there with his mouth open.

"I would hate to inconvenience you, dude. Your romantic relationships are far more important than the money we could make." I'd worked myself into a royal rage.

I knew what drove me to rag on him. My relationship with Em. It was going nowhere. James picked women up like litter by the roadside. He tripped over relationships every day of his life, but I had the love of my life and she couldn't get past the fact that I was emotionally immature. She hated the fact that I was tied to the dreams of James Lessor, and not really motivated to go out and find someone willing to pay me megabucks for having no real skills. And, truth be told, she was probably right. But life is a bitch.

"Skip, I—"

"Just go. You already blew her off on the ride. Don't blow her off on anything else. I'll deal with Winston."

"She's a bright girl, Skip. A Bluffton Beaver."

"A what?"

"It's not a joke. She's a Bluffton Beaver."

"Well, I'm glad I'm not standing in the way of that relationship. You and a beaver."

"Graduated from some school in Ohio. Bluffton University. Their mascot is the beaver. Do you believe that?"

I didn't.

I could hear music from the midway, '80's rock, "Don't Stop Believing," a 1981 hit by Journey. Long before I was born. Maybe I had more at stake than James. Maybe I needed to believe more than he did that I could make something of myself.

I turned around and walked into the bedroom. Three steps. But at least there was some distance. I needed the money, and I felt like I needed a relationship that would settle down. And deep down inside, I knew I needed to find out what Winston Pugh knew. The little guy had invited me over, and I was sure that there would be a couple of free drinks. With no other plans, that seemed like a pretty good idea. Free drinks and a chance to find out what made a Moe Show tick.

"Skip, I'm going over to Angie's trailer."

I flopped down on the bed, hands behind my head, and didn't say anything.

"Remember what Moe said."

"About what?"

"Don't tell this guy what we're here for. Somebody in this show is apparently a killer."

"Oh, yeah. Thanks for reminding me."

"Hey, pard, we're going to be trained on the rides at eight a.m. tomorrow morning. By ten we'll be running a couple of them."

"No shit? Eight a.m.?"

"That's the time, Skip.

Life just got better and better and better.

I had a slight headache, probably from the two mimosas, so I drank a beer, popped two aspirin, and walked over to Winnie Pugh's Petting Zoo.

The dusty ground inside the ring was covered in hoof prints, and three glass-domed gum dispensers were mounted on metal poles by the fence posts. They were crammed with some kind of brown pellets, fifty cents for a handful of pressed processed grain to feed the head-butting goat or miniature donkey, or even the black pig that huddled by the rail. The pig eyed me warily.

Pugh was directing a stream of water from a green garden

hose into a metal trough, and the tiny, bedraggled, gray donkey was wetting his thick pink tongue and taking long swallows of the liquid.

The dust-covered pig approached me, a longing look in its eyes, and I knew right away I should have had fifty cents worth of pellets in my hand. Did Pugh even feed the animals, or did he just depend on the customers? Oh well, I'd learn.

"Get's hot like this and I can't keep enough water in this trough." He looked up at me and again spat tobacco at my feet. "How you doin', young man?"

I nodded as a mangy chicken strode to the wet tobacco stain and took an inquisitive peck of the offensive brown spit.

"Kiddies be comin' in tonight. Linda will be out here makin' sure that all the animals behave themselves."

"Linda?"

He gave me a sideways glance, then leered at me, the gap between his stained teeth mocking me. "Linda Reilly. She's not fond of the chicken or the ducks, and she hates pigeons and most other birds, but she's pretty good with all the other animals. They like her. She respects them and they respect her."

I couldn't build a lot of respect for the butt-butting goat, the deer, or any of the other animals on the lot. They were animals for God's sake. But then, I'd never owned a pet in my life, so I didn't understand animals.

"So, this Linda, she works for you?"

Garcia, the sheepdog, strolled out from behind Pugh's trailer, stopping short when he saw me. Finally, he walked over, rubbing against the short guy's leg. The dog was almost as big as Winston. He eyed me with distrust. I don't respect animals, and they don't respect me. It is mutual.

"Linda lives with me, young man. She's my paramour. And she does other stuff."

I wasn't sure what paramour meant. I'd check it out at

dictionary dot com tonight, but I assume it meant that Winston slept with her.

He walked back to the pipe sticking out of the ground and turned off the faucet. "Why don't you come on in and you can meet sweet Linda. Okay?"

A radio played inside and I could hear an off-tune warbling voice singing along with Kenny Chesney. No shoes, no shirt, no problem.

I nodded to Pugh.

The trailer was smaller than the Airstream that James and I shared and it listed slightly from what appeared to be a low tire.

"You like tequila?"

It contained alcohol. How could I not like it?

As we walked up the wobbly wooden stairs, the big dog let out a low growl. Looking down at him, I saw him snap at me. I vowed to stay away from him for the next three days. Or for the rest of my life.

I was hit with the odor of greasy fried food.

"Burgers, fish, or chicken. The girl loves to fry meat."

She turned from the stove with a big smile.

"Hi, honey." He reached up and threw his arms around her waist snuggling his head under her bosom. As he squeezed her tight she leaned down and kissed the top of his shiny bald scalp.

"This here is—" He paused. "What is your name?"

"I'm Skip, Linda. Glad to meet you."

She released the little man and grabbed my hand. Dazzling me with her green sparkling eyes, she held my hand for several seconds, then let go with a sigh and turned to her skillet.

"Skip, you're just in time for some early dinner. Winston and I get busy with the zoo from five to nine so we always eat early. Do you like fried frog legs?" She pushed a limp lock of brown hair from her face, never losing that smile.

I hesitated. Over the years James, a culinary grad, had

cooked up some adventurous dishes, but he'd never fixed anything like that. I'd never tried frog legs, but I was certain I would hate the taste.

"I just had lunch, Linda. I'm stuffed." A weak lemonade and a beer. It was preferable to her early dinner offer.

Pugh set three paper cups on the small kitchen table and poured from a gallon jug of Jose Cuervo. "Nectar from the desert fruit, young man." He eyed his cup, then threw it back, smacking his lips as he swallowed the cactus juice.

I followed suit.

My eyes watering, I watched as Linda swallowed her shot, poured herself a second and in record time swallowed that as well. She continued to flip the coated frog legs in the frying pan.

"Let's talk about the Moe Show. That is why you dropped by."

I nodded. "It is. And to be neighborly."

"Neighborly?" Linda adjusted the heat on her stove.

Pugh poured himself a second shot and leaned back in the cheap wicker kitchen chair. "There's no such thing as neighbors here, is there Linda?"

"No, honey."

"You and me, young man, there's no real friendship here. No close relationship. Understand?"

I thought I did.

"Don't get close to anyone. I tell you that for your own good."

It seemed like everyone wanted to make that point. I didn't say a word.

"So you're only with us for this weekend, right?"

"Right."

"They're all a bunch of crooks. Lying, stealing, thieving scoundrels. From the food vendors to the management."

"Moe?"

"I said all of 'em didn't I? They're *all* in it for themselves."

Well, I thought, aren't we all?

"I'm the biggest draw they got, boy, and they're tryin' to push me out."

"Yeah?"

"First off it's Disney, tryin' to get me to cease operation. You saw that attorney's letter?"

I nodded.

"Now it's the ride guys."

"The ride guys?"

"They're pushin' me, boy."

"Why would the ride guys want you out?"

"More room for their rides. Whatchu think? Put another big DT-type contraption here. And then where are the kiddies gonna pet a goat or feed a pig?"

"DT?"

"Dragon Tail."

"So, you're getting forced out because of space? For another ride?"

"Oh, they haven't said it yet, but Moe and the sisters— Schiller and Crouse—they want me out so the ride guys can put another machine in. It's just as obvious as it can be, son. I ain't gonna let it happen. Ain't gonna."

Linda eyed the tequila bottle, and I was certain she was going to take one more shot.

"Winston is quite certain that they're going to try to move him out this summer." She poured her third shot.

"All the signs are there," he paused. "What was your name again?"

"Skip."

"All the signs are there, boy. I asked for a new arena, a new water tank, and they can't come up with the bucks. For God's sake man, it's a *drop* in the bucket. I asked for a little more money to fix this trailer up just a bit and again, they can't come up with

42

the money. It's a drop in the bucket. But when it comes to a new ride, well then they're tryin' to raise all kinds of money. I'm bein' pushed, boy. Pushed."

Linda Reilly nodded her head. She raised the paper cup of tequila and poured it down her throat. Cast-iron stomach.

"You see, we hear the sisters talking. Schiller and Crouse. And their brother, Moe Bradley. You know, there are coconut telegraphs out there and people hear stuff. People tell me things."

The little guy jumped from his chair and grabbed my hand. I stood up and he marched five or six steps to the door. Flinging it open, he pointed.

"You see it out there? The other animal on the grounds?"

The green Dragon Tail was waving in the sky, to the left, to the right.

"They're talkin' about some ride that's even bigger than the DT. They're figuring out how to afford it and get it on the summer tour."

"Don't forget about Disney, Winston." Linda's voice got louder and she slurred her words. "You know, how they're trying to shut you down, too."

"I mentioned Disney, Linda. I did. It's all part of it. A damned conspiracy, that's what it is." He glared out at the ride, slammed the door, and went back to his chair. Huffing and puffing, he slammed his fist on the cheap vinyl table.

The little man was getting wound up, and I thought it might be a good time to get to the heart of the matter.

"It just seems like everyone is against him." She stood there for a moment with a greasy spatula in her hand.

"Winston, you're talking about the rides, and I was curious about them." Now was the time to confront him about the death. Just ease into it. "I heard there have been some accidents in the last year. Pretty serious accidents. Am I right that someone died after falling off a ride? I believe I read that somewhere."

The only sound in the small trailer was the radio playing softly. Pugh stared up at me with a puzzled expression on his face.

"Winston, you know about the accidents, right?"

I'd apparently stepped over the line. I don't know how, but it was obvious I'd crossed a boundary.

"Accidents? You want to talk about accidents? You're brand-new here, less than a day, and you want to talk about accidents?" He stared up at me and searched my face with his mournful eyes.

This little man had been with the show for a long time. He had to know everything.

"Winston, I read about some accidents. Some of the rides that maybe jumped the tracks? A seat belt might have broken? A safety bar—"

"So you're here to ask me questions?" He stared at me.

Linda turned from her skillet, the dripping spatula in her hand.

"I'm here because James asked me to be here." Be low key. Don't let them know you're investigating them. "That's all." This didn't seem to be a good idea, but I kept on. "I'm sure someone was killed. I feel certain that I heard that." Heard it from Moe himself.

The two of them sat there, staring at each other, then at me. The tension was as thick as molasses.

"Winston?"

"Who are you, young man?"

"I told you, I'm Skip." The little man was having trouble with my name. "I'm James's friend. You mentioned it earlier. James is my roomate. He's the new marketing director."

Pugh licked his lips, staring into my eyes.

"Uh-huh." Nodding in patronizing fashion, he said, "Young man, I think you'd better leave now."

It was my turn to stare. I'd missed something here. "Did I say something to offend you?"

"No." Shaking his head he stacked the paper cups on the table. "But Linda and I have to get ready for tonight's show."

"You need to go." The lovely Linda, now frowning and her eyes shooting daggers at me, held the spatula in her fist like a weapon, and I got the message.

Winston stood up, walked to the door, and pulled it open. He waited while I pushed back my chair and took three steps to the exit.

"You stop back again sometime." He said it flatly, coldly.

"Or don't." Linda looked ready to fry *me*.

As I walked away I knew I'd overplayed my hand. What started out as a tell-all on the Moe Show turned out to be a chilly rebuff. My first act as an official Florida P.I. was a miserable failure.

CHAPTER NINE

The Dragon Tail was half full and shrill screams broke through the loud music, AC/DC playing "You Shook Me All Night Long." The tight curl of the green and gold cars mounted on the tail, then the snap to the left in midair, a snap to the right, followed by that deadly drop. The tequila in my stomach burned, and I turned away from the smoke-breathing monster.

There was no sign of James or the girl as I approached the Bar-B-Que Pit trailer, with its cartoon drawing of a pig's head smiling at me. Nothing like personalizing your food product. I thought about the kids feeding Winston Pugh's pig, then stopping here and having the pig feed them. I'm sure the irony was lost on the public.

"What'll you have?"

I looked up at the man's grizzled face bearing three days' growth. His stained apron gave credence to the small hand-lettered sign plastered on the glass window of his trailer.

*We've got the thickest, tangiest, hottest, **messiest**
barbecue sauce in the south. Guaranteed.*

"What do you recommend?"

The man shrugged his shoulders, looking bored with the whole process.

"How about a sandwich?"

"Pickle?"

"Sure."

"Extra fifty cents."

"Fine. Sandwich and a pickle."

He slopped the pork and sauce on a bun, laid the fifty-cent pickle spear on top and held out his hand.

"Six fifty."

"Six fifty? For this sandwich?"

He pulled it back, and I felt the tequila burning deep in my gut. "I'll take it. I'll take it."

The thickest, tangiest, hottest, messiest barbecue sauce in the south joined the tequila and helped stoke the fire down below.

Kids with faces full of cotton candy paraded by, and mothers with sun hats and strollers, along with fathers in shorts with diaper bags on their shoulders and babies in their arms, shepherded small children over the dusty ground.

He was staring at me from the rifle booth. The one where you shoot BBs at a paper target with an air rifle and have to punch out its center. It can't be done, but stupid people keep trying. I know that for a fact. I spent thirty bucks one time with Em at a small fair.

I glanced at him and he honed in on me, his eyes searching mine. Not the kind of look a carnie gives you when he wants your business. Not like the guy who calls you over to guess your weight or age. There was more to it than that. Like he knew me from somewhere.

"Kid, come here. Try your luck."

I stopped, tempted to take him up on his offer. I knew better, but as I said, stupid people keep trying.

"Nah, I'm no good at that game."

"Come here." He motioned and I walked over. "No one's good at this game. Why the hell you think we keep it in the show? 'Cause we make all the money and the rubes walk away with nothin'."

I never heard a carnie use the word rubes before.

The painfully thin man turned, grabbed a furry snake, and tossed it to me. "Here. Pretend you won." He grinned and I could see several front teeth missing. It wasn't a pretty sight.

Turning from him, I scanned the grounds looking for a trashcan where I could eventually throw the snake. Two teenagers stood at the booth to my right, trying to toss wooden rings onto bottle tops. To my left was a pint-sized train, the faded blue and yellow cars filled with bored children going round and round in a tight circle while the acne-scarred operator chewed his fingernails and stared into space.

"You're part of the Show, right?" studying me with a quizzical look.

I wasn't. At least no one was to know. As James had said earlier, I was just along for the ride.

"The Show?"

He ran a hand through his greasy black hair, the pale skin on his bony face stretched tight. His faded-blue wrinkled T-shirt was draped over his puny chest and shoulders and a pair of faded jeans hung loosely from his hips.

"This dung heap. You know what I mean." He waved his hand in a sweeping gesture, alluding to the rides and assorted trailers.

"No. I'm just helping out a friend. James is going to be the new marketing director, and—"

"Don't kid a kidder, son."

"Pardon?"

"You're a spy. Word's gettin' around."

"A spy?" Had Moe gone out with a memo?

"You're checkin' out the players, tryin' to see if any of us was involved in those accidents. Am I right?"

I tossed him the snake and took a step back. "Look, I don't know anything about that." The truth was, I knew very little. "What's your name?"

"My name?"

"You're accusing me of something. Of being a spy. At least I need to know your name. I'm considering going to Moe, and telling him that you were threatening me." I needed to know how this guy knew we were investigating the Show.

"You watch your step, kid. There are people here who don't take to outsiders. You never know what could happen to you."

And there were outsiders who didn't take kindly to carnies, speaking from personal experience.

"Give me your name."

"Boy, don't get yourself involved. Somethin' may happen to you, and it might not be pretty. You got no stake in this game, so you and your friend should just mosey back to wherever it is you come from."

"I have no idea what you're talking about."

He stared across the grounds, then walked up to the counter and leaned over. I could smell strong alcohol on his breath. "Son, there are no friends here. We tolerate each other—sometimes. You learn to never trust anyone here. However, I'm doin' you a huge favor. I'm givin' you a very friendly warning. Walk away."

No friends. The same message I'd heard from Winston.

"Are you listening to me? This job could be your last." There was almost a pleading in his voice.

"Look, I'm here to help my roommate this weekend. He's

going to be marketing the . . ." I hesitated—may as well use the lingo—"Show. Marketing the Show. That's it."

He studied me, a thin trail of moisture on his upper lip. The skinny man wiped at it. "It's your funeral." He reached under the counter and pulled out a wooden-stocked air rifle, one that wasn't chained to the counter. Casually aiming it at me, he pulled the trigger.

I felt my heart jump. Nothing happened.

"Go home, little boy. Go home. We'll take care of our own problems."

To be truthful, I was scared to death of this guy. But I hung in there. "What's your name?"

"Kevin. Kevin Cross. You take that to Moe. I'm the most loyal employee he's got and he knows it. I look out for him and the Show. And I know what's going on here. You tell Moe, you hear me? I got it all figured out. You and your friend. Checkin' up on us—well you be sure and let me know what you find out, okay?"

Walking away I heard him over my shoulder.

"Hey, kid, before you go, want to try one for free? One at no charge, okay? Maybe I'm wrong about this. Maybe this is your lucky day."

And then again, maybe it wasn't. I walked back to the trailer, past the little roller coaster, jerking over its tiny orange track of hills and valleys, by the brightly colored Fun House with amplified guffaws and belly laughs blaring from huge speakers, by the greasy smell of the chicken-on-a-stick trailer, the Bar-B-Que Pit, the Ferris wheel, and five other rides, half expecting to see James and Angie. There was no sign they'd been there.

Reaching our Airstream trailer, I grabbed a beer, plopped down on the sofa that would be James's bed later on tonight, and I thought about the mission. What the hell had we been thinking? We were so far out of our league. Private investigators? This wasn't the kind of job we should have been involving ourselves in. I mean, these were some pretty rough characters, and people had been injured on those rides. Actually, someone had gotten killed at this show. Not only that, I'd pretty much been threatened by the air rifle guy. Maybe James and I should discuss this a little further.

I downed the beer and had a second before I ventured back out to the show. With a little liquid courage I wanted to see Winston and Linda work their magic, and I wanted to see the Dragon Tail close up. If we were putting our lives on the line, I needed to know what the rules were.

CHAPTER TEN

There was a line at the Dragon Tail, and a young guy with a striped, collared shirt and buzz cut took tickets and stuffed them into a wooden box. The second guy looked vaguely familiar. I couldn't put my finger on it. Standing tall, hair hanging down over his forehead, he escorted the older couples, the teens, and youngsters into the gold-green cars and pulled down a shiny metal bar, locking it into place with the flick of a switch. There didn't seem to be any way the bar could spring free while the Tail was going through its contortions, but then what did I know about carnival rides?

The cars spread out flat and when all of them had been bar-locked, the ticket taker walked back to his seat and pushed a button on a dull gunmetal gray control box. The dragon exhaled his smoke and the jointed, sectioned metal tail started wagging. It was that simple.

I approached the operator and he held up his right hand.

"Whatchuwant?"

"Hey, I'm Skip. My partner and I are going to learn the ride tomorrow morning, and I just thought I'd see how you operate it."

"Oh, you're gonna learn the ride?" He tilted his head back with skepticism. As if he didn't believe me.

"Yeah. In the morning."

"Like hell."

"What?"

"This is my ride, buddy. Charlie and me. This is ours." He pointed his thumb to the other young man and for a minute I knew why he looked familiar. Charlie looked like James. Same build, hair—

"Don't even think about messing with us, bud."

I realized I was threatening his livelihood.

"No, not to run it full time. I mean, not to run it at all. Well, just for the morning. A couple of hours, you know. My partner is the new marketing manager and—"

"You?" He planted himself in front of me and I could tell from the start that I was not worthy. "You? You're gonna learn the ride? So you could do it by yourself? Is that what you're sayin'?" The tail rose in the air and whipped to the left. The riders screamed.

I knew how to address this situation. Whenever you're not being understood you just speak louder, right? So I spoke louder, almost shouting. "No. I am not going to be operating the ride. I mean, maybe we'll operate it for a couple of hours, but that's all. We're not permanent. Please understand that. I'm—we're just supposed to be learning how it operates."

He shook his head. "I seen this happen before. But never to me. I can make waves. Yes sir. Waves."

AC/DC's Brian Johnson screamed over the sound system, *You shook me all night long.*

"Look—whoever you are—"

"Bo."

Yeah you, shook me all night long.

"Look, Bo, please understand that I'm never going to run the ride by myself. I have a full time job." Well, selling security systems wasn't much of a job, but it was one hell of a lot better than being a carnie. Most of the time.

He paused, rubbing his right hand over his chin. The tail dropped like a ton of cement and once again the riders screamed, their shrieks and the music almost breaking my eardrums.

"You think you can just waltz in here and learn the ride in one morning?" This guy was pissed. "If Moe is thinking about replacing me, he'd better think real hard."

Taking a deep breath, I tried again. "Listen, Moe isn't thinking about replacing anyone, and no, I doubt if I'll ever figure it all out. But with your help—you and Charlie, I'll at least have an understanding of what it takes."

He eyed me cautiously. "It's not easy. Not easy at all, you understand?" Now the tail rose, whipping to the right, curling, then rising even higher.

"I'll bet it's not. What all is involved?"

He paused. "I shouldn't tell you."

"Just let me see the basics."

Pursing his lips, he stared back at the Dragon Tail. "Well, for starters you push this button." Motioning to a green button.

"Okay. Then what?"

"That starts it." He pointed to three large plastic buttons mounted on that gunmetal gray pedestal. Green, yellow, and red.

"The red stops it?"

"Yeah." He gave me a questioning look.

"And the yellow is?"

"The yellow is your panic button. If something goes wrong—say, have you done this before?"

He was serious. "No."

"Just that you knew the buttons and all."

"I was just guessing on the red button." Carnies.

He frowned. "You know it takes some trainin'. It's not like you can just come up and push the button. I'd have to show you precautions."

"Precautions?"

"Who are you, anyway?"

I was tired of people asking me that. "I already told you. My partner and I are just trying to get a feel for how the ride works."

He glanced up at the screaming riders as the tail snapped to the left.

"That's got to strain some necks and backs." It hurt just to watch the tail as it snapped back and forth.

"*This* takes care of *that*." Bo pushed the red button and the tail froze in midair. Gently swaying, it slowly came down, like a helicopter, gently floating to earth. As the cars softly landed on the ground, I saw the operator's eyes getting bigger and bigger as he stared over my shoulder.

I spun around and there was Moe Bradley.

"Hey, Skip. Kevin said you were over at the rifle booth."

That was quick.

Bradley put his arm around my shoulder and pulled me along as he walked away from the Dragon Tail.

"Everything okay?"

I was taken back. "Uh, yeah. I was a little confused when Kevin—"

"When Kevin what?"

"Well, when he accused me of being a spy. I mean—"

"Hey, hey, Kevin tends to be somewhat of a worrywart. He calls me daily with three or four concerns. They never amount to much. I don't know where he picked up this spy thing, but just ignore him, okay? Nobody knows anything. I'm keeping it quiet.

You and James, you do as I ask, and if you're successful, if you figure out who's trying to sabotage our show, I'll not only pay you what I offered—I'll bonus you. Okay? A bonus."

I nodded my head. He'd startled me and I wasn't sure how to respond.

"So, what do you say?"

I studied him for a moment, the silver hair combed straight back, the starched collar on his pale blue shirt, and the sharp crease in his gray slacks. Not the look I would have expected for a carnival operator.

"Let's just get back to the project at hand, okay?" He raised his eyebrows. "We got a deal?"

"Uh, yeah." And me, wondering why he was offering even more money. Wondering why he was hiring two wet-behind-the-ears private detectives to help save his show. But hey, I needed the money. Don't look a gift horse in the mouth. Whatever that meant.

He removed his arm from around my neck and walked toward his trailer. And as he walked away I still wondered where Kevin Cross had heard I was a spy.

Winston's zoo was crowded, youngsters and parents wandering around the dusty ring, clutching handfuls of the pressed food pellets, gingerly holding out their palms as the donkey, the goat, the pig, and assorted other animals sucked up the food, several taking nips at the children's hands.

"Hey, Linda." I shouted, and she briefly raised her head.

"Skip." Glancing up briefly as she kept her main focus on the small children and the animals.

"I'd come in, but it's five bucks a head."

"It is."

She made no effort to cut me some slack. I thought maybe there was a carnie discount, but apparently not. The big sheepdog approached the fence, pausing as kids petted his thick coat. When he got close to me, he gave a deep growl. The kids were all right. I wasn't.

I hung around for five minutes, thinking maybe Winston would appear and I could make amends, but he never showed up and Linda ignored me the rest of the time.

Dust from the animal ring rose around me and with my tongue I could feel the grit on my teeth. My partner had deserted me, and I had no idea what or who I was looking for.

Wandering back to the trailer I watched blue, red, orange, and yellow lights flashing in the dusk. The Tilt-a-Whirl with its spinning white lights threw long shadows on the ground, and the cacophony of clashing, crashing music and screams came from everywhere, congregating inside my head.

One more beer, then I was going to pass out and worry about all of this in the morning. Trying to get a grip on what exactly we were to do was impossible. I needed to talk to James and tell him what had happened tonight, but apparently he and Angie had other plans. I was afraid this was going to cost me my paycheck and my bonus.

Popping the beer cap, I put the bottle of Yuengling to my lips, sipping the bitter brown liquid and washing the dust from my mouth.

Sounds from the show drifted in and out, and as the light faded, I heard footsteps outside the trailer. I kept expecting James to walk in. I was anxious to talk to him about the strange encounters I'd had.

The first beer went down smoothly and I opened a second, listening to the sound of someone or someones outside the trailer. There was a crunch, like a person's footsteps on the gravel where the trailer sat. A muffled cough right outside I thought.

Twice I opened the door and once walked into the dusk to

see if someone was there. There was this eerie feeling in the air, like someone was out there, listening. I'd already had threats from some of the carnies. I wasn't sure I could trust anyone. Then I dozed off in the middle of the second beer.

When I heard steps on the wooden landing my eyes snapped open. It was dark outside and the raucous carnival sounds had subsided. It must be after nine. Finally a chance to run the day's events and frustrations by James. The sharp rapping on the door surprised me.

"James?"

"It's Winston."

It took me a second. Winston Pugh. I stood up and opened the door.

"James isn't it?"

"No. No. It's Skip. Come on in."

The little guy still had his overalls on, no shirt, and I could detect the odor of animals. Maybe it was Winston's sweat. Hard to tell.

"You're a cop, right?" He worked his jaw, chewing hard.

"What?"

"You're a cop."

"No."

"I was told you were." He stared at me accusingly. The little guy was breathing hard, his jaws working furiously on a wad of tobacco.

"It's not true." What I was was pissed. I wasn't a cop. I wasn't a spy. At this point I wasn't exactly sure what I was.

"Then what the hell are you?" He looked up at me, and in the dim light from our trailer I could see sweat on his forehead.

"I've been through this with you before."

"Yeah, yeah, you're the marketing manager's friend. I remember. And your first question to me is about the accidents that have been happening at the show? About somebody who was thrown from a ride and was killed. Not the type of question a bystander casually asks, is it?"

In the dim light I saw him roll his beady eyes.

"People here, they don't like busybodies. People who are lookin' into other people's business. But listen, boy, I don't care who or what you are. The point is, I need you to come with me. Right now." He spun around and marched down the three wooden steps. "Well?" He looked over his shoulder. "Are you coming or not?"

I squinted into the darkness and hesitatingly followed the short man. I thought about leaving a note for James, but he'd probably never show up to read it.

We headed across the lot, past the now quiet and dark rides and booths. The Bar-B-Que Pit was shut tight, the painted pig on the side leering at me. In the distance I could see lights shining softly in Moe's showplace trailer. And someone was walking with a flashlight on the show grounds. The light bobbed in the distance.

"Where are we going?"

"You'll see. You'll see." The determined guy walked faster, his short legs moving like pistons, heading toward the air rifle trailer. I heard him spit tobacco in the dirt as he walked.

And then it hit me. I knew where we were going and I really didn't want to see the skinny guy again.

"Winston, hold on. Are we going to see Kevin Cross?"

He stopped abruptly, turning and planting his floppy rubber boots in the dirt. "You remember I told you that there are no neighbors here?"

"I remember."

"Well, the closest to any friend I have is Kevin Cross. And Kevin's got a story to tell. You seem to be the likely person to tell it to."

I only wanted to go back to my trailer. I only wanted to go back to my apartment, and forget this thing had ever happened.

"I met Kevin Cross already. I don't think he wants to see me again."

"Linda says he's got a story to tell you. Just listen, okay?"

"What kind of a story?"

Two men walked by, puffing on cigarettes, heads down, talking in muted tones. They moved on toward a distant row of four trailers, the pungent odor of smoke trailing behind them.

"I don't know exactly. He's got some information on what you referred to as the accidents."

"And he hasn't shared this with you?"

"After Kevin's talk with you tonight, he said he had some things he wanted to come clean about. He called Linda."

"Your Linda?"

"Yes, whose Linda did you think it was? Do you and I have another Linda in common?"

He had me there.

"Cross told Linda that he had a pretty good idea of who was behind the accidents. She said he sounded almost sinister about it."

"So why am I going along?"

"Linda said he wanted to see you, and he asked me to be there." Pugh stood there, chewing on his plug. "Is that okay with you?"

I hesitated. "The guy practically threatened me, Winston."

"He did?" Pugh looked back at me. "Probably just looking out for your best interest."

"I don't know that anyone is looking out for my best interest. You were the one who told me there are no friends here."

"Just see him, okay. Linda says he wants to talk."

"Yeah. Well, I'm surprised." Cross had grilled me. Let me know that he didn't trust me. So why the hell was he asking to see me now? "You didn't talk to him?"

Exasperated, he spit on the ground. "Linda did. Okay? She's

my business manager. Kind of takes all my calls and stuff like that. He told her he wanted to see us. Now let's go."

The trailer was closed, a metal shutter pulled down over the opening. I wondered if I could shoot the center out of that target in the dark. I certainly had never been able to do it in the daytime.

"Kevin." Pugh shouted his name.

The night was eerily quiet, a stark contrast to the earlier noise and activity.

He called out again. "Cross, it's me, Winston."

"Maybe he went out to dinner or something."

"Nah. I told you, he talked to Linda. Said he'd be here tonight. He lives behind the trailer."

There was a stillness in the stale night air, and I was aware of the musty odor of moist bare earth. Dew was settling the fine dust that covered the ground at the show.

"Kevin likes to drink. Probably had a couple back there."

"Maybe you should check back with Linda. Maybe you got the information wrong."

"She's out tonight. Left a couple of hours ago." The little guy spit. "Oh, he's here. I'll find him."

We walked around the trailer and there was a minicamper covered in pale green and white vinyl siding. Pugh stepped up on the landing and pounded on the door.

"Cross, damn it. Open up."

Nothing. He pounded again. There was no sign of life.

"Might have passed out." He turned and looked up at me. "Been known to happen with him before."

Pulling open the squeaky door, he stuck his head in. "Kevin!"

"Winston, he's not here." I just wanted to go back to the trailer. Or jump in the car and drive three miles to my dingy little apartment. I wanted to be anywhere but here at the Moe Show.

The little guy walked in. I stood outside and heard a lone bird singing in a nearby tree.

Thirty seconds later he hadn't emerged. I decided to give him another thirty and I was gone. This was too creepy.

Some night animal made a croaking sound, and I could hear the hoot of an owl in the distance. The faint odor of frangipani hung still in the air, and I took a deep breath, trying to remember where I'd smelled the fragrance recently.

Thirty seconds later Pugh walked out. He trudged down the steps and looked up at me with a frown.

"He's in there. Kevin's in there."

"Is he coming out? He's going to tell me his story?"

"Nope. Somebody shot him. Kevin's dead."

CHAPTER ELEVEN

"Are they going to shut it down?" Along with a group of twenty-five or thirty people, James was staring at the green and white minicamper, his arm around Angie Clark's shoulders. I saw her shiver in the early morning air. Apparently the noise of the sirens had disturbed the happy couple as the cruisers descended on our little show. It was just too bad that my best friend had his evening ruined by the sirens. Poor James. Poor Agent Hot Pants.

"Shut what down?"

"The show?"

"Well, James, they haven't asked my permission at this point."

He removed his arm from Angie's shoulder and pointed at me. "Hey, hey, pardner. A little sarcasm there?"

"If you had a clue as to what's been going on this after-noon—this evening—"

James frowned and turned away.

"You're one of the guys who found the body?" The dead guy reminded me of my father, the last time I ever saw him. The beginning of a beer gut, a cheap-cut sport coat that was about half a size too small, and a bald spot on the top of his head.

"I was here when Winston found him."

"So you saw the deceased's body." It wasn't a question, it was a statement.

"I did." Sitting on the toilet, pants at half-mast, and a hole above his right eye. A Rorschach pattern of blood spattered behind him, and gray and yellow globs of brain-matter stuck to the cheap vinyl wall. I'd seen him. Someone had hit the target. Bull's-eye.

"Now you and Mister Pugh, you both discovered this body at the same time?"

James stood to the side, his eyes going from the detective to me, like he was watching a tennis match.

"No. I mean, Winston, Mr. Pugh went in, found Kevin's body," I shuddered. It wasn't pretty. "Then he asked me to go in with him. And I saw—"

Two men in white carried the stretcher from the camper, the assembled crowd parted, and they slid it into the back of the ambulance. Rotating red and blue lights from two cop cars colored the scene in an eerie purple hue as the detective jotted down notes on a handheld pad.

"I'll have some more questions. Are you staying here? On the grounds?"

I pointed to the Airstream. "Tonight."

"You think of anything, you let me know." The detective handed me a business card. Detective Bob Stanton.

"I'll definitely do that."

"We're going to interview anyone who's still on the grounds, so I'll be around for a while." He eyed James and Angie. "You two hear or see anything?"

James shook his head. "We were both asleep."

"You vouch for each other?"

"We do." Angie nodded and hooked her arm around James's. Almost too much.

"Yeah. I was out like a light. And Angie must have joined me within minutes." James smiled at her.

"Yeah. Well—" Closing the notepad, he shoved the pen in his jacket pocket and started walking away. Over his shoulder he said, "Lock your doors."

"That's comforting." Angie visibly shivered, and James seemed to hug her tighter.

"How about if I stay the night? It might feel safer."

She gave him a slight smile. "I think you *were* spending the night."

"Oh, yeah." He looked at me, then back to Angie. "Listen, I really need to talk to Skip for a little while. Why don't you go back to the trailer, and Skip and I will sit outside on those two lawn chairs. I'll be in shortly."

She nodded. "I'm a big girl, James. I can stay by myself."

He smiled. "You know, I wasn't worried about your protection."

"Oh?"

"I'm worried about mine."

CHAPTER TWELVE

They didn't shut it down. In fact, other than the buzz of carnies over their cardboard cups of hot steaming coffee, the next morning seemed uneventful. Of course I've never seen a carnival this early in the morning, but everything seemed low-key, aside from the yellow crime-scene tape in back of the air rifle trailer.

James was outside Angie's trailer, drinking *his* coffee from a china cup. There was a smug, self-satisfied look on his face.

"She made me breakfast, amigo, and some coffee. Pretty sweet. Want me to get some for you?"

I shook my head. My stomach was already in knots.

"From what you told me last night, this should be a piece of cake. Three buttons and that's all we have to know. Am I right?"

I nodded. "Listen, James, this Bo and Charlie, they seem to take a lot of pride in operating the ride, so don't make light of it, okay? I don't think we need to piss these two guys off."

"Hey, you know me."

That was the problem. I did.

We walked toward the DT, James sipping his steaming beverage. "So, we're now on a bonus, plus our guarantee? He keeps throwing money at this thing. Boy, Moe really wants us to solve this doesn't he?"

I'd explained everything until three in the morning when he'd finally gone back into Angie's trailer and I'd stumbled back to the Airstream.

"This guy was in a rush to make sure we didn't bolt, James. It's the only explanation I can come up with. I mean, he was practically begging me not to leave. It's like I told you last night, I don't understand why. It doesn't make any sense. We're not the team I'd choose for this project, believe me."

"Skip, it's good money. First day we get licensed we get a job. Why can't you just accept that?"

"Yeah, you're right." Always the optimist. I guess we balanced each other pretty well that way.

"So, let's make a plan, do our job, and make the money. It's not that difficult, Pancho."

"I called Jody this morning."

"Jody?"

"Yeah. Jody Stacy. Our private investigator friend. You remember. We supposedly used to work for him?"

"Oh. That Jody."

I'd actually gotten him out of bed at about seven a.m. He'd been a little groggy, something about surveillance until the early morning hours on some cheating wife. No murdered carnies, just a wayward spouse.

"You woke him up this early?" Early to James was any time before ten a.m.

"Jody is a pro, James. He's been doing this for how many years now? And he's the reason you and I are in the P.I. business. Am I right?"

James glanced at me as we marched toward the Dragon. "You're right, amigo. He's a pro and he's the reason. So what?"

"Do you know what he charges?"

"For a job like this? I have no idea."

"A hundred twenty-five dollars an hour, James. And if you buy a block of ten hours he'll bring it down to a thousand. A hundred dollars an hour. You can get a pro, someone who actually knows what they're doing, for a thousand."

"And your point is?" We were approaching the Dragon Tail and I saw Bo and Charlie, cigarettes dangling from their mouths, rags in hand wiping the morning's dew off the seats, dropping ashes back onto the seats.

"James, pay attention." He knew what the point was. He just didn't want to admit it. "If you can get a pro to come in here and investigate this case for a thousand, why would anyone pay the two of us two thousand plus a bonus?"

The two operators saw us at the same time, and I caught the hostile frowns on their faces.

Stepping up to the guardrail, I waved. "Bo, Charlie, this is James."

They glared at us.

"Hey, Bo, like I told you yesterday, we're just here to learn a little bit about the rides and the show. We're not here to take any full-time jobs."

"Uh-huh." Charlie took the cigarette out of his mouth and blew a stream of smoke in my direction. His physical resemblance to James was uncanny. "You actually going to operate the ride?" He glanced back at the evil looking Dragon, green and yellow fiberglass and steel, the tail poised to toss riders around like a hurricane.

"We're just doing it for a couple of hours."

Bo raised his eyebrows. "That's all?"

"That's all."

"But you are gonna learn all there is to operate it. Operate it at any time, right? So you could run the DT full time?"

"Guys, we are really excited to be here. To see how two professionals do this." James raised his cup of coffee as if giving a toast. "Moe said you were his top ride guys and we want to learn from the best."

Charlie stroked his chin. Now that James was standing right next to him the resemblance wasn't quite as—

"Moe said that? That we were his top ride guys? Me and Bo?" He glanced at his cohort.

"He did."

"Well, I would hope so. After all—" Charlie glanced at his partner, a sly smile on his face.

"Moe should say that," Bo said.

"Well, boys," Charlie glanced at his watch, "come on in here and let's get started. It's eight o'clock and our ride starts at ten so we've only got a couple of hours to show you two the ropes. Let's go. Time's a wastin'."

And just like that, James was Charlie's new best friend. Bo, standing by the controls, a scowl still on his face, didn't seem quite so sure.

By five after eight we'd pretty much mastered the ride. Safety bar the rider, click the lock, push the green button. Two minutes later, push the red button, unclick the lock, unsafety bar the rider. And remember that the small metal switch activated the smoke from the dragon's mouth. Talk about complicated.

"You all should probably take a spin so you'll know what it feels like. Charlie and I had to ride it a couple of times."

James gave Bo a weak smile. "Nah, that's not part of the deal. All we need to do is operate it for a couple rides."

"No, you need to ride the tail, Jim." Bo wasn't making any points. James hated the name *Jim*.

"Don't need to."

"Well, Jim, if you're gonna run this ride, then you're gonna ride the tail. Let me call Moe in on this."

"You do that."

He didn't need to. I could see the head guy walking toward us, his impeccable tan jacket and slacks set off by a pair of brown tooled cowboy boots.

"Hey boys, have Bo and Charlie got you up to speed?"

"We're up to speed, Moe." James smiled at him, reaching out and shaking his hand. "And now, Skip and I are going to get some breakfast before the first riders get here."

"They don't seem keen on riding the tail, Moe." Bo frowned, a concerned look on his lean face.

"Oh?" Bradley looked accusingly at James.

"I don't think that's necessary, Moe. We learned how to operate the ride, and I don't see any reason—"

"It is necessary, James. Skip. I want you to have a feel for what this is all about."

I stared once again at the monstrosity that was the DT. Bo flipped the switch that caused smoke to belch from the monster's mouth, and for just a moment, I felt that the creature's red glowing eyes were watching me.

"Moe—"

"No, James, you've got to ride it once. It's part of the job."

James bit his upper lip, I chewed on my lower one. This was not something either of us had anticipated.

"Well, I'm happier than a tornado in a trailer park." James stared at me, daring me to remember that one.

It took a moment to digest the quote. Mater, from the Pixar animated movie *Cars*. And that was probably what we were about to experience. The feeling of being right in the middle of a tornado in a trailer park.

Bo flashed a bold smile, leering at me. "We'll just give you half a ride. How's that? Just half a regular spin on the tail."

A regular ride was two minutes. Have you ever counted slowly to 120? It's longer than forever. And counting slowly to sixty takes forever. Especially when you've seen the tail do its thing.

"You boys enjoy the ride. It will open your eyes." Moe gave us an engaging smile. "Me, I'm having breakfast with my sisters at Denny's. It's a toss-up as to who will endure more torture. You or me." He winked at us and walked away.

"We're screwed, Skip." James stared at the cars on the tail.

"We are, James. We really are."

CHAPTER THIRTEEN

James motioned to me to go first and I did. I walked back to a car about midway on the tail and stepped in. Each car, or pod, held three people comfortably on the cold, hard plastic seats. Four people if you squeezed them in. I saw our potential number three walking toward us the second I sat down.

"James. You two are going for a ride? You didn't tell me." Angie Clark had a surprised smile on her face as she headed toward us, the early morning sunlight bouncing off her long golden hair.

"It's a test run for us." It was obvious he didn't want the company. "Just, you know . . ." he was stumbling, looking for a reason not to invite her, ". . . for the two of us." James avoided looking at her.

She glanced at me and put her hands out, palms up in supplication. "Hey," shifting her gaze to Mr. Romance, "you promised me a ride. Remember?" She stopped short of the car, a little pout on her full lips. She wore a pair of shorts and a halter top that showed off her figure. Very well I might add.

Bo gave James a slight push, and he moved in beside me. "Bo, can I ride?"

The carnie leered at her. "Anything for you, Miss Clark."

She walked back to the car and gazed down at my roommate. "I'm going for a ride, James. I promise I won't be a problem." She scooted in, and I inhaled the faint odor of her perfume. I could tell James was far from happy.

Pulling down the safety bar, Bo clicked the lock and walked away as James grasped the thick metal rod, his knuckles almost white.

From seemingly nowhere, the sound of Poison jump-started the speakers, the voices shouting out *Ain't nothin' but a good time.*

"Don't be too stiff, James." She raised her voice to be heard over the music, rubbing her leg against his, giving him a sly smile. "These rides have a tremendous g-force." She was shouting. "If you're too stiff, you could injure your neck or spine. Or something else."

James usually had a snappy comeback for a soft-ball comment like this. But he swallowed hard and had no response at all. And neither did I. We both just kept our eyes straight ahead as we felt the tail start to rise in the air, and from the corner of my eye I saw Angie put her hand over his.

"This is going to be fun. Just relax."

Fun and relax were words I was not familiar with at the moment.

I spent my money on women and wine—the music was pounding in my head.

Higher and higher. I'd closed my eyes, but when I squinted I could see Pugh's little zoo and the animals feeding from two troughs. Winston and Linda were down there, puttering around the fenced-in area. The top of the rifle booth and Kevin Cross's trailer were off to the right, and in the distance I could see

Bradley's American Eagle trailer and our Airstream. I shuddered, thinking of Cross's dead body on the toilet. Never mind he was a carnie, it was not the way I'd want to end my life.

A black-and-white cruiser slowly circled the show grounds, and I wondered if they were looking for clues.

Higher, the tail gently rose, and if you didn't look straight down, it wasn't too bad. I could gaze out and see the strip of shops, The Bauble Brigade, Baby Bonanza, and Fabulous Fabric. I secretly wished we were all three in Harry's Hideaway, having an early morning boilermaker.

Beyond the strip I could see the road. Slowly, steadily we rose in the air, and I glanced off to the left and saw the Dragon's head and the beady red eyes. Steam was pouring from his nose and mouth and I laughed out loud.

"James, look."

But his eyes were shut tight. Angie was squeezing his hand and there was a ruddy glow on her face. A thrill junkie.

I'd almost forgotten about the snap, the whip to the left. I was lost in the lofty view of the land below. That dusty, dirty ground that sprawled beneath us and the people walking below as they went about their set-up chores for the amusement rides. And then the cart lurched, along with my stomach. I squeezed hard enough to crush the safety bar, accidentally squeezing James's hand.

"Holly shit." He grunted out the words, and Angie screamed, that excited girly kind of scream that you hear in the movies when a girl is feigning fear or terror. And the tail whipped to the left.

Ain't nothin', but a good time.

I couldn't breathe. I tried and found myself choking, my throat closed tight. The small car jerked again, a short, abrupt move, and my back felt like it would snap. We flew at lightning speed, the tail sailing through the air. I knew the rest of the routine. Straightening out, the tail curled and suddenly whipped to the right, moving at an incredible velocity and I closed my eyes, summoning up every childhood prayer I could remember. We were flying, shooting out above the grounds below, a hot early morning breeze stinging my face and I thought for sure the pod was going to spin off the tail and we'd be hurled into deep outer space.

Angie screamed again, her silky blonde hair flying back against the seat. James muttered, "Holy Shit," and I still hadn't drawn a breath. Couldn't. Daring to open my eyes, I saw Bo and Charlie, sitting on a small bench far below, smoking cigarettes and looking up at us. I swear they were smiling, a devilish wide-eyed glare on their pasty faces.

"It's done, right?" James coughed out the words. "Half a ride? Please. Say it's done." He wasn't opening his eyes, but he was ready for this torture to end. I had a fleeting thought that he was sorry he'd ever taken this job. I knew I was. Every time I get involved with one of James Lessor's projects—

Opening my mouth, my chest aching from lack of oxygen, I finally caught some air. "Should be." Oh, God, let it be over. I promised right then and there I'd stop drinking, watching porn on the Internet with James, and I'd find a church. Somewhere. Whatever it took.

The tail straightened out, and then I remembered the deadly drop we'd witnessed every time the tail settled to the earth. Screaming in anticipation, Angie shattered my eardrum as our pod plummeted to the ground. It had to be moving at two hundred, five hundred miles per hour, and I felt my chest caving in, with absolutely no room for oxygen. In just a second this would all be history. I couldn't last more than that.

When we were about one inch from the ground (I exaggerate), the brakes slammed on and I felt this huge sense of relief. We went from 499 miles per hour to zero miles per hour in a matter of seconds, and I believe we all three breathed a sigh of relief. I know I did.

Opening my eyes wide I saw Bo and Charlie still sitting there. Still smoking their cigarettes. Smiling at us. And it hit me. No one was pushing the red button. The button that would stop this infernal machine.

"Bo." I screamed at the bench, trying to be heard above the raucous AC/DC music now playing. Brian Johnson screaming *You shook me all night long.* "Bo, you said half a ride. Push the button. Push the damned button."

The son of a bitch sat there and smiled at me as the tail slowly rose in the air and straightened out, then whipped to the left. My body slammed into James's and I thought I was going to lose everything in my stomach.

"Bo, you son of a bitch, turn it off," my shrieking having no effect on the smiling duo below.

"Ohhhhhhhhhhhhh shit."

James wasn't dealing with this well. Angie screamed that high-pitched girlish wail, and I gripped the bar as tight as possible. This was going to be a long morning.

The tail snapped to the right and we were flung the other way like rag dolls, our limbs out of control. Hurled against each other, fingers frozen to the bar.

I wondered if this was reason enough to back out on all my promises. The drinking, the porn—

And then, as we plummeted toward the ground, sure to crash and be buried in the sandy, barren soil, Angie Clark lifted her hands in the air. Screaming at the top of her lungs, the crazy lady raised her hands high above her head, proving she had no fear, and no sense.

I closed my eyes, scrunching up my forehead, and waited for the brakes. As we slowed, I opened them again and saw Charlie by the buttons. I knew I would be eternally grateful.

I took a deep breath, my chest aching. James didn't open his eyes as the pod settled softly down on the platform.

Everything was peaceful for a moment, except for the raucous music. Charlie strolled back, a smirk on his face as he flipped the lock on the bar.

James sat frozen as Angie lifted the unlocked bar and scooted out of her seat.

Bo was now standing at the button station, hunched in deep conversation with a third party. I knew who it was. The woman and Bo both straightened up, and she shot me an evil glance, stalking off.

James had finally opened his eyes looking white as a clean sheet. Shaking his head, he stared at the lady. From the look of his face I thought he was just like I was about two minutes ago. About to lose the contents of his stomach. But he took a deep breath and swallowed. I saw some color return to his cheeks and he shook his head again, trying to clear the fog.

"Skip, who the hell was that?"

I stared after her as she headed across the grounds, puffs of dust clouds rising from her shoes.

"Did we do something to piss her off?"

I wasn't sure. "That's Linda Reilly. She's Winston Pugh's girlfriend. I told you about her last night."

Angie was running up the platform, grabbing Bo and giving him a great big hug. "What a great ride, Bo. Thanks for letting me go."

James shook his head again, obviously not sharing her unbridled enthusiasm. "Thought we were gonna die."

I'd had similar thoughts.

Angie turned to us with a big grin. "Anybody want to go again?"

Turning from her, my roommate watched Linda Reilly's vanishing form. "Dude, that lady—"

"Yeah?"

"She was seriously mad at somebody."

"Looked like it."

James shivered, took a deep breath, and slowly eased himself out of the seat. "Looked like she was seriously mad at you."

CHAPTER FOURTEEN

Detective Bob Stanton was back with a couple of uniformed police officers and we could hear them peppering the show's employees with questions about the night before.

"Did you see anything suspicious?" "Where were you between the hours of—" "How long have you been employed by Moe Bradley?" "Did you know the deceased?" "Did you have any close relationship with the deceased?" "Did you have any issues with the deceased?" And on and on and on and on. No one admitted to anything as far as I could tell.

They finished their questioning before the show's opening, and I watched as Stanton grabbed a uniformed officer by the arm and marched off to Winston Pugh Charlemagne's fenced-in domain. I wondered what new questions they would ask the little man. Or were they questioning Linda? Winston had found the body. I'd been second. But so far, all I'd had were a couple of vague questions.

To be honest with them, I'd mentioned that the entire evening was a blur. Pugh had pulled me out of the trailer in the middle of an alcohol-induced sleep, and I'll never forget seeing the bloodied corpse hunched over on the toilet, lifeless and stone cold.

Moe Bradley, some guy with thin, wispy white hair, and Bradley's two sisters, the team of Schiller and Crouse, watched anxiously, sitting in a black Cadillac Escalade, hoping any signs of the police were gone by the time the show opened up at ten.

I wondered how this would affect the attendance. Some people would stay away out of fear. Some people would show up to see where the murder took place. Some people would try to go right into the trailer and see the bloodstains. We live in a very sick society.

"Brother," James looked at me and brushed his hair from his face with his right hand. "I drink now and then because—" He paused. We were sitting outside the Airstream on two cheap webbed lawn chairs, and my roommate still seemed pretty shook up. The ride had obviously had a lasting effect on him.

"Because?" I've always wanted to know James's excuse for drinking. "What's the reason, James?"

"Well, I don't know." He was genuinely frustrated. "I don't usually open a sentence like that. How the hell do I know why I drink? I never really analyzed the act before. Never really thought about it. But the point is this. Right now, I need a drink. *Need* a drink. I usually don't need one, but I *need* one now."

I don't think I ever drank because I needed to. Wanted to, yes. Needed?

"I believe there's a beer in the fridge." It was my beer, and it wasn't a good idea, but I offered. I was glad when he didn't take me up on it.

"No, you're not listening to me. I just went through hell and I need a *drink*. A real drink, Skip."

I nodded. "Yeah, a drink would be good right now. And there's Harry's Hideaway right up there on the strip. That's pretty tempting, isn't it? They've been open since six a.m., and we've got forty minutes till the Moe Show opens for the rides."

"You're reading my mind, compadre."

"One thing is wrong with this, James."

"What? We've just been through one of the most harrowing experiences in our lives and—"

"James. We've got to operate the Tail this morning."

"Operating the Dragon Tail consists of pushing two buttons, Skip." He was on his feet holding two fingers in front of my face. "Two. We just have to push two buttons. A third if there's an emergency." He stared at me. "Okay. Another one for the smoke. But it's a total of four, count 'em, four buttons. Come on, amigo. We can do that in our sleep. Don't push *my* buttons, okay?" I saw the excitement in his eyes. "Let's go. Harry's is calling."

I eased myself out of the chair. "James. If there's an accident, if someone is injured, or killed, and we've had a drink, even a beer—" I let the sentence hang. He had to understand.

"Damn."

He stared at me, squinting with a frown. Hell, someone had to be the professional, someone had to be the grownup, and it obviously wasn't going to be James. We were on our first P.I. mission, and this wasn't a time to screw it up.

"You're right," he said. "I hate that about you."

"Maybe we drink too much, anyway." I shrugged my shoulders.

He stood there, stretching and looking over the grounds. Finally, "Fat, drunk, and stupid is no way to go through life, son."

There was no hesitation on my part. "Actor John Vernon who played Dean Wormer said it to John Belushi in *National Lampoon's Animal House.*"

James usually used more esoteric quotes. But this one I knew I'd nailed. I'd seen the movie about twenty times. And

Dean Wormer was right. Belushi had proved himself fat, drunk, and stupid. And then he died.

"Easy one, pard. But it was apropos."

And he was right. It was apropos.

"After that ride, do you think you've got the hang of it, Jim?"

James scowled at Charlie. There were no more words between them.

We operated the Dragon Tail ride till noon. Bo and Charlie strolled over to Harry's Hideaway at 10:01, and from a distance we watched them slap each other on the back as they walked in. James gave me a dirty look. I stood by what I believed. It just wasn't a good idea to drink, then try to run a show ride.

Those two didn't seem to care at all that they could later be impaired with their alcoholic intake. And maybe, just maybe, that was part of the problem. After my short trip to Winston's trailer where the tequila shots were plentiful, after the visit to Moe's American Eagle, where mimosas ruled the morning, after hearing Pugh tell me that Kevin Cross drank to excess, and seeing Bo and Charlie head off to Harry's, I figured that this Moe Show was fueled on champagne and grain and cactus alcohol. A wicked combination.

But other than the occasional accidents, the death of a customer, and the shooting of a guy who ran the rifle booth, maybe that didn't mean much. These were carnies. Carnies, for God's sake. I *expected* them to act in an irrational manner.

"Get me a rag and disinfectant, Skip. Damn."

We'd just emptied our fourth group of riders from the Tail, and for the second time James had found urine on a hard plastic seat. I told him from the beginning, I wasn't going to clean it up. It was his business, and I reminded him that I was just along for the ride. If these people had the piss scared out of them, that was his problem. I just kept thanking God that I didn't have to ride this beast again.

He wiped and sprayed, and cursed the whole time. Two hours of this work was wearing on both of us. A mother screamed at us about allowing her thirteen-year-old daughter to ride the Tail. The girl had gotten dizzy and vomited as soon as she exited the perimeter. Another job for James.

Of course Mom hadn't even missed the teenager for thirty minutes. And then an elderly couple claimed that the man had suffered a severe stroke while on the ride and they wanted to know who to sue. The guy took meticulous notes while I pointed out Moe Bradley's trailer.

Two women who professed to be married lesbians threatened us with a sexual harassment suit because we wouldn't allow their fourteen-month-old baby on the ride, and a group of eighth graders from Delray attempted to take thirty water balloons onto the Tail. Of course we denied the request. I could just imagine thirty water balloons reining down on the unsuspecting people below as these cocky middle schoolers laughed it up above the masses. And the worst thing was they were young kids and could all probably withstand the crazy tail gyrations.

As the sun soared high in the heavens, we kept glancing at our watches, the minutes slowly approaching noon. There was no sign of our replacements. Charlie and Bo appeared to have disappeared into Harry's Hideaway, and we wondered if they'd ever come out.

"Son, it appears we may be at our post a little longer than anticipated."

I glanced at the strip mall, peering through a steady stream of customers. No sign of our full-time operators.

"So what are our options?"

I looked again. Nothing.

"Skip?"

"*Our* options?"

"Amigo, you stand to make a couple of bucks on this project. Correct me if I'm wrong."

I glanced at my cheap Timex. We had one minute left on our shift. "I've about had it with the Tail, James."

I had a college degree, for God's sake. This wasn't what I'd signed on to do. Operating a carnival ride? It was like flipping hamburgers, or emptying bedpans at a nursing home. Pushing buttons at an amusement park was not a job for me. These were jobs for people who—people who had fortitude. Stamina. People who were a whole lot braver than I was. Thank God for people who could do those jobs. I wanted to hide behind a desk, never ride a Dragon Tail again, and make two or three hundred thousand dollars a year.

People who flipped burgers, emptied bedpans, ran rides? They were the backbone of our country.

"Compadre, we can't just walk away from this." He glanced out at the line starting to form for the next ride. There were probably forty people, and we'd see another forty before it was over.

"No, *you* can't walk away from it. It's your training program, James. Me? I'm just here for the—" and I finally got the joke, "the ride."

Charlie and Bo stepped behind the railing, from where I do not know. Walking up to me, Bo stood two inches from my face. "Thanks for taking over, guys. Maybe you appreciate the Tail a little more now?"

There wasn't a trace of alcohol on his breath.

"We do. We really do. Boy, do we appreciate what you go through." James was almost sobbing.

Charlie pulled a rag from the stand that housed the four buttons. He ran it over the red, yellow, and green switches. Heaven forbid he would get any of our germs on his fingers.

"So you guys are private investigators, eh?"

I glanced at James and just shook my head. This was getting old.

"I'm the damned marketing director for this operation. That's all there is to it." James folded his arms across his chest.

"Well, if that's what you want us to believe."

Charlie took up his position behind the buttons. "We'll take over now."

"And by the way," Bo stepped back and eyed the Tail with the eye of a trained surveyor, "did anyone piss their pants? Should have warned you guys about that." He chuckled and joined his partner at the button station.

CHAPTER FIFTEEN

An older gentleman with wispy white hair walked into Harry's Hideaway, wearing a dark jacket and trousers and black T-shirt. I thought for a moment he was a priest by the way he was dressed, the way he held himself. I know, it sounds like a joke. *This priest walks into a bar*, but it was far from a joke.

He surveyed the thin crowd, then made eye contact with me at the end of the bar. I thought I might know him, but I didn't know from where.

Keeping an eye on the man, I nudged my partner with my elbow. "Who's that guy, James?"

He looked up from his beer, studying the elderly man. Giving it about ten seconds, he said, "Not sure. Maybe I saw him with Moe's sisters, earlier today. Yeah. That's it. But," he paused, staring at the guy, "I have no idea who he is."

As the man walked down the bar toward us, I felt like making a quick trip to the restroom. He was ramrod straight, his teeth were clenched, and it was obvious he was on a mission. And I wasn't in the mood for any confrontation today. Or any other day. He reached us before I had a chance to make my getaway.

Grabbing the barstool next to me, he hoisted himself on it and stared into my eyes.

"You two are the private detectives?"

Damn. I swear, everyone in town knew who we were.

James raised his hand. "Excuse me. I'm the marketing director for the Show." Taking a sip of beer, he gave the man a cautious look.

Turning to me, he asked, "So *you're* the P.I. then. Am I right?"

"What is this all about? I'm James's friend, and all he's doing is—"

"Yeah, yeah. You're the two."

"And who are you?"

"I'm Ken Clemens."

The name meant nothing to me.

James nodded. "And what does Ken Clemens want with us?"

"There're a couple things you need to know." The man raised his arm and signaled to the hefty girl behind the bar. "Draft. Whatever is cheap."

"You'd be surprised at all the things we need to know." I took a long swallow of my cold Yuengling and slapped the mug back on the bar. "What are you going to teach us today?"

"First of all, Judy Schiller is my . . ." he hesitated, "my girlfriend. Do you know who she is?"

I nodded. It didn't sound right. A man and woman at that age calling each other boyfriend and girlfriend.

"And?"

"She's the reason you two are working here."

Judy Schiller was Moe Bradley's sister. I had no clue how she was responsible for James and me having a job. I didn't even know the lady.

James glanced up at the TV over the bar above his head. The broadcast was a classic baseball game from several years ago. "I thought we had this job because Angie Clark decided that I was the most creative applicant in the group." He paused. "Was I wrong?"

The stoic bartender shoved a full beer mug in front of Clemens and moved down the bar, wiping at imaginary spots on her vinyl countertop.

"No, Angie is why you have the *marketing* job. I'm speaking of the *P.I.* job." He stared at James with an evil glare in his eyes. "You do know what a P.I. is, right? Do you even know what they do? Because I have this impression that you boys are brand-new to this line of work."

Taking another long swallow, I waited for James. It was the perfect opening for one of his witty comments. Instead he kept his eyes on the ballgame—the Marlins two and the Indians nothing, bottom of the sixth. I sensed he was seething.

"Look, Mr. Clemens, even if we were working a second job for Moe Bradley, we probably couldn't admit it." I met his gaze. The old guy stared right through me. Very confident, very composed.

"Let me lay it out for you." He pushed the beer mug to arm's length and took a deep breath. "You know there have been some serious accidents at this show. I would think you would have studied every one of them, being professional private investigators." He shot it at me with disdain. Folding his arms over his chest, he glared at us. "You do know about the accidents?"

"We're aware of the accidents. And the death."

"Are you more than aware? Have you studied these accidents?"

It hit me that we knew very little about any of the accidents. Except the short newspaper article I sort of remembered, and that Moe told us there had been several incidents and someone had died. The truth was, we hadn't done any research at all. None.

We were probably in the wrong line of work here.

"Judy and Virginia have been very concerned about the future of this enterprise, and they pushed Moe, forcing him to hire a private detective agency."

"They forced him?" Moe Bradley didn't seem to be one who could be forced to do anything. I immediately wished I hadn't asked.

"They did. They should have been more explicit. Hire someone with experience. But Moe doesn't really care about that. This was just to placate them."

"Wasn't there an official investigation?"

The older man threw his hands up. "You see? You don't have a clue. Of course there was an official investigation. The question is, have *you* done any investigation at all? Have you two as much as researched the lady who was killed?" he hesitated. "Do you even know her name?"

We didn't.

"Of course there was an official investigation. And even though there were some very mysterious circumstances, the investigation stalled out. There was no proof of any foul play."

"So what's your point?"

"It was too easy. One accident, maybe. But that many in a row, and one of them involving a death, well—"

"So you have questions about the official results?"

"Oh, my God. You two are clueless." He picked up his beer mug, then placed it back on the bar. "Judy and Virginia had a lot of questions. And they *demanded* that Moe launch a private investigation."

"So, let's say he did," I said. "Moe seems to be a reasonable man. Let's say he launched a private investigation."

"Oh, he resisted. Didn't want to do it. He made it very clear that he didn't want anyone snooping around the show. Especially private investigators. He said that accidents happen. It's part of being involved with the show, and maybe the show was just going through a bad stretch." Clemens never blinked. Cold and calculating. I never met anyone who could keep their eyes open for minutes. Maybe longer. He just kept staring.

"It's possible." I stared at him, trying to break his steely gaze. "It's possible that they were just accidents. You just said that the official investigation didn't turn up any sign of foul play."

"Mr. Moore, Mr. Lessor, here's what you need to understand. When Judy and Virginia decide they want something, they always get what they want. Always. Believe that. So that's why Moe hired *you*. It was quick and it was simple."

"We're still not admitting that we hold any job that deals with investigating these accidents you are referring to." James finally turned his head and stared into Clemens's face. "I really don't know what you're talking about."

"Fine, fine. I want you to hear me out." Clemens pulled the mug to him and took a sip of the beer. Making a sour face, he set it back down. "We—the girls and I—thought that Moe would hire a *real* detective agency."

"Pardon?" He now had James's full attention. "Did you say a *real* detective agency?" His voice was somewhat strained.

"As I said before, young man, someone with experience." He smirked. "Unlike you, I did a little research. Unlike the two of you, I know what I'm talking about. It's not my *impression*, son. I *know* what's going on. Since you got your license less than a week ago, this has got to be your first official case. You've got no experience at all, do you?" His voice was cold, hard, and accusing.

"That doesn't mean that—"

"And you're doing this crackerjack job of investigating by sitting on your ass in this sleazy hole of a bar. Of course this is the place where all of the criminal element hangs out. You've probably decided to just sit here and wait for guilty parties to come to you. Am I right? Am I?"

"Mr. Clemens," James was ready to explode.

"Mr. Lessor and Mr. Moore. I'm here to inform you that if you don't come up with an answer in the immediate future, your services here will no longer be required. Immediate future."

James glared at him.

"Immediate future being by Sunday. In case you weren't aware, there was a shooting here last night. You are so far out of your league, I can't begin to tell you."

"Look, you son of a—"

"Ah ah, Mr. Moore. My girlfriend and her sister own the majority stake in this business venture, and no matter what your arrangement with Moe Bradley, they can take you down in a matter of minutes."

I cringed. I didn't even know the ladies and they were ready to take us down.

"These are very strong women, gentlemen. Am I understood?"

I flashed to dollar signs in my mind, and they were disappearing as I sat there. The harrowing Dragon Tail experience may have been for naught.

James took a deep breath. The entire bar could hear it. "This may surprise you, Mr. Clemens, considering that we are rank amateurs, but we have a suspect already and it shouldn't take the rest of the weekend to prove this person was responsible for the accidents and the death of a rider." James gave him a sly smile, took another slug of his beer, and turned his attention back to the television.

"Oh, really?" Clemens's disdainful tone was condescending, but there was a question mark at the end. He wasn't ruling out the fact that James had a suspect. I had the same question mark.

"Really." James was emphatic.

I sat silent, afraid to say anything at all.

"Just so you know, Mr. Lessor, Moe Bradley is trying to buy

controlling interest in the Moe Shows. From his own sisters."

I had no idea what that had to do with James's statement. We had a suspect?

"What does that have to do with the accidents?" James asked the million dollar question.

"He kind of runs the show anyway, doesn't he," I asked. I just pictured him as the owner type. The girls seemed to show up on rare occasions.

"Have you been paying attention?" He raised his eyebrows, a very sinister expression on his face. "Moe does not have controlling interest, and because over the years he has proven to be an unscrupulous businessman, my girlfriend and her sister have no intention of selling any of their stock to him. Your employment as investigators is simply something he's doing to appease them as he tries to convince the ladies to divest of their shares."

"I really don't care about the business end of this enterprise." James had his dander up. "I told you we'd have the case solved in a couple of days."

"What?"

"You heard me. We'll have the case solved."

"You said you don't care about the business end of this enterprise?" He'd raised his voice and customers at the bar were watching.

"You're the marketing manager, Mr. Lessor. You should care very much about the business end of this enterprise. That's your other job," he hesitated, "that you're obviously not qualified for."

James blinked. Trying to be cool, he'd played his hand without reading all the cards. But that's James.

The gentleman pursed his lips, tapped his fingers on the bar, and stared at James. The big lady behind the bar strolled down to him.

"You want something else, bub?"

Clemens gave her a slow look. "Bub? That's not my name. And no. The beer you served me was warm and tasted like piss. I assume any other drink you serve will taste equally foul."

Her eyes grew wide, and even in the dim light I could see her face flush. "That'll be two fifty, *bub*, and you are not welcome in this establishment again."

He reached for his wallet, pulling out three ones. "Don't worry. I would never have come here in the first place, except it seems to be the place where these two inept private investigators do most of their work."

I thought it was an unfair comment. It was the first time either of us had ever set foot in the bar.

Clemens stood up and looked at me with a cold, hard glance.

"People who work for a carnival are private people. They don't like folks snooping or looking into their affairs. I've seen these people take matters into their own hands, Mr. Lessor."

"And your point is?"

"My point is, you'd be better off quitting. Right now. Quitting and going back to whatever little hole you and your friend crawled out of."

James stood up, his eyes wide. I held my hand up, hoping he wouldn't do something stupid.

"Someone paid a price last night, boys. In case you haven't noticed. Someone who apparently knew too much. Kevin Cross was shot while relieving himself. Pretty nasty stuff."

"Are you threatening us?" James was ready for some physical contact. And that scared me to death, because he lacked any physical prowess.

"Threatening you? This operation needs a *real* investigation. A *professional* detective agency. Boy, I'm giving you a warning. Don't you understand?"

He finally blinked.

"When the carnies figure out that you're investigating them, when they understand that an amateur duo like yourselves is bumbling around their domain, you're liable to disappear. You boys are an accident waiting to happen."

Giving his delivery just the right pause, he finished with, "Threatening you? Right now, with me giving you that information, I may be the best friend you have with this show."

Clemens turned, and without a glance back, walked out of Harry's Hideaway, pushing two patrons out of his way.

"James? We're going to solve this case in the next couple of days?"

"Damn it, Skip, he was—"

"Telling us that we may be killed?"

"Sounded like that."

"You think?"

He sat back down and stared at what was left of his beer. "Skip, I don't really think that our lives are—"

I cut him off. "And what the hell was that bit about we already have a suspect?" I wasn't certain that he was sane at this moment. "Are you out of your mind? What the hell was that all about?"

"Amigo, I wasn't going to let him—"

"What kind of pressure are you putting on us?"

James was quiet, sipping on his beer, watching the game on TV but not really seeing anything at all. I could tell.

"James?"

He studied me for a moment.

"Are you going to answer me?"

"What's so great about telling the truth? Try lying once in a while. It's the currency of the world."

"What?"

"The Marx Brothers. *A Day at the Races*."

"James, did it ever occur to you that you use movie quotes to cover yourself? On a regular basis?"

"It's sometimes easier than coming up with original thought, Skip. You of all people should understand that."

He drained the last of his beer, slid off the stool, and headed for the door. I should have been upset. I'd just gotten slammed. Instead, I realized he was probably right.

CHAPTER SIXTEEN

We wandered through the show, watching the carnies weave their magic, selling cotton candy, drawing a sparse crowd to the dart booth, pulling a senior couple to the Ferris wheel, and tantalizing customers with the smell of greasy meat, popcorn, and deep-fried elephant ears. It was two p.m. and there was a handful of people on the grounds. Maybe the normal carnival public had heard about the shooting and they were staying away for fear of their lives. That was a strong possibility. Murder at the Moe Show was a good reason to stay away. Maybe the Bayview Mall just didn't attract a whole lot of people. That would have been my guess. A runway of useless shops and a bar. Anyway, the crowd was meager. It wasn't really a crowd, just a handful of people wandering listlessly. I could have rolled a bowling ball down the center of the Show and never hit a single person.

Some new heavyset punk with a bandana tied over his head was working Kevin Cross's air rifle booth and he looked bored with the process. I kept thinking about the dead body we'd discovered directly behind the concession.

"Hey, lady, want to win a teddy bear?" He threw the line off to a young woman and man passing by. They ignored him and kept on walking. Perched on a wooden stool, he seemed to nod off, only to wake up when the next possible customer came near. "Hey, lady—"

Lame lines, for an impossible game.

He stared at me as we walked by and then spit on the ground in what appeared to be a deliberate comment on James and myself. I couldn't wait to get out of here.

"You remember what Moe said, James? Keep it low-key."

"Yeah."

"Hell, I think everyone here knows we're investigating them. And I don't think we did anything to telegraph it."

Glancing at the zoo, I saw Pugh working the small arena, coaxing the obnoxious goat to stand still while a six-year-old boy about Pugh's size tried to pet him. Linda was nowhere to be seen.

"Hey, boys, over here."

The skinny bald man motioned to us from Freddy's Fun House, the trailer with the painted flames. He stood on an elevated porch, pointing to the opening of the Fun House.

"Come on, don't let your friends tell you about the Fun House. See it for yourself."

James shook his head. "No. Got things to do."

"Hey, are you the new marketing guy or what?"

James snapped to attention. "Yeah. I am."

"Then how the hell are you going to market the Show if you don't know the show?"

James looked at me for the answer. Of course this was the same guy who had told me I had no original thoughts. So I kept quiet.

The thin man pushed the sleeves of his T-shirt up on his shoulders, exposing his bony arms. "You probably don't think much of this little attraction, do you?"

"The Show?"

"No. The Fun House."

I was unimpressed, but again kept my mouth shut. This was James's gig.

"Come on up here. For free. There's nobody here right now, so go on in and see for yourself. What have you got to lose?"

James walked to the Fun House trailer and I followed behind. I had no interest. Didn't care. But there was James, boldly mounting the stairs, standing on the porch and motioning to me.

"Spooky, crazy. The most fun you'll ever have in a trailer, my friends. Something special for everyone." He motioned with his hand, and I walked up on the porch. Together James and I walked through the dark entrance.

"I hate these things." James muttered under his breath.

A blue lightbulb mounted immediately inside cast an eerie pall and an iridescent arrow painted on the wall pointed to the left.

"Having fun yet?" I asked.

"I don't like going places I can't see."

We followed the arrow to the left, two, three strides and the space was pitch black, I felt the roller bars under my feet just as James shouted.

"Whoa. Hold on, man." He reached back and grabbed me, trying to steady himself.

"Stand still, James. They're just some rollers. Walk slowly, they probably end in a couple of feet."

He let out a breath and sure enough, a couple of steps later we were back on a firmer footing.

Ghoulish noises resonated from tinny speakers. Wailing and a whooshing sound.

"Damn, Skip, sounds like bats."

"Sound effect, James. Man up."

We took several more steps and the flashing face startled

both of us. Almost three dimensional, the monster's face snarled, larger than life, its mouth opening right in front of us as if it was going to swallow us whole.

The path abruptly turned to the right as a dim red light clicked on to show us the turn.

"Never should have done this, amigo."

"It's a kids' amusement, James. They apparently have a different sense of humor.

"I was a kid. Once."

A life-sized skeleton dropped two feet in front of us, and James froze as I ran into him. A jangling piano played rickety music as the bones danced and we waited for four or five seconds until the animated thing retreated to some hidden place.

Five more steps and I saw James in front of me. His head was bloated, his body as skinny as a rail and right behind him I saw myself. Fun house mirrors. Now what could be more enjoyable than this?

"Tell me, Skip, how much more of this do we have to take?"

I'd already thought about it. A turn to the left, then to the right. As wide as the trailer was, they could take us one more path to the left and probably another to the right. Then right again to the entrance/exit. Maximizing the space. I'd learned that in business school. Little things kept coming back.

"Keep walking, man."

We stepped past the mirrors, six in all, showing us in contorted shapes and sizes. One had us upside down, and never once was I tempted to laugh.

A yellow light popped on as we hit the wall, showing us the turn to the left. I caught a glimpse of James as he made the turn into the narrow passage and I heard his surprised gasp. Turning the corner I stumbled over something, gasping as well.

"James?"

Nothing.

"Hey, buddy. James? Not funny."

I couldn't see my hand in front of my face. Knowing it wasn't a good idea, I reached down to see what I'd stumbled over. I prayed it wasn't James. Whatever it was appeared to be narrow, long and soft like a pillow. Definitely not James.

"James?"

The next instant the floor slipped, like an earthquake knocking my feet from under me, and as I careened from one cushioned wall into the other, a hideous laugh played over the speakers. Grabbing at the walls I felt the floor shift again. Moving steel plates. I took a broader step and the plates slid again, throwing me against the other wall.

There appeared to be no James in front of me. And if my plan was right, I still had another right turn and half a right turn before this torturous amusement was over.

Two more steps on the shifting floor and once again I was on solid ground.

I wanted to double-time it, move as fast as possible, but when you can't see one inch in front of yourself, you tend to take it very slowly. Another two steps, three, and I felt something in my face. A spider's web, stringy and strange. Clawing at it, I kept moving.

"James. Come on man, you've got to be out there."

Faster now, calling his name every four or five seconds. An animated rat the size of a dog crossed my path, baring his teeth. A storm came up, with loud claps of thunder, flashes of lightning, and the sound of rain pouring all around me. I patted my shirt and hair, but all was dry.

I stopped for a moment. Someone, something behind me now. A paying customer who had followed behind us, or maybe James, having doubled back. I sensed them, even the floral scent of a sweet perfume, and not knowing who it was I started moving again, stepping up my pace, moving away from the manufactured thunderstorm.

And something hit me from behind, harder than a fun house effect. Hard enough behind my knees to send me crashing to the floor. I kicked back and heard scurrying behind me.

Jumping to my feet I made the final turn.

"James." At the top of my lungs now.

A full-sized clown puppet dropped from above and I froze for an instant. The eerily painted face mocked me with a red slash mouth and dark brooding eyes. Heath Ledger as the Joker. A shiver went down my spine as he danced for me just for a couple of seconds. Five steps, then ten, and I found myself at the exit.

Breathing hard, I blinked at the bright daylight. No one was on the porch. Not the skinny, bare-armed carnie and not James. I shuddered, the memory of the attraction almost as bad as my memory of the Dragon Tail.

I closed my eyes for a moment, and when I opened them I saw the crudely lettered sign by the steps. CLOSED TILL FURTHER NOTICE.

And there he was. Standing below, looking up at me.

"Where the hell did you go, James? This wasn't fun."

"Dude. We're in deeper than I thought we were."

I blinked again. "What are you talking about?"

"Somebody grabbed me in there."

"Yeah?"

"Grabbed me. Pulled me to the side. Said we needed to leave the show. Now. Quit messing with everyone's lives."

"I got knocked down."

"You too? I'm out here because they pushed me out of—" and he pointed to a closed door halfway down the trailer, "that door."

I stepped off the porch and went down to the door. Two feet above the ground, it was labeled with stenciled letters, EMERGENCY EXIT ONLY.

It hit me that the closed sign and emergency exit sign were signs we should probably pay attention to. The signs that this wasn't a good venture for us were everywhere.

James brushed himself with his hands. "We were set up, Skip. Pisses me off. Damn it, we're here to do a job. And I'm not going to leave until we've done it."

"This is too much. Someone highjacked you in the Fun House, threatened you, then pushed you out the door?"

"They did."

"Someone attacked me in the Fun House, knocked me down—"

"Apparently."

"Let's get the hell out of here, James."

"Come on, amigo. Admit it. It's just starting to be fun."

CHAPTER SEVENTEEN

"I want to meet Winston Pugh." It came out of nowhere.

"Because—"

"Because I think the little son of a bitch has a lot to do with this."

"Just like that? You want to meet him?"

"Why not?"

This entire gig was James's idea. Why not indeed? He should have been the one who met Winston in the first place.

"I don't think Winston is up to it," I said. "He and his girlfriend are not the type. But the girl—the one who seemed pissed off when we got off the Dragon Tail? I told you, her name is Linda—she's Pugh's girlfriend. The tequila shooter." I'd told James that she and Winston seemed to really like drinking shots of the cactus liquor.

He nodded. "Yeah. I remember. There's some reason that she stalked off like that, Skip." James was finally engaged. "You didn't do anything to offend her, at least that you can think of, right?"

"No."

"Well, it just adds to my theory."

"It's not Pugh, James."

"Look, Skip, someone shot this guy in the trailer. Someone shot this Kevin Cross. Am I right?"

"Of course someone shot him." What a stupid question.

"Well, someone sabotaged the rides, too. It makes sense that both of these things were an inside job. So it's probably Winston Pugh." He tossed it off like there was no other solution.

"What?" I was dumfounded, and at the same time I had this sudden epiphany that we could do this. Both of us working together, we could make it happen. Find the culprit. James finally seemed to be focused. That was the positive.

And as soon as I had that thought, I knew I was—*we* were—way out of our league. There was no way. James was crazy.

He had a way of driving me nuts.

We walked by the Ferris wheel, spinning in the sky with only five of the brightly colored carts full. I wondered if the riders knew someone had been murdered fifty yards away.

"Skip, I seriously think Pugh is the guy. And because he knows we're investigating the show, he tried to threaten us at the Fun House."

"You can't be serious. Was it a short guy with a whiny voice who threatened you?"

He paused. "I don't know. It happened fast and the voice was a low whisper. But I bet it could have been Pugh."

We had no business at all being private investigators. "Pugh was at the zoo when you got attacked at the Fun House. I saw him there."

"If I had to name the suspect, it would be Pugh." Matter of fact.

"You've never met him. You don't know him at all."

"Nope."

"Then how could you—"

"He's the perfect match."

"So no one else could have done it?" I asked.

"Well, I think that Bo and Charlie are persons of interest."

James watched way too many movies. "James, you really just said that? Persons of interest?"

"You hear it on TV, *Law and Order* and stuff, and anyway, yes. I said it. Okay? Bo and Charlie, they've got access. They are persons of interest, but Skip, we don't know what their motive would be. They'd have an idea how to do it, but with Pugh, we've got a motive. And this Linda, his girlfriend, she thinks we're investigating him. As soon as you asked Pugh about the accidents, she figured you were trying to pin them on her boyfriend. So she's afraid we're going to figure it all out. That's why she's pissed off at you. It all makes sense, Skip."

I stopped and shook my head. Now he was telling me that we had to watch out for Linda Reilly and Winston Pugh. "What the hell are you talking about? How do you know it's an inside job? And Pugh? That's impossible. I told you, he was working the zoo when you got pushed out of the Fun House."

He took one more step, turned, and said, "Makes no difference. He could have put someone up to it." James was pushing hard. "You told me this guy feels threatened. Winston Pugh thinks that everyone is against him. Now that sounds to me like a guy who is out to protect his world."

"Well, he does, he does think that people are out to get him, but I don't think he's out to protect his world. I just think he's paranoid."

A young couple dressed in shorts and T-shirts approached us, staring at each other and holding hands, paying no attention to their surroundings, lost in only themselves. They almost ran into us, then split, the girl in tight shorts walking around James, the guy walking around me.

James turned his head and watched them for a second.

Either he was staring at the girl, or thinking it was another threat. Turning back to me he said, "You told me Pugh is worried about keeping a position with the Moe Show. He thinks they are going to let him go. Am I right?"

"Yeah. So what?" I was shouting. There were at least three songs blaring over the loudspeakers and it was next to impossible for us to hear each other talk. Barenaked Ladies were singing *Brian Wilson*. I could make that much out. "And if you want to find me, I'll be out in the sandbox . . ."

"Pugh *is* paranoid, James. He thinks Disney is after him. He thinks that Moe is after him. The ride guys too. But it's just his personality. The guy is paranoid. I'm sure of it. But come on, he's not a killer." I was trying to be heard over the music.

"The rides, the threat of new rides coming to the Show, he's concerned about losing his job because of the rides." James gave me a smug look. "Think about it, amigo, it makes perfect sense."

I'd explained it all to James, even though his involvement in the clue department was minimal. But he'd grasped it all.

And there was Green Day, singing "Wake Me Up, When September Ends." A song about the lead singer's father. I didn't need this, remembering my father's hasty exit from our family.

"So, this Winston Pugh," James continued, talking above the music, "he sabotaged the rides. He attacked us in the Fun House. It has to be him. I was right. I *am* right. We have a suspect and given two days we should be able to—"

"Two days? Winston Pugh? No way. James, you are totally wrong, man. This little guy is a . . ." I paused, trying to remember the word, "a Munchkin." That was the perfect description of Pugh. A Munchkin. A little guy from the *Wizard Of Oz*. "He wouldn't hurt anyone."

"Then we're going to follow the yellow brick road, pard. In two days or however much time is left, we can prove that your little short buddy is responsible for the accidents and for the deaths.

It's the perfect answer. He's the perfect villain. I feel this, Skip. In my bones. Let's go with it."

I took a breath, trying to clear my head. "You're only saying this because you promised Ken Clemens a suspect. That's it, isn't it?"

"An emphatic no."

"You haven't even met the guy. You don't know either of them."

"Doesn't matter."

"It does matter. I don't believe you. You've lost your mind."

"Skip, I'm only saying it because it makes the most sense. You know it does. Now, we just have to prove it. The short guy thinks the rides are driving him out. He sabotages the rides."

"Someone was killed."

"Maybe he didn't mean for that to happen. The injuries, the death, they were collateral damage."

I could smell the tangy barbecue and smoke coming from the pig wagon, and got a whiff of hot buttered popcorn as we passed by. The guy in the stained apron was ladling on the sauce for three young kids. He looked up and gave me a frown.

"The air rifle guy finds out about it and threatens to turn him in. Winston Pugh kills the air rifle guy."

"Kevin Cross."

"Who?"

"The air rifle guy," I said.

"Whatever. Perfect solution."

"You forget that I was with Pugh when he found the body in the little camper."

"Pugh shot him, then went to get you. Skip, don't you see? It is so perfect. And think how happy detective Bob Stanton will be. Our first case and we turn over the murderer to him."

"Not to mention how happy Ken Clemens and the sisters will be."

"Let's not forget Moe."

"James, you're crazy."

"We'll call Jody, get some recording equipment, bug Pugh and Linda's trailer and we'll solve the case."

He was brighter than that. Nothing was that easy. However, it was a place to start. I had no better idea. In fact, I had no ideas at all and James actually made some sense, in a crazy, perverted way.

"Are you with me, pally?"

"Sure, James. If for no other reason than to prove to you that it couldn't possibly be Pugh."

"Oh, it's Pugh. And we're going to make that money, pardner. It's as good as in our pockets."

CHAPTER EIGHTEEN

I drove to Delray in the late afternoon, windows down and the hot humid air rushing in . The air conditioner was on the blink and this was as good as it could be. Jody Stacy has a shop that sells retail spy stuff over on West Atlantic Avenue, and even though I didn't have a clue what we needed, I figured that he'd give me some idea of what to look for.

The rusted yellow Taurus struggled, the engine coughing every once in a while and if I floored the thing, it still only got up to about fifty-five. Any money I made on this deal was going into a newer automobile. Then, if there was anything else left, James could get his used box truck.

Seeing the cop car, lights flashing in the rearview mirror, I instinctively braked. No need. I couldn't speed if I wanted. The car went screaming by, obviously concerned with something far ahead of where I was.

I thought about Kevin Cross and the lady who'd been mangled by the Cat's Pajamas. There was some nasty stuff going down and we were just floundering around, trying to tie up a bunch of loose ends. And then I noticed the black Escalade, lagging back about six cars.

Occasionally the elegant Cadillac would pull out into a passing lane, move up a car, then drop back. And I remembered very clearly that I'd seen Moe Bradley, the two sisters, and Ken Clemens all sitting in a black Escalade. They'd been parked out by Kevin Cross's trailer after his body had been found.

There must be thousands of black Escalades, but this one seemed to be hanging around a little longer than it should. Any self-respecting driver would have passed me by now.

And then I started to wonder if it was Ken Clemens. Or was it the sisters? Or just one of the sisters? Or was it Moe, checking up on me? The mind plays strange tricks when you're in over your head.

I pulled off at the exit and slowed down, watching the rearview mirror to see if the Escalade followed, but I never saw it.

When I entered the shop, Jody was on the phone so I browsed, checking out the flat screen monitor with ten different camera shots of me. Then it was a game to see where the ten cameras were.

The big fuzzy teddy bear was easy. The lens was in the bear's eye. That was the original nanny-cam, where parents would set the stuffed animal up in a child's room and monitor what the nanny was up to. And I figured out the camera in the wall calendar, the fake motion detector, the sprinkler overhead, and a couple others, but the one that kept moving had me confused.

On the monitor, my head was jerking all over the place even though I was standing perfectly still, then for a moment I was gone from that section of the screen, replaced by the store window, then a wall. I looked over the entire room, trying to figure out where the camera was located. Nothing was moving.

"Confused?"

I spun around, and he was looking over my shoulder, staring at the same monitor that I was.

"Yeah. I am. Where do you keep the moving camera?" I turned and he stepped back. Jody is an ex-cop, with the tough-guy physique, a square jaw, and looks the girls used to drool over in high school. The last time I'd been in the store, Em had been with me, and Jody had made it very clear that he was interested in her. I had a brief moment, wondering if she'd seen him at all during our break.

"First of all, congrats to you and James. I mean now that you guys are official." He gave me a broad smile. "Real private investigators."

I thought there might be a hint of sarcasm in his voice.

"Thanks to you."

"Glad to help."

"We may take jobs from you."

Our high school classmate smiled. "Plenty of room for competition, Skip. Plenty of room."

"Jody, where is the camera?"

"Camera? The one that moves? Not just a camera, Skip. An audio recorder, too. Pretty cool, right?"

"You're not going to tell me?" I stared at him. "Remember, I'm a paying customer. If you want to sell it, you've got to show me how it works."

He nodded. "Speaking of selling it, you guys still owe me seventy-nine bucks, Skip. Seventy-nine."

"I thought James—"

"James? You should know better." He screwed up his face in disbelief. "It's for the smoke alarm video cam. You guys never finished paying it off. You do remember the smoke alarm cam?"

We'd used it for a job at a software company. It helped solve the case, but our client never paid us. Maybe that's the reason James stalled the payments to Jody. Still— "I'll make sure you get it."

Jody nodded. "I know *you* will. It's James I'm concerned about."

I had firsthand knowledge of how it worked. Jody would suggest equipment, vaguely hint at a price and a possible return of undamaged goods, then do whatever he wanted to do. He and James would have made a good pair.

"Look, Jody, we're in kind of a tight spot. I think I need another hidden camera, something that could be put in a small camper. Where the heck is that camera that keeps moving?" I was getting frustrated watching the bobbing image on the screen. Now the video image was a close up of my shirt.

"You're looking at it, Skip."

What I was looking at was Jody. Front and center. I checked out the buttons on his shirt. That seemed possible. Maybe it was his eyeball. I remembered the scene from the movie *Angels and Demons* where they scanned eyeballs as a security process and the bad guys had carved out someone's eyeball and used it to gain access to a secure room. It couldn't be. An eyeball camera? There were a lot of weird things in The Spy Store, but even Jody wouldn't go so far as to—

"Right here."

He pulled a gray ballpoint pen from his shirt pocket.

"Three hours of video and audio, and it downloads to your computer. Very simple to operate."

"Wow."

"The quality is superb, man. I mean top-notch." He was showing off. Proud of his equipment, proud of his knowledge.

"So I could walk into someone's home—"

"Have this baby in your pocket, and you'd get it all. Or, you could leave it. Set it on their kitchen counter or table, then call them and say you'd pick it up later. Chances are they would leave it there. You come back in, pick it up and download the video and audio."

"Yeah. I like that." I did. "But what if they try to—"

"Write with it? Here." He moved to the counter, clicked the top of the pen and started scribbling on a pad of paper.

"It really works."

"Well, of course, it does." He sounded offended. "Everything in here is pretty much what it appears to be. Except that it's not."

I worked that around in my head.

"Take the pen. Pay me when you get the bill."

"Oh yeah? How much?"

"I'll get you a price later, okay?"

Damn. He was doing it again. Dodging the question. But what was I going to say? I needed equipment.

Jody pulled a box with a new pen from the shelf and dropped it into a bag.

"And then there's the Cell Sleuth."

"The what?"

"Look, if you want to pick up on what's going on in a guy's life, you need to know what's happening on his cell phone. This is the Cell Sleuth. You can track all of his phone calls and text messages."

I'd met Linda and Winston. My guess was that they didn't even own a cell phone, but I could be wrong.

"Hey, don't worry about this. If you don't need any of these things, send them back, Skip. I'm just making suggestions." And as he walked behind the counter and I watched him punch in some keys on his computer, I did worry. I had no idea how we were going to pay for any of this, but if we didn't have the equipment, we couldn't complete the job. He walked back out, stepped to a counter, and pulled another box from the shelf.

"Finally, you need the EMT. I'm telling you, it will help solve the crime. I don't care what the case is, chances are excellent that the people you're watching are keeping some sort of record on their computer. And e-mailing information you need."

That was it. I waited for an explanation, but he kept punching keys on his computer. He seemed to think I knew exactly what the EMT was for. I said, "Jody?"

"Yeah."

"What the hell is an EMT?"

"E-mail Trap."

I had no idea what he was talking about.

"A what?"

"E-mail Trap. This device sends out messages to a computer. When the owner of that computer clicks on the message, you have total access to everything on that person's unit. Total access, Skip. All the e-mail, Web sites, you name it, you've got it. It's worth its weight in gold."

Again I questioned whether Winston and Linda even had a computer. I'd seen no sign of one in their tiny trailer.

"So I need all three of these things?"

"You do."

"Are they all legal?"

Jody smiled. "Skip, come on."

"They're not, right?"

"What you do with them is your business."

I nodded. "Jody, we're not making a ton of money on this case." I didn't want to ask for favors, but—

"Not to worry, dude. I'll get you an itemized bill. It's not going to be that much. You guys are friends, so I'll give you a professional discount."

Again, "not to worry." I wondered if he'd helped us get a license just so he could sell us all the equipment. It wasn't going to cost that much, but what exactly was *that much*? I mean, he said the E-mail Trap was worth its weight in gold, and I knew that gold was a little pricey right now.

"But of course I'm going to add the seventy-nine for the smoke detector video camera." He gave me an accusing look. "Plus a past due fee, Skip. I don't care what your good friend tells you, he didn't cover it all."

I was certain that Jody would add the past due amount. James had sworn to me that he would take care of that bill. I should know by now you can't always trust James with money. And I wasn't sure about Jody Stacy.

"Hey, Skip, one more thing."

He laid the bag with my three purchases on the counter.

"Yeah?"

"I heard you broke up with Emily."

Son of a bitch.

"True or not true?"

I let it sit for a second or so. Technically Em and I were on a break. Not broken. There was a difference. Definitely a difference. Break. Broken up. He wasn't going to get me on a technicality. No way. Finally I looked him coldly in the eyes.

"Not true. Sorry, Jody."

"Hey, dude, I just wanted to know if you were all right. You surely understand that, right?"

It was comforting to know that my new best friend was looking out for me. He had my best interest at heart. And I thought about his closing line: "You surely understand that, right?"

I turned and walked out of the store, into the teeming, hot Florida summer. I understood more than he thought I did.

CHAPTER NINETEEN

On the drive back to Carol City I kept an eye out for the black Cadillac SUV, and actually saw two that passed me at high rates of speed. Well, high rates, considering how fast I was able to go, but I was certain those Escalades weren't keeping tabs on me.

I steered the sputtering Taurus onto the dirt road that circled the barren patch of ground where the show performed and pulled onto the gravel next to the trailer. James was walking out with a good-looking blonde. Not Angie Clark. My engine sputtered and died.

"Hey, babe." She walked to the open window and rested her elbows on the door, staring right into my face.

Smelling her hair, the light scent of her perfume—

I didn't answer. Couldn't. I had no idea what to say. I was sure she'd never come back and afraid that if I said anything at all she'd turn around and walk out again. I was shell-shocked.

"You do remember me, right? It hasn't been that long." A little sarcasm, a little humor.

I finally found my voice. "What—?"

She turned to James. "He's a man of few words. Not the loquacious charmer that you are, James, but I get his drift."

Backing off, she let me open the door and step out. Then she ran the few steps to me and threw her arms around my neck, pressing that warm curvy body into mine. God, she felt good.

"I missed you, Skip."

"Yeah, well—"

"I know. At least I think I know." She hesitated. "I wanted to see you again to be sure."

"Sure of—"

"Sure that we should get back together."

"And?"

She pressed her warm moist lips to mine and we held that position for seconds. Minutes. I had no grasp of time. Finally we broke.

"Skip. Here you are, up to your butt in more trouble. You and your miscreant friend. I miss that."

I stood back and took a good look. Silky blonde hair, a faint spray of freckles that dusted her cute nose and cheeks, a crooked smile on her lips, and a red top featuring cleavage that showed off her full breasts. She wore a pair of tight jeans and sandals with just a little bit of a high heel. I'd missed everything about her.

"You miss me being in trouble?"

"No," she said, "I think I miss not being here to get you out of trouble." I couldn't believe she'd actually said that.

James stood off to the side, a frown on his face. "Miscreant? Skip's miscreant friend?"

"Do you even know what it means, James?" She glanced over at him. "Miscreant? Obviously it's not good."

He was silent, squinting his eyes. Em's relationship with James was part of the problem. A big part of the problem. And I knew he'd look up the word miscreant the minute he had a chance.

"Anyway," James said, "I told Em what's been going on here and she agrees with me, pard."

"Em has never agreed with you. On anything."

"She's never met Winston, but she thinks there's a good case to give the little guy a hard look."

God I'd missed her. We'd dated off and on since high school and the off had always been her idea. I was *on* 100 percent of the time.

I reached into the car and pulled out the bag with my purchases.

"Great," James said. "Stuff to work with, right?"

"We'll see." I was feeling less than confident about the buys I'd made. "Jody suggested three different things we could use."

"Let's look at them in the trailer." James furtively glanced around, then grabbed the bag from my hand and climbed into the Airstream.

I let Em go first, and I have to admit I admired her cute little butt in those tight jeans. I couldn't help grinning. Why she'd come back I had no idea, but I certainly wasn't going to question the motive.

"I've got coffee on the stove," he said. "I'll just heat it up." James turned up the gas burner on a cheap tin pan full of brackish looking liquid. I immediately thought of dirty dishwater.

Opening the bag on the small table, I pulled out the Cell Sleuth. Time to explain all of the spy paraphernalia. "Jody had these suggestions." I wasn't going to take all the credit. Or all of the heat. "This Cell Sleuth tracks a client's cell calls, even text messages. We'll know all about his communications."

"Oh, yeah?" James took the small device out the box. "How does it work?"

"I, uh, have no idea. Somehow it lets us bug his phone, and I guess we can hear all of his calls on that little receiver there."

James held up a small black box. "This thing?"

"You know, I'm not even sure that Pugh has a cell phone." What had I been thinking?

"Everybody has a cell phone, amigo. We'll figure out how it works later. Okay, what's next?"

"This gizmo," I said, feeling like I'd been had, in the light of day, in front of my friend and girlfriend. None of this stuff seemed to make any sense. Stuff that Jody had convinced me was a good idea. "It's a program that sends a message to a computer. If the operator opens it, we have access to everything on the computer. Everything. According to Jody we can open any of his programs."

"Well," Em looked at the box suspiciously, "if this four-foot killer Winston Pugh doesn't have a cell phone, he and his Linda may not have a computer either."

I knew that.

"But if they do have a computer, we could learn a lot," James said. "And if they don't, I could send a message to Angie and get a complete profile of the girl. Would that be cool or what?"

Em and I both glared at him.

"Got another package there, Tonto."

"Yeah. This is a pen." I removed it from the box and James studied it for a moment.

"And what does it do?"

"Writes." I took it back and clicked the top. Writing on the back of my hand I printed "Video. Audio."

"Oh, cool," Em said. "A video camera with sound?"

"Amigo, this is something we could really use."

"Yeah." At least they were impressed with something I'd brought back. "We can plug it into a computer and download everything on a disc."

"How much?" James was eyeballing the assorted spy devices and appeared to be concerned.

"Apparently it doesn't matter."

"What does that mean?"

"We don't pay our bills anyway. Jody says you still haven't covered the smoke alarm camera that we used on our last case."

"Ah, let me check on that."

"James?"

"I can't remember, Skip. Seems like, you know, I'm pretty sure—"

"This is what I missed." Em shook her lovely head. "You guys just bumbling along. You need guidance, boys."

"And just what kind of guidance," James asked, obviously relieved to be let off the hook.

"You need someone to lay out a plan."

I picked up the pen, pushed the record button, and aimed the invisible lens at her. "Okay, Em. You're back. You've got most of the details, so come on and give us the plan."

She smiled, her eyes bright and her lips moist. "You're recording this, right?"

"I am."

My on-again, off-again girlfriend pulled a pen from her purse. "Since your spy pen is already in use, I'll use this."

James handed her the roll of paper towels that was sitting on the sink.

"What am I supposed to do with this?"

"Write on it. We don't have a lot of colorful tablets lying around."

"Okay, boys, pay attention. You've apparently got until Sunday night, and I think it's probably impossible to figure this thing out. I stand on that statement. This is probably impossible. But," she hesitated, "but, if we're going to make a stab at it, here's how I think we play this out."

It was great to have her back. Great to have her getting involved with our caper, even though she had no clue what she was doing and even though she was putting us in more trouble than we could possibly imagine.

Seven o'clock and all the lights were on. Our carnival, Moe's Show, was twinkling in the early dusk, like fairy dust from a Disney movie. The crowd had grown and as the three of us sat on lawn chairs outside the trailer we sipped the watery, stale coffee that James had manufactured. I took a taste and grimaced.

"James, what did you put in this? It tastes like watered down gasoline. The cheap grade."

"Dude, you said we drink too much alcohol. I'm figuring out ways we can be sociable and not have a beer."

"We're heading out to introduce you two to Winny Pugh's Petting Zoo. Probably better that we don't have a beer." I was thinking our meeting should be sober. I was also thinking that our meeting could cost fifteen dollars if Linda stuck to her five bucks a head rule.

"If we hit it off," Em gave her cup of brackish liquid a look of contempt, "we may get invited in for tequila. Right?"

"If," I said.

"Better than this garbage."

"I looked up miscreant." James spat a stream of coffee out of his mouth. "Something about being a villain?"

"Villain, immoral, lots of low-life references, James." Em tossed the rest of her coffee on the ground and stood up. "I'm ready to meet the famous dwarf and his girlfriend. Anybody want to come along?"

James and I followed suit, tossing our foul tasting drinks on the dirt and rising from the cheap plastic woven lawn chairs.

"Gentlemen," she turned and faced us, "I'm sorry," she paused for a moment. "Gentleman and James, let's conduct ourselves in a professional manner. If James is correct, we may be confronting the man behind the equipment failures, the injury, and death of a Moe Show patron, and the murderer of Kevin Cross."

"Could be." I nodded.

"No question. It all goes together, team. Let's travel."

Traveling would take all of ninety seconds. I was apprehensive, but we had Em's plan and come hell or high water we were going to stick to it. Except that we didn't.

Couldn't.

CHAPTER TWENTY

The lights burned bright in the early evening, casting a colorful glow over the dreary piece of dirt we now called home. The three of us trudged across the barren ground, watching the growing crowd line up for the main event. The Dragon Tail was obviously the premier attraction, and even those who had no intention of mounting the green and gold monster huddled nearby to watch the gyrations and marvel at the brave—or stupid— people who rode it. Not once. Not twice, but sometimes three times in a row. As crazy as that sounds.

"It's a phenomenon, bro." James kept shaking his head, shaggy hair hanging low on his forehead.

"What is?"

"The DT."

"DT?" Em looked at us with a puzzled expression.

"Dragon Tail." James nodded toward the ride.

"Well, yeah, it is. So phenomenal that I would only ride it once." I glanced back at the huge beast. "In respect."

"Bullshit." Em turned and gave me a sly smile. "James told me you two had negotiated half a ride."

"But that didn't happen."

"What did you expect? These two guys—"

"Bo and Charlie," James chimed in.

"Bo and Charlie were worried you were stealing their jobs. How can you blame them? Two college educated guys like you come along and," she hesitated, "well, barely college educated."

James and I had partied a little too hard during our four years at Samuel and Davidson, better known as Sam and Dave University, and to Em's credit, she was right. We'd barely graduated. And personally, I didn't feel any smarter, more intelligent, or more mature for the experience. But there were some great times. I mean some really great times.

"And these two guys," she continued, "they take over the ride. What do you expect Bo and Charlie to do? They want to scare the crap out of you. They want to scare you off. Warn you that if you interfere with their job, they will screw you."

"They did an admirable job," I said.

Em smirked. "Of course they did."

I countered. "Could they be the bad guys? The ones who messed with the rides? It would make more sense that Bo and Charlie were the ones who tampered with the rides than to blame Winston. I mean—"

"No reason, Skip." James kept walking, his head bent low.

"We haven't figured out a reason yet, but there may very well be a good reason. They know the mechanics of the rides. As dumb as they appear, I have a feeling they know a lot more than they let on."

"Those two?"

"Yeah. Those two." I kicked a loose stone, sending it two feet in front of me. Like a soccer ball, I kicked it again. "I think they might have an axe to grind with the Moe Show."

"Winston Pugh is trying to protect his job, his business,"

James said. "He's the obvious villain in this scenario. You can make up all the scenarios you want to, Skip, but Pugh is the culprit."

We ended at the petting zoo railing. Linda was gently prodding the goat to move away from a small boy. Maybe he'd just butted the kid, or maybe she was afraid that he was about to butt the kid.

"Linda." I called out and she raised her head.

"I want you to meet some friends of mine."

That frown again. "I'm a little busy right now."

I heard a low growl and saw the sheepdog staring in my direction. I wasn't sure that he couldn't leap the fence so I backed off just a bit.

"Is Winston around?"

Linda put her foot on the goat's flank and pushed. The animal stumbled, then slowly walked away from the small child. Linda walked over to the fence and leaned across the upper rail, staring at the three of us.

"So what do you want?"

"This is my good friend, James. He's the new marketing director for the Show, and this is—"

"That's not what I heard."

"I'm sorry?"

"I heard he's a P.I., trying to find out if someone is sabotaging the rides."

"Well, that rumor has been traveling around like a—"

"It's what I heard." I could smell tequila on her breath. She could probably smell dishwater coffee on mine.

"I'm the marketing director and I just wanted to meet you and Winston." James stepped forward and offered his hand over the railing. She just stared at it as the dog walked up by her side. There was that low, throaty growl again accompanied by a snarl as he looked at James.

"Oh, what a good-looking dog." Em was all bright eyed and bushy tailed.

Linda gave her a cautious glance.

"What's his name?"

"Garcia."

I kept thinking it should be Monster.

"Garcia, come here." Em knelt and put her hand inside the fence. The evil dog stopped his growl and walked to Em's hand.

"Em, you could lose that hand. I'm serious, that dog—"

He extended his long pink tongue and licked her palm. Then with a gentle yip, he licked her arm and started panting.

Em glanced up at me and smiled. "I have that effect on a lot of males."

I bit my lip. She was being truthful.

"Winston is inside sleeping. You know he was up rather late last night with the police and everything." A snide, almost sinister look on her face.

"You know I was with him when he found the body?"

"Oh, I know."

The trailer door squeaked open and Winston Pugh Charlemagne stepped out onto the small step. He wore his trademark blue overalls without any shirt underneath. His exposed chest spouted tufts of white hair and he scratched his almost bald head. I noticed he was barefoot as well and I wondered if he dared walk into the compound. Several fresh piles of manure were scattered around the fenced-in area and the five or six families inside were taking great care to avoid them.

"Hey, young man." He pointed in my direction as Linda turned to him.

I didn't think she appeared too happy.

The little man smiled at her, waved at a mother and father with their infant son, and stretched, raising his stubby arms in the air. He had a huge brush of hair under each armpit.

"Winston. I wanted to introduce you to two friends." I shouted to him as he walked down the steps and over to the fence, skillfully maneuvering his way through the minefield of animal waste.

"Linda, why don't you clean up the shit, hon?" He reached up and laid a hand on her arm.

Linda's head flew back and she glared down at him. "Clean up the shit yourself, *hon*. Seems like it's time you took a turn out here. I can guarantee you that you don't have a clue how much I do for you. Not a clue." Linda stormed off, up the steps and into the trailer.

"She's got a snootful of Jose Cuervo, that one does."

"This is the new marketing director for the show. James, this is Winston. And this is—" I never knew how to introduce her, "this is my good friend—"

She frowned.

"My favorite—"

She squinted her eyes.

"This is my girlfriend, most of the time. This is Emily. Emily, Winston."

"A looker," he said.

"Thank you." I swear she blushed. "We were hoping to come in and talk. Skip told us you've got some really good tequila, and I'd especially like to talk to you about the sheepdog, Garcia."

"Oh?" He smiled. Just a little. Talk to a man about his girlfriend and it's trouble for everyone. Talk to a man about his dog and there are smiles all around. "Let me have a quick word with Linda. Need to get her back out here with the customers. Then we'll go inside and have a conversation." His gaze lingered on Em, and I saw his eyes travel up and down and back up her body. I didn't blame him. He turned and trudged back up to the tiny trailer.

A father put his quarter in the pellet machine and pressed a handful of the tiny food nuggets into his eight-year-old daughter's hand. She tried to feed the black pig, but porky wasn't buying it. Apparently the man-made nutrition didn't have much appeal.

"When we get inside, I'm going to ask him some questions about the dog. I'll write down the answers, and when I'm finished, I accidentally leave the pen. Tomorrow I'll realize that I left it at their trailer and I simply go back and retrieve it."

I shook my head. "Why do you two think that Pugh and Linda are going to sit around and spill all their secrets about the rides and the shooting last night?"

"Because," Em smiled, "you told us that they drink."

"To excess," James said.

"Well, I can't be certain that it happens every night, and so what if they do?"

"Skip, when you've had too much to drink—"

"Like that ever happens."

"—I can get you to tell me anything." Em had a smug grin on her face as she glanced up at the trailer. Linda was just walking out, giving us a cold shoulder.

It was true. But I'd tell Em anything all the time, drunk or sober.

"So there's a good chance they'll talk over cocktails," James said.

"Cocktails?"

"Shots. Whatever."

The angry woman stomped to the railing and lifted a shovel, stepping back to the piles of manure.

Winston walked out on the tiny porch and waved us in. We made sure we were a safe distance from the woman with the spade.

"Pretty nasty stuff last night, wouldn't you say so, son?"

I agreed. The same words I'd used. We were all seated at the table, a paper cup of tequila in front of each of us as Pugh swung his short legs back and forth, never touching the ground. He had a half grin on his face, and I figured he had a snootful of the amber-colored liquid as well.

"Cops talk much to you, boy?"

"Just some general questions."

"What did they say? They wonder about me, finding the body and all?"

"If they did, they didn't tell me."

Pugh shot Em a hard look. "Lady, I don't know exactly what your involvement with these boys is, but I'm just gonna say what I think."

"And what do you think?" Em raised her eyebrows.

The short man cleared his throat. "What I think is that these two boys are investigating the rides here."

"Oh?"

"I pretty much figure it's the reason they didn't get many questions last night. They're in cahoots with the police. You see, they got a couple of questions and that was it. Now me, I spent an hour with those policemen. I thought I was goin' to jail."

"What are you trying to say?" I asked.

"You boys, you are part of the investigating team. They left you alone, didn't they?"

I had to admit that I didn't spend an hour with any detective. Still—

"They are," he pointed his finger at Em, "private investigators. Hired by Moe to pin blame on somebody."

"What if they were?"

"What if they are? What if they are? Well—"

He paused and pounded down a shot, pouring another immediately.

"Well, it would mean that somebody didn't want Kevin Cross to tell his story to the private investigators here. Somebody knew that I was bringing this young man to Kevin's camper. That's why the man was shot. It could mean—" he had nothing left to contribute.

It was pointless to argue with Pugh, especially since he was correct. We were private investigators. We had a license. Almost anyone, with a minimum amount of investigation could prove that we were in fact private investigators. Private investigators sounded very strange to me.

A synthesized version of "La Cucaracha" blared from somewhere on the kitchen counter.

"Is that your—"

The tinny song repeated itself.

I glanced up and saw the phone, complete with the Bluetooth earpiece, lying by the sink.

"It's the phone."

The irritating melody played again and I was ready to answer it myself just to stop the music.

"Are you going to answer it?"

Pugh glanced at the door. "No. No. Linda does that. I don't—" he didn't finish the sentence.

Mercifully the tune did not play again.

"Mr. Pugh, I came because I'm considering buying a dog." She gave him a sexy smile and his eyes lit up.

"What kind of dog?"

"Possibly an Old English sheepdog, like yours."

He forgot about the P.I. question immediately. "Any special qualities you want in your dog?"

"I don't want a dog that sheds too much."

He slapped his hand down on the table. "Well then, this here is your perfect dog. They have hair like humans, not fur. They don't shed more than you do." He paused and scratched his chest. "Not that I am saying you shed, miss."

"Oh, great. Very little shedding." Em reached in her clutch

purse and pulled out the pen. The gray pen that offered three hours of video and three hours of audio. She jotted something down on a sheet of white paper.

"And make sure you get a puppy who's been vaccinated and wormed."

Em scribbled another note.

"Oh, and I don't know what you do for a living, missy, but these dogs eat you out of house and home. You'd better plan on a pretty big budget for food. Course, we buy all of our food wholesale. I could probably get you a pretty good deal." He strained his neck to see what she was scribbling.

Em kept writing.

James had downed his shot and cautiously poured himself another. Pugh was busy talking to Em and never seemed to notice, or care.

"Come here, missy." Pugh stood up and walked to the door, pulling it open and yelling, "Garcia. Garcia!"

The shaggy dog loped over to the trailer.

"Well, come in here you big ol' sweetie." Pugh, barely taller than the dog, kneeled and placed both hands behind the ears of the creature. He scratched the hairy dog until the animal was whining. It beat the heck out of a low growl.

"You see? You can't find a friendlier dog." Pugh motioned to Em to scratch the dog behind his ears as well.

"Hey, Garcia." She knelt as well, the big hairy dog pushing his fuzzy head into her stomach.

She wasn't a dog person. I don't care that the dog fell under her spell, I knew she wasn't a big dog lover. Didn't hate them, but would probably never own one. This was all for show.

"Hey there, Garcia. How are you, huh? You big old guy." The dog scrunched his face and buried his head in her lap.

I noticed the pen was still in her hand as she reached to scratch the furry mutt.

Taking a step back, Garcia looked her in the eyes, his tongue hanging from his mouth. Em's spell seemed to overwhelm him. Then, in a split second I saw the eyes spark, the tongue gone from his face and his jaws open wide. He snapped down on the pen in Em's hand and with a jerk, he yanked it from her grasp.

"No." Em shrieked.

The dog leaped from the step, kicking up a cloud of dust as he hit the ground. His legs pumping as he ran for the railing, he stopped on a dime as he plastered himself flat on the ground. Then one, two, three, four maneuvers, scooting as he went and he squeezed under the lower railing, surfacing on the other side. A prison break had never been done so convincingly.

"I never." Pugh stood there with a stunned look on his face. We all stood there with stunned looks on our faces.

Garcia turned and gave us a head over shoulder gaze, as if to say "try and get me now, suckers."

"Well, I guess that plan is pretty much out the window." James stared accusingly at Em.

"James—" I was ready to deck the son of a bitch.

"What? This was the big idea?"

Pugh was out on the step yelling for the dog to come home. "Garcia. Garcia. You get back here." And the three families in the ring were glancing back and forth to the dog as he disappeared from sight and to the trailer where the short guy was begging his dog to return to the compound.

"Garcia. Come back, boy. You get back here, do you hear me?"

Linda ran to the fence, screaming at the top of her lungs. "Garcia. You damned dog, you turn around right now."

"If you think I'm paying for half that pen, you have another think coming, amigo." James crossed his arms and watched the carnival turned circus outside Winston Pugh's door.

CHAPTER TWENTY-ONE

"I've changed my mind." Em sat on the sofa/bed with a cold Yeungling in her hand. Cool and calm.

"Regarding what?" James spoke from a dining room table chair. He was leafing through the instruction manual for the Cell Sleuth.

"If I ever buy a frigging dog, it will not be an English sheepdog. You can't trust that breed."

"You had no intention of getting a dog," James said.

"If I ever did—"

"Nobody could have seen that coming." I seriously believed that. I never would have put that pen on the line if I'd had a clue.

"How much was the pen?" Em showed some concern. She could have paid for the pen with pocket change, no matter what the thing cost. I ignored the question. It was somewhat embarrassing to admit I didn't know the price.

The dog had not surfaced. Pugh and Linda paid a couple of the carnies twenty bucks each to go on a search-and-rescue mission, but it was ten p.m. and no one had brought him back. Forty bucks to find this stupid dog, but Garcia the thief had vanished.

"Skip. How much?" She stared into my eyes.

"Jody said he'd bill me."

My guess was that the price could be anywhere from one hundred to six hundred bucks. And who knew what it was worth with dog slobber all over it? I didn't want to tell her that I didn't even know. And I didn't want James to know that I had no idea "how much." I'd screwed things up royally, and I vowed to send James out for the spy equipment from now on.

"Skip?" She was getting angry.

"He never told me."

"He never told you what?" James kept his eyes on the printed page.

"All right. He never told me how much the damned thing cost. Okay? I don't have a clue." There. I'd said it.

"Damn." James looked up from his reading. "You don't even know how much this stuff was?"

"As I pointed out, you never paid him the last time. I mean, if you don't pay for it, it doesn't matter how much it was."

James scowled at me.

"Look, we can return it if we don't like it, James."

"Think about that statement, my friend. Return it? We don't know where the hell it is."

Oh, yeah. The pen was missing.

"Well, we should have a very good record of where the pen went. If and when we ever get it back." James rolled his eyes. "Em, you did turn it on, right?"

Em in turn rolled her eyes back at him.

"Well, I just wanted to be sure. With this great plan of yours, I never know." He flipped a page in the manual and kept on reading.

I didn't figure it made much difference at this point. If the pen was on and we found it, we'd have video of the show grounds, bouncing as the dog ran from sight.

"And we get, what? Three hours?" Em was still engaged in finding the pen. "Three hours of video?"

"Three hours," I said, "but that's if we find the thing."

Pugh was going to call me. On his cell phone. To let me know if the damned dog ever showed up. I was certain the pen would not be in Garcia's mouth.

"Skip," James lit a cigarette.

Normally I'd say something about smoking inside, but the windows and door were open, and I really didn't care. I just kept thinking about how much money this was going to cost me. I needed to make some sales. Some poor, unfortunate soul needed to buy a security system. I had bills to pay. It was obvious that this P.I. thing was not going to work out.

"We know Pugh's got a cell phone," he said.

"Yeah?"

"With one of those ridiculous ear pieces," Em said.

"Bluetooth." I shrugged my shoulders. "So what?"

"He's got a cell phone. Everybody understand that? And we've got the software and receiver, pard. The software to track every communication he makes on that phone." James had that smug, arrogant tone to his voice.

"So what do we do?"

James took a long drag on his cigarette and let the smoke escape his lips in a slow stream. "Listen, according to this manual, all we have to do is load the software on your laptop, plug in the antenna that came with the system you bought, and get close to Pugh and his phone."

"Close?"

"Maybe ten, fifteen feet."

"Then what?"

"The computer and the antenna automatically connect with his phone, assuming the Bluetooth device is on. We can download text messages, conversations, e-mail. Hell, we could check his tweets."

"I seriously doubt that Pugh and Linda use Twitter."

"But pard, according to this," he tossed the brochure down on the table, "we can do it. No problemo. And this receiver picks up all the calls. It's called Bluesnarfing."

"It's even got a name?"

"The process. Bluesnarfing."

"It automatically connects to his phone?"

"Kind of like your computer picks up a wireless signal."

"Jeez."

"I say we try it. What do we have to lose?" He walked to the door and tapped the cigarette ashes onto the dirt.

"Pugh is a nice guy, James." Bluesnarfing. It just sounded nasty. "We really shouldn't be messing with stuff like this. I'm sure it's illegal."

"You bought it, dude. You made the purchase. So I'm thinking that you thought it was a good idea at the time. Am I right?"

Em took another swallow of her beer. "He's right, Skip."

"What? For the second time today you agree with him?"

"We're looking for specific information. It's not like we're hacking his phone for personal information. We're not going after bank accounts, or a mistress that he's texting."

"Pugh? A mistress? He's very lucky he has Linda." This whole conversation was absurd.

"I still say that Winston Pugh is our guy." James took a puff on his cigarette. He'd hit up the guy with the pretzel cart, offering to buy a pretzel and Pepsi if the guy would give him a smoke. Given the cost of a pack these days, it probably was a great deal.

"If there's nothing on Pugh's cell phone, no harm done." Em leaned toward me. I couldn't believe she was on board with this.

"We won't even look at the personal stuff. We're simply trying to see if there's any mention of sabotaging rides."

"Or what? Shooting a carnie? I doubt if you text about killing someone."

"Skip." She put her hand on my knee and I knew I was going to agree with her. "Do you want to be paid or not? I would bet you money that there is incriminating evidence on Pugh's cell phone. Text messages that he had with your rifle guy, Kevin Cross. Calls he made to someone outside where he talks about how he's scared they're going to kick him out of the Show."

"Calls he made to Linda, if they're in this together." James's eyes were wide. He was getting into this spy thing.

"All right, fine." Walking back to the small bedroom I reached under the tiny bed and pulled out my company's laptop. If they ever found that I was using it to spy on some dwarf zoo operator, I'd probably get fired.

"James, you load it." I was washing my hands of this entire event. "You can put the Cell Sleuth software on the computer."

He already had the disc in his hand. "This is going to be so cool. You know, if Angie Clark has Bluetooth on her phone I could listen to her—" he let the thought hang when Emily shook her finger at him.

"How are you going to get close to his phone?" It seemed like something we should think about.

James slipped the disc into the computer and hit enter. We could hear it whirring inside the laptop, then a menu appeared on the screen.

"We go over to Pugh's trailer later tonight," he clicked on the menu, "when it's dark and the Show is closed. All we have to do is sit outside the trailer for a couple of minutes and the computer takes care of the rest."

"So it just connects?"

"That's what the instructions say."

It just sounded too easy. And too smarmy. And what happened if we got caught? In the middle of the night, outside Pugh's trailer with a computer? What would happen then?

"Skip, it's not like we're breaking and entering," Em said.

It was exactly like we were breaking and entering, but if Em was on board, then I guess I was too.

"Okay. Then it's a go." James keyed in on the menu items, then handed the computer to me. "Okay, amigo, when it gets really dark, you just—"

"Oh, no. Absolutely not. You're not going to hang this on me, *amigo*."

"It's *your* computer, Skip. I just thought you'd—"

"You just thought wrong."

"Oh, for crying out loud. You two are so childish, so asinine." Em reached out and grabbed the laptop from James.

"Name calling doesn't get you anywhere, Emily." James shot the comment at her as she tucked the computer under her arm.

"Screw you, James. I'm going over there right now, and I'm not only going to do some Bluesnarfing, but I'm going to find out if they have a computer." She stood up and walked to the door.

"Boys, watch me and learn."

We did.

CHAPTER TWENTY-TWO

We watched her brisk walk as she headed toward the zoo, computer tucked under her arm. She didn't even wait for me to grab the case. Puffs of dust exploded from her heels as she walked. Turning her head and shouting over her shoulder she yelled, "Skip, get your ass in gear."

I jogged to catch her while James stood in front of our silver trailer, shaking his head. Emily was going to show him how to run his P.I. firm.

"What are we going to do? It's still daylight. I mean—" I was gasping. Lack of exercise and too much beer will do that to you.

"You've got a very limited timetable to figure this thing out. If we work on James-time this will never get solved."

I didn't give it any hope to be solved no matter whose time we worked on. James-time or anyone else's time.

Em handed me the computer, put one foot on the zoo fence, and with little effort lifted herself over.

"Well, come on."

I handed her the computer and made the same maneuver. My foot caught in the rung and as I struggled to free it, I almost fell into the ring. Finally, wriggling it free, I stumbled into the animals' domain.

They were lined up on the far side of the fence, dipping their heads into a long trough. I never would have climbed the fence if Garcia had been watching his flock. But Garcia had broken the law and was on the run, criminal that he was. Thank God.

"Linda. Winston." Em was shouting as she walked to the trailer.

Winston stuck his head out of the door. "We haven't seen hide nor hair of Garcia, young lady. I would have called you in a heartbeat." He ran his hand through the sparse hair that sprouted from his head. "You don't have to keep pestering me. If I see him, you'll hear from me."

"That's not why we're here."

"Oh?"

"No, it's something else right now."

He looked relieved. "Ah, got a question for you, missy. I've been wondering. What the heck is so important with that pen?"

"First of all," Em strode up to the little porch as Pugh stepped out, "that pen belonged to my father. It's very expensive and I know he wants it back."

"Uh-huh. Looked to me like it was expensive. Very fancy lookin'."

"It means a lot to him. I really hope we can get it back."

"Okay. We're trying."

Em touched his arm with her free hand. "It's very important, Winston. I can't begin to tell you."

"There something else you wanted?" The short, stout zookeeper scratched his left armpit, glad to change the subject. Tugging on his overalls, he shifted his shoulders, maybe getting ready to square off with me and Em.

"Yes there is."

"You and the boy there?"

Em held out the computer. "You, Mr. Pugh, seem to be a guy who knows how to run a tight business. Therefore I'm guessing you have a computer that keeps your organization on track."

The little guy ducked his head. "Well, I do have one but I don't, you know, it's not so much—" as if he didn't want to discuss it.

"You've got a computer?"

"I do own a computer. It's a laptop, kind of tiny, and Linda uses it sometimes."

"I thought so. Can we see it? Skip is thinking about getting a new one, and I just wanted a professional opinion."

He stepped back through the doorway as he studied us on the ground. Finally he nodded.

"You brought *your* computer over here because?"

"To compare," Em smiled, that disarming smile of hers. The one that makes your heart kind of jump. "I told Skip," she looked at me and gave me a wink, "that you'd have a good idea of what computer he should get and probably what kind of software to load. Was I right?"

Pugh blushed. "Well, of course, you were right. Linda could probably give you some advice. Why don't you two come on in?"

We stepped up onto the landing and squeezed into the tiny camper as he motioned for us to sit at the table with the bottle of golden Jose Cuervo. "I'll get my Dell. You two stay right there."

He walked back into the tiny bedroom, and I grabbed Em by her shoulder. "You're brilliant," I whispered.

"I am, aren't I?"

"You can download the cell phone information right now."

He returned with the laptop clutched under his arm. "Here 'tis."

"Great." Em glanced around the room. "Where is Linda?"

"Oh, she's off for the night. She goes out with her girlfriends sometimes and they don't roll in until three or four in the morning. They play cards or something like that."

Em and I nodded.

"I can pour you some tequila while you're looking at the computer." He motioned to the bottle.

"You were going to call us if you found—when you found Garcia, when he came home. Remember?"

"Well, we haven't found him."

"But if he did come home?"

Pugh stood, stepped up on a three-step stool, and took three paper cups down from a shelf above the sink. Pouring from the bottle on the table, he smiled at us. "I'd probably have to come over to the trailer and *tell* you he'd come back."

"You've got Skip's cell phone number, right?"

"Well, Linda's got it. And she's got the phone."

We were quiet for a good thirty seconds.

"So, there's only one phone?"

"Yep."

Em was tight lipped. Finally, "So you don't have the phone?"

"Nope."

"And you can't really help us with the computer?"

"Linda and I could."

Em looked at her cup, lifted it with her right hand, and pounded down the beverage.

"Will you have another?" Winston asked.

"Nope. That's the computer you need, Skip. That frigging Dell laptop. Okay? Now it's time to go."

She grabbed my laptop and headed out the door. I didn't touch my drink as I ran after her.

"Damn."

"Hey, you couldn't have known."

"Skip. That shrimp can't operate a computer or a cell phone. No wonder he keeps Linda around." She was shaking with anger. "First the pen, now the cell phone. I'm screwing this whole thing up."

"No, you're—" I raced to keep up. She was walking straight toward the row of shops, the laptop held tightly under her arm.

"I am too. I really thought I'd be able to help you guys. You were better off by yourselves. Jeez. I thought we'd waltz in there and load the cell phone information in a few seconds. What was I thinking?"

"Hey, slow down. I can only move so fast."

"We're almost there."

"Where?"

She headed for the bar halfway down the strip mall, and waited for me outside the open door to Harry's Hideaway.

I staggered to the doorway. "You . . . walk . . . really . . . fast when you're—"

"What?"

"Mad."

"I just think we both could use another drink."

Out of breath, all I could do was nod. A drink and some oxygen.

"You've got till tomorrow night," she said. "If you have any chance of figuring out who is sabotaging the Moe Show, we have to get some information. And now—"

Walking into the dingy, dimly lit barroom I heard the din of voices and country twang coming from the old jukebox. A female duet harmonized about their exploits, the chorus lyrics resounding with, "Hey Thelma, you're gonna need a Louise."

I could vaguely make out some of the people at the far end of the bar. The place was hazy with smoke—one of those liquor establishments that didn't pay any attention to the no-smoking ordinance—and raucous laughter rang from the table next to us.

"Kind of like you and James," Em kept the laptop tight by her side as she surveyed the crowd of revelers.

"What's like me and James?"

"That song by Molly Reed. You two are like the male Thelma and Louise."

I ignored the comment.

"More like Laurel and Hardy. Or the two guys in *Dumb and Dumber*." She shook her head.

Surveying the small establishment I saw open seats at the bar.

Em read my mind. "Should we sit up there?"

I watched the chubby lady behind the counter as she slammed beer bottles on the cheap vinyl counter, pouring shots of straight alcohol and an occasional mix. This was raw drinking. No fancy Florida cocktails at Harry's. You'd get laughed out of there if you as much as ordered a Margarita.

I headed toward two open seats when she grabbed my arm.

"End of the bar. Four ladies. See them?"

"Oh, yeah." Boilermakers in front of them, and empties off to the side, it appeared that they'd been drinking for a while. I definitely recognized one of them.

"There's a seat right next to her. Stay here."

I watched as Em marched up to the lady. Over the noise I heard her.

"Hey, Linda. Remember me? Emily. Skip's girlfriend. I just wondered if this place has wi-fi."

Looking puzzled, Pugh's girlfriend watched as Em opened the laptop and tapped a couple of keys. Em stared at the keyboard for several seconds then back to Linda.

"Guess not." She closed the lid. "You ladies have a nice night, and Linda," she put her hand out and covered Linda's, "I sure hope your dog comes back home soon. Preferably with my pen. I really need that pen."

She got up, grabbed me by the arm and pulled me out of the bar.

With a self-satisfied smirk on her face, she waltzed across the parking lot toward our Airstream.

"Got it, Skip. We can tap into her cell phone anytime we want."

CHAPTER TWENTY-THREE

James was sitting on the step, a big smile on his face.

"Good news, amigo. Great news, even."

"Well then, ours can wait." James always trumped me. It never failed. "What's so great?"

"I found a truck. The spymobile is back in action."

"You what?" He didn't have a dime saved and had yet to cash his first paycheck from Moe. We had unpaid bills, and Jody Stacey had just informed me we owed him seventy-nine bucks. I knew all of this, and I knew there was no way he could afford a box truck.

"Same make and model as the old one, Skip. The one you blew up."

I let it slide.

"Lower mileage, and the owner swears it doesn't use as much oil."

"James—"

"It was in the paper. Call it serendipity, call it chance."

"What? An ad?"

"Box truck for sale. Skip, it screamed out to me."

"Do we need—"

Interrupting me, he glanced at Em. "I already know what your girlfriend is going to say, being the judgmental type that she is, but Angie is lending us the money."

"This is the girl who works for Moe?" A tone that maybe was just a little judgmental.

"Angie?" I couldn't believe it. And I couldn't believe that she was lending *us* the money. James, maybe. Definitely not us.

"I've been telling her how much we need the truck."

"*We* don't need the truck."

He stood up, walking down to meet us. "We need it, pally. If we want this business to succeed, we need the truck. And Angie Clark is lending us the money. I told you, she believes in me. Look, we can write it off to the business."

"James, I don't want to be a part of this *we*. And we don't need a write off. We don't make enough to even qualify for—"

He put his hand up, fending my comments off. "I pick it up in an hour."

Looking at my cheap Timex I realized that would be ten p.m.

"And where's your banker?"

"Took off for an appointment. She'll be back. But come on, pard, isn't it very cool that we're getting another truck?"

The truck had been the bane of our existence. In just the past year we'd tried to use it as a moving van and we were almost killed. We'd turned his former truck into a traveling kitchen for a salvation show and almost been killed. We'd turned the now destroyed truck into a spymobile and—

"You're that close with this girl, after one day, that she lends you money?" Em couldn't leave it alone.

"See what I mean, roommate?" He glared at me, then at Em. "As hard as this may be for you to fathom, the majority of women find me charming, Emily."

"Then the majority of women are idiots, James."

"How much did she—" I never got to finish the question.

"Twelve grand, my man." He held up what appeared to be a check. "I figure two or three jobs and we'll pay for it all."

"We?"

"You're on the P.I. license, dude. So yes, I say *we*. You and me, Tonto. We need this truck."

I was with Em. He knew Angie Clark for a couple of days and she lends him twelve thousand dollars? Maybe this lady really did work for a bank. Or recently robbed one.

"We need to talk about this, James."

"Let me repeat myself. We need a truck, Skip." He gave me a very hard look and that was that. "Now, tell me your good news." He folded his arms and waited for our story.

It wasn't over. I hadn't signed on to James's latest scheme, but I decided to let it rest for the moment.

"Em hacked the cell phone, James. She hacked Pugh's and Linda's cell. It was slick. As long as Linda and Pugh stay in the area, we'll have access to all their communication."

"No kidding?"

"No kidding. You should have seen her."

"Well, my hat's off to you."

"And," I took my laptop from Em, "Pugh has a computer."

"They're wide open to our intrusions, right? So all your purchases from Jody are paying off except—"

"No one has found the dog."

"Or the expensive pen. Well," James nodded to Em, "let's go in and have a celebratory drink."

"As long as it's not your coffee." Em stepped up and entered our humble abode.

She had the computer up and running in seconds.

"Text messages to her girlfriends. Ruth, Margie, Kathy. About meeting at Harry's tonight."

"Pretty incriminating evidence." I couldn't help but lend sarcasm to the text.

She didn't respond. "Here's a message to her mother in New Hampshire."

"How do you know?" James sipped his beer, sprawled on the couch.

"Know what?"

"She's in New Hampshire."

"It says 'How are things in New Hampshire?'"

"Ah."

"I thought we weren't going to read the personal stuff." The two of them had made a big deal of telling me there would be no screening of personal messages.

"Skip," Em looked up from the computer screen, "how are we going to find the ones that are relevant if we don't read the rest of them?"

I glanced over her shoulder. "Oh, there's a damning message. A note to their veterinarian." I studied it for a second. "About changing the formula for the deer's medicine." I stepped away. "Well, now I know that they're guilty."

"Skip—"

"I just don't know what you two thought we'd find."

"Hey, we've got tonight and tomorrow, pardner. That's it. We've got to pull out all the stops or Ken Clemens and the team of Schiller and Crouse will stop us. Cold."

"This could take a while." Em was scrolling slowly, scanning each text message for clues. And I was sure there were none.

"If they make a call, or take a call, then what?"

James picked up the instruction manual. "According to this, we can intercept them all on the receiver. We're covered."

"So," I quit spying on Pugh's messages, "these tools are sort of our weapons?"

"That's probably a good way to look at it." Em kept scroll-ing.

"You remember the quote, 'A weapon unused is a useless weapon?'" James asked.

I did. "*Spies Like Us.*"

"Dan Akroyd, Chevy Chase."

"A terrible film."

"Most of theirs were. But, the line works. A weapon unused is a useless weapon."

"Hey, here's a message. Linda did send a text to Kevin Cross. She asked him if he'd be home last night. She says, "Winston can come over and talk to you." She got that smug look on her face.

"Means nothing."

"Means that she set up a meeting with Cross and her boyfriend."

A knock at the door startled us, and Em slammed the lap-top screen down. It's funny how paranoid you get when you're breaking and entering.

"Yeah?" James and I called out in unison.

The screen door creaked open and Pugh shoved his little head through the opening.

"Hey, Winston. What's up?" My eyes went from the little guy to the computer sitting on the table.

Em's eyes shifted to the little man, probably wondering the same thing I did. Had he heard us discussing his cell phone?

"Garcia's home."

"And?"

"No pen. Sorry."

I wished that I'd gotten the price on that pen.

"Any idea where he was?" Em was thinking about the pen too.

"Yeah. The boss brought him home."

"Boss?"

"Moe. Seems the dog was over there most of the time. Moe always gives him a treat, these cheese crackers he keeps, so—"

"Well, thanks." I was trying to figure out how I was going to pay for the pen video camera.

"Hey, is that your computer there?" He walked in, and Em froze. Pugh walked to the table and touched the case.

"It's on the blink, Winston. Not working. That's one of the reasons that we asked you—"

"Here. Let me see. On the blink, I'll go get Linda. She can probably fix it."

The short man made a grab for the laptop and flipped it open. "I'll just take it over to—"

"No." Em shrieked.

James and I froze, waiting to see Pugh's reaction.

"Seems to be on." He glanced at us with a frown then stared at the screen. "Course, Linda could tell you for sure."

"It's just in the sleep mode. See? It's not on the blink at all." Em reached out and yanked it from his grasp. As I told her, she's really fast when she gets mad.

Stepping back, Winston stared up at her with his mouth wide open.

"Missy—"

"Look here, Mr. Pugh. I've got some personal information on this screen, and I can't let a stranger just see everything that I—"

He studied her for a moment, a look of puzzlement on his face. His personal cell phone messages were two inches from his fingertips. Linda's text to Kevin Cross was within reach.

"Okay. Okay. Just wanted to be of some help." He frowned and turned toward the door. Looking back at us he said, "Remember, you came to me. You wanted help. So next time don't come lookin' for any of my expertise. 'Cause you won't get it. You just figure it out for yourself." He stomped out of the trailer, letting the door bang behind him. The last time he'd left this trailer, I was with him and we were on our way to find a dead body.

Em set the computer back on the table and took a deep, ragged breath. "Well that would have been interesting."

We were all quiet for a moment.

"Never saw it coming," James said.

"There's a lot of things we don't see coming." I shifted my eyes to Em and she avoided them.

"Hey, pard. He doesn't suspect a thing. Okay? I think we handled that situation very well."

Em had handled it very well.

"Got to grab Angie and go get the truck, amigo." We walked outside and heard Angie shouting to James from Moe's trailer.

"Come with me. Em, you can meet Angie and Moe."

We walked across the lot, making out the luxury trailer in the dusk.

Moe and Angie sat on the porch and she jumped up and hugged James.

"Angie, I want you to meet Em, Skip's off-again, on-again girlfriend."

Em smiled a smile she didn't really mean and shook Angie's hand.

"And Em, this is Moe. Moe is our employer."

"Glad to meet you, young lady."

"So Garcia was hanging out with you this evening?"

He laughed. "He was. He likes my cheese crackers. Never knew a dog to eat cheese crackers, but he does."

"Moe," Em was staring at him, "is there any chance Garcia had a pen in his mouth when you found him?"

"A pen? Nope."

"That pen in your pocket—"

He glanced down at his shirt.

"It looks very much like one my father gave me. One that Garcia took from my hand a couple of hours ago."

"Ah, this pen." He pulled it out and handed it to her. "Found it on the ground over there. Dog must have dropped it."

"Yeah. This is it. Thank you so much. This means a lot to me."

Moe smiled, charming Em from the start. "I'm glad I could help such an attractive woman. You are truly a beautiful lady."

I know Em was blushing.

"James, we've got a truck to pick up, remember?"

Angie grabbed his arm and pulled him toward her trailer.

"Thanks, Moe." I didn't know what else to say.

"How you coming on our special project, Skip?"

"Fine. Just fine. Lots of things happening."

"How about you and James give me a short report tomorrow morning, about eight a.m.?"

"Um, sure, we can do that."

He smiled, stood up and walked into his plush home, the door slamming behind him.

We stood there for a moment looking at each other.

"Fine? Just fine?" Em gave me a weak smile.

"It's better than saying we don't have a clue."

"Then we'd better get a clue by tomorrow morning. You just agreed to a meeting at eight."

"All right. We'll go back and keep reading phone messages."

Em smiled at me. "Did you ever stop to think that whenever there's work to be done, whenever there's heavy lifting—"

"James is somewhere else."

"That's what I was going to say."

"But, hey, we're better off than we were ten minutes ago."

"How's that?" She looked puzzled.

"We've got the pen and I don't have to pay for it if I return it."

We started back to the Airstream.

"And, Skip. Just think how good things are going to be in about an hour."

"You are talking about you and me?" I had a feeling she was alluding to an all-nighter at the trailer.

"No, no. Don't get all excited." She shook her pretty head. "I'm talking about you and James."

"Me and James?"

"Hey, boy, you're going to have another box truck."

"Oh, yeah." That took all the excitement out of me. "Now we're sure to solve the case."

CHAPTER TWENTY-FOUR

Em grabbed my hand and for the first time in months we walked together, hand in hand. We walked without talking, not really paying attention to where we were going. Just walking.

"And maybe I will stay the night." Her voice was soft and sexy. "I've never made love in an Airstream before."

"You know something? Neither have I."

Long shadows lay on the show grounds, cast by a pale half moon as it lit up the rides. In the distance I could see a light bobbing around the perimeter. A flashlight from Moe's security patrol. Actually, the patrol was made up of two of the ride operators who split the late shift for an extra fifty bucks apiece. Cheap security.

"Skip?"

"Yeah."

"You know you really should put together a plan."

"I thought we had one. You know, bug Pugh's phone. Put the pen in Pugh's trailer. Bug Pugh's computer."

"But you think there might be other suspects."

I was quiet. Duh.

"You don't believe that Pugh is behind this, do you? Even though he does have a terrific motive?"

"No. I thought I made that clear. He's harmless. But I'm even more puzzled by something else."

"What's that?"

"Why you're involved. I thought by now you'd know better than to get into anything that James has going on."

"Maybe I'm just looking out for you."

"So what else do we do?"

"Find out how those rides were tampered with. Maybe go over and talk to that security guy who's bopping around the show grounds. Maybe talk to Bo and Charlie and let them know who you are and what you want."

"But that blows our cover and I'm not sure that Bo and Charlie—"

She let go of my hand and stopped in front of me. "If you haven't figured it out, Skip, your cover is blown. Now you've got to start asking questions."

We reached the trailer and I stepped up to open the door. Before I could get my fingers on the handle the door swung out hard, banging my head, and I stumbled off the landing, crashing into Em. As I pushed myself to my feet, a shadowy figure leapt down from the step. Whoever it was seemed as surprised as I was, and in the faint light I saw him duck his head, taking one step toward me. I felt a fist go deep in my gut, clear to my spine and when I doubled up that same fist caught my jaw. My head snapped back and I remember crumpling to the ground, the world spinning out of control.

Em was shouting my name as I blacked out.

CHAPTER TWENTY-FIVE

She was shaking me, awakening me, and I struggled to open my eyes, finally staring into her face, which was highlighted by the distant moon. And maybe a couple of show lights that burned in the distance.

"Skip."

Now her face was brilliant, hot white with a bright spotlight and I thought for just a moment she was an angel. And she was no longer looking at me, but staring up in the air. And with a great deal of pain I turned my head and saw the lights of heaven, twin lights, with a yellow blinking light.

The yellow blinking light threw me off.

Em was on her feet, jogging to the light.

"Did you see someone running?"

"Almost hit 'em." The voice was James's.

"Whoever it was broke into your trailer, ran out, and had a rather nasty run-in with Skip."

"Whoa."

I struggled to a sitting position—and realized the twin head-lights and blinking yellow light were part of James's new truck.

"Pard, you okay?"

I shook my head, and spit on the ground. It felt like my front tooth was loose. "I've been better."

"Almost ran over the guy just a minute ago."

"Did you recognize him?"

"Never got a good look."

Em glanced around. "Where's Angie? Did she get a look at him?"

"I doubt it. I dropped her off at her trailer."

"James, at least you got a truck that has a turn signal." The blinking yellow light finally registered.

"Don't get too excited, amigo. It never goes off. We're perpetually turning left. But I'll get it fixed. I'll get it fixed."

Em was stroking my hair, not knowing exactly what to do.

"Let's get you inside." James turned off the engine and it coughed and hiccuped. Not a good omen. He helped me up the steps, my legs feeling like Jello.

Pulling the door open, he caught me as I stumbled in, planting myself on the couch.

"What the heck did he want?"

"Are we sure it was a 'he'?"

"Hit pretty hard if it was a she." I rubbed my jaw.

Everything seemed to be in order. The computer still sat on the small table, and there wasn't much else of value in the tiny unit.

Em walked to the small refrigerator and opened it. She pulled out two of the last four beers and handed me a cold bottle.

"Opener?"

"No. You put the bottle on your jaw. If you don't, that's going to swell up to where you can't even talk."

I put the bottle on my jaw and Em poured half of the other beer into a stained coffee mug. She handed the mug to James and took a swig from the bottle.

"This is a good thing, amigo."

"And just how is this a good thing, James? I get smacked around, someone breaks into our trailer—"

"Skip. We've stirred something up. Last night, the guy from the air rifle booth wants to talk. Before you get to him, someone has killed him. Tonight, someone thinks we're close to solving the case, and they break in trying to see what information we have. We're making things happen."

"And we have absolutely no idea what happened."

"Start eliminating."

"Like how?"

James took a slug of beer from his coffee mug. "There must be someone we can eliminate."

Em sat down on a vinyl kitchen chair and we all thought about that for a moment.

"Well," I knew who wasn't our break-in artist. "It wasn't Winston Pugh. He's not the guy who broke in."

"And how do you know that?" Em asked.

"Come on, Em. He hit me in the jaw."

"Oh, yeah. Winston couldn't reach your jaw."

"But that doesn't eliminate him from being the guy who sabotaged the rides. He's still got the best motive we know of." James made his point.

I got the point. It was just that I couldn't picture the little guy actually killing anyone.

"He wasn't happy when he left here." Em knocked back another swallow.

"Reminds me of the dwarf I rear-ended with my truck last year," James said.

"I don't remember that."

"Oh, yeah. He gets out of his car and he yells, 'I'm not Happy.' So I said, well, then which one are you?"

I didn't bother to smile.

"We can rule out—"

"Angie Clark." James nodded his head.

"Are you sure? What do you really know about her?" Em pried.

"It's just that she gave us a pile of money. If she's guilty why would she want to help us?"

"To throw us off the track," Em said

"That's an expensive decoy."

"Or maybe it was to throw us off the truck," I suggested.

"Hey, the truck is going to pay off, amigo. I promise you."

"Yeah. I'm sure."

"Guaranteed."

"James, the first truck never paid off. And you didn't have to pay anyone back for that one."

James licked his lips. "This one's got some built-in cabinets in the back, Skip. We can haul some of the gear."

"You could put the gear in the trunk of a car."

"Yeah, but this truck comes complete with an extension ladder, pally."

"An extension ladder?"

"Yep. Big, long aluminum ladder. Probably goes up twenty, thirty feet. Rides right on top of the truck."

"So we can raid second-story sorority houses?"

James turned away and ignored me.

"Well, we've got the computer and we can still track Pugh's calls." Em pulled the computer over to her and clicked. The screen came to life.

"Well here's something interesting." She frowned. "Someone read the screen with Pugh's calls."

"Uh-oh." James's eyes got big and wide.

"It appears they just scanned a few of them so I'd bet they didn't know what they'd found."

"Let's hope."

"And whoever was here typed in a message of their own."

"They did what?"

"Keyed in their own message," Em said. She shoved the computer to me and I glanced at the screen.

Another reason it couldn't be Pugh. He obviously didn't know how to operate a computer.

In big bold type it said, **PRIVATE COPS, GO HOME.**

CHAPTER TWENTY-SIX

James walked out from the bedroom. "Nothing I can see. I think you guys scared them off. And my guess is that whoever it was just wanted to scare us."

"They succeeded." I wondered where the next attack would come from.

The three of us looked around the tiny space, all of us feeling a little paranoid.

"Let's take a walk outside." Em opened the door and motioned to me. I walked out, followed by James.

"Someone may have bugged the trailer." She looked back at the silver bullet-shaped trailer. "I say we call the cops." I expected that from Em.

James was firm. "No way. The cops get involved, we're screwed. I've never known it to fail."

"So, do we call Moe?" I already knew the answer to that one.

"Hell no." James was adamant. "We'll see him at the meeting and we can bring this up if we want to."

He was right.

"I'm going to Angie's place. Grab a couple of beers, and I'll be back after I talk to her. He walked out of the trailer and we were quiet for a moment. Em cracked the last two beers and made me put ice on my jaw. And I've got to tell you, it's tough to drink beer when you're pressing an ice bag on your face.

She read some more text messages from Linda and Pugh, but no one ever made a call on their phone, so around midnight we decided to pack it in. Em and I retired to the minibedroom and even though I was a little sore, we fell into a comfortable routine.

Despite what happened earlier in the Fun House, I found that you can have fun in a trailer.

She drifted off to sleep and I tossed for half an hour. I would have tossed *and* turned, but the bed was too small to do both.

Finally, I got up and went to the kitchen. The computer sat on the table where we'd left it. I opened the door and looked outside, watching that bobbing flashlight in the distance. It stopped down by the Dragon Tail and seemed to disappear. I wondered if the guard was taking a break.

James's new used truck was parked beside my car and Em's T-Bird, and I questioned how he was ever going to pay for it. His last vehicle had come from the money he inherited from an aunt he didn't ever remember. I wondered if he had any other aunts or uncles in the family who were inclined to leave him a small inheritance.

There was a warm breeze blowing across the show ground, and I left the door open. I figured James was probably right. No one was coming back tonight.

Picking up the empty beer bottles, I tossed them in the trash, and thought about Em in the next room. Probably the best thing that ever happened to me, and it was all just like something floating on the breeze. It could disappear at any moment. One breath of air and it could all be gone.

In the small kitchen mirror my face looked puffy, and I saw

the angry red skin where someone's fist had collided with my jaw. My stomach muscles were sore from the blow and I rubbed the tender section with my hand.

And then I saw the pen on the kitchen countertop. We'd forgotten all about it. I picked up the silver cylinder and smiled when I realized how concealed everything was. I'd seen it working live when Jody had it in his pocket. That was the only time I'd seen it. Live.

Now I wanted to see how it played back the recording in the computer. I unscrewed the top as if to put in a new ink cartridge, and there was the plug, as simple as that. Almost like the antenna that we'd plugged in to tap Pugh's cell phone. I plugged it into a port and heard the chimes on my laptop.

Turn up the volume, hit play on the menu. Could it be that easy? It was. Screen popped up and there was the jerky picture of Pugh, then the table, then someone's fingers, then a piece of fabric and maybe a chair as the moving picture swept back and forth, up and down, in and out. I felt my stomach turn, and for a minute felt like I was back on the Dragon Tail.

I moved the cursor ahead and the video was bouncing, racing at full tilt, and I knew the pen was in Garcia's mouth. I couldn't watch. I moved it ahead, maybe ten seconds.

And it was perfectly still. The lens was a little dusty, but the picture was still, quiet almost, a blurry, dusty image, and I could hear a voice in the distance.

"Hey, old man. How are you? Working a little far from home aren't you?"

Moe, talking to someone.

"Well, you come on up here. You know I've always got your cheese crackers."

And I knew where the pen had ended up. Standing up I stretched and reached to shut the lid.

"What's that?"

I turned around, thinking someone was talking over my shoulder, but it was Moe walking closer to the microphone.

"What is that? Looks like somebody has gone and left a perfectly good pen lying here."

And it started moving. A good picture of Moe's face, then a blur and a shot of Garcia, chewing crackers as fast as he could.

Then a bounce and step after step as the pen in Moe's pocket jumped up and down and sideways and back, with sweeps and swoops. I tell you, it's not for the weak of stomach to watch.

Finally he was on the steps, and I could tell he was moving into his American Eagle trailer.

"Come on, Garcia. Get in here."

The dusty, mangy sheepdog with the vicious growl was now inside with Moe, and I felt like an intruder. I was inside as well.

"Let's get you some water, boy."

The pen moved to the kitchen, then I heard the faucet running.

There was a pounding, and the camera turned and made a stop before approaching the door, probably for Moe to put a bowl of water down for the criminal canine.

The door opened, and I heard Moe's voice.

"So, you decided to visit me after all."

The pen was picking up the material of someone's shirt. It was blurry, so close that I couldn't make it out.

"Well come on in, if you want to know what's going on. I'm not going to talk to you out there."

I heard that familiar growl and I knew that the sheepdog had it out for other people besides James and me.

"Garcia. You calm down. Go eat your crackers." Another blur and Moe said, "Sit down."

A rustling of fabric and leather, and the pen was cocked toward the blank screen of the big-screen TV. Most of what I could see was the TV. I couldn't make out the guest, but whoever it was hadn't uttered a word.

"You were right. They're looking at you as a, let's say, a person of interest. I think they suspect you and your partner. And I'm warning you, you'd better be able to cover your ass. Understand?"

Then I heard the voice. Two words.

"I understand." Whoever it was had turned from the microphone and the voice sounded like it was in a cave.

And that's when things got very, very interesting.

CHAPTER TWENTY-SEVEN

The camera was focused on the dark big-screen TV. When Moe sat still I could see the room reflected in that monitor. I caught a quick view of Garcia, off to the side of the room, not a good image, but it was obviously the dog. And the white-haired Moe, although it was tough to make out his features. And the man sitting next to Moe. As soon as I tried to study him Moe moved, and the camera moved. I swear I was going to be seasick.

Cursing, I continued to watch as the camera changed its angle. I was now viewing the kitchen from the plush leather sofa. That wasn't going to get me anywhere. And then it hit me. I could back up the video, freeze frame a picture and enlarge it. I knew I could do that because the menu said I could.

I carefully rewound the video back to where the big-screen TV was visible. Freezing the picture, I worked the mouse and arrow, and sure enough, the TV screen got larger and larger and larger.

"What's that?"

The video wasn't playing, but I stared at the screen, trying to figure out where the female voice came from.

"Skip, what is that?"

I turned quickly. "You almost gave me a heart attack."

"What are you doing?" She stood there in a T-shirt that barely covered her cute little butt.

"I'm watching the video from the pen." It sounded dumber than heck, but that's what I was doing.

"At this hour of the morning?"

"I couldn't sleep."

"And what have you found?"

"Em, somebody just knocked on Moe's door and he let them in."

She put her hand on my shoulder. "Maybe we should see a doctor about a possible concussion. What do you think?"

"Listen, I know this sounds weird, but Moe told whoever it is that they are a person of interest."

"Are you listening to yourself?"

It sounded crazy. "Em, he said the person had better be able to cover their ass. His word."

"So you think this has something to do with you?"

"With us?" I looked back at the screen. "Maybe."

"So Moe is warning someone that they are a person of interest? What does that mean?"

"Like a suspect. You know."

"So who is this person? Did you hear the voice?"

"Muffled."

"All I see is a screen. A TV screen. What do you possibly intend to find with that? There's nothing there."

"Watch this."

I brought it closer and closer. The resolution was bad and the reflection lacked any mirror quality—just dark and grainy, but I zeroed in on the suspect. I glanced behind me to make sure she was watching.

"There he is."

She leaned in close and I could smell her perfume.

"Moe said that this guy and his partner were suspects and that they'd better be able to cover their asses.

"Skip, it's not a good picture. How can you tell? I mean if the camera was right on him, maybe, but—"

"Come on, Em. Don't you recognize the guy? Who does that look like?"

"I don't know. I don't believe that—"

"I'd swear it's him, Em."

I knew now why Garcia was growling at him.

She studied it for several seconds. "Now why would Moe accuse James of being a suspect? And for what?"

I didn't have an answer, but I did have the rest of the pen video to watch.

CHAPTER TWENTY-EIGHT

There they were, sitting side by side, and I forwarded the video to where I'd left off. Moe was talking and I could see into the kitchen.

"He's got orange juice and champagne in that stainless refrigerator."

"And that's not helping us at all."

I would have liked some orange juice and champagne. Would have tasted good and maybe eased some of the pain in my jaw.

"You and what's-his-name, people are starting to talk about the two of you. Maybe we just need to distance ourselves right now. Take a break." Moe sounded concerned. Telling James to distance himself?

I stopped the video. "Did you hear that? He's going to fire us. I really needed the money this time, Em."

"Distance yourselves? What does that mean? I didn't hear 'fire.' Skip, where do you get the idea that someone is going to fire you?"

"You heard him. He said people are talking. Everyone

knows that we're private investigators. It's the worst kept secret in the world." Private investigators. The title sounded so phony.

"Maybe." She was skeptical. "Keep it going."

I hit play and heard a growl. The camera shifted and I could see Garcia's head, filling my computer screen.

"Hey, what do you want? What do you want?" Moe's hand extended and he ruffed up the dog's head, scratching him behind the ears. And as he leaned over, the camera lens tumbled, bouncing with a thunk and a thud.

"What happened?"

The video took off, and I saw carpeting, at least I think it was carpeting and a swish and a swirl and dark wood, a flash of white, a flash of yellow, and again it was making me nauseous.

"What the hell—"

And then everything was quiet and there was just a white screen.

"Skip, was that the—"

"Dog? I think so. Your friendly canine stole the pen again."

"Well, damn."

"That's it? Damn?"

"What was James doing there?"

"We've got another hour to watch."

And we did. Except for some very distant, unintelligible conversation, there were no more clues. Finally, at the end of the video, I could hear Moe. His voice got louder and louder as if he was approaching the microphone.

"Come on you thief. Give it up. Where did you put that pen, huh? Where is it, big guy?"

And it came to life, bouncing, moving with a dizzying speed, and then there was Garcia's big face, his tongue hanging out and what appeared to be drool running from his mouth.

"We've got to get you home, pal."

And just like that, the video stopped.

"Three hours, my ass."

"What?"

"Jody said three hours. I don't think the whole production lasted more than an hour and a half."

"Skip, what did it all mean?"

"I'm tempted to go down to Angie's trailer and find out." My roommate had some serious explaining to do.

"It's four in the morning."

"Oh, yeah."

"So, you'll come back to bed?"

"It's Sunday, Em. Today we either find out who is sabotaging the show, or we lose our jobs."

"It sounds like you may have already lost them."

"Then four a.m. is simply a time. And it is the precise time to wake up my roommate and find out about his clandestine meeting with Moe."

I was surprised she answered the door. Who knows, it could have been Kevin Cross's killer. It could have been whoever broke into our trailer and punched me. But she opened the door, dressed in at least a pink terry cloth robe. I had no idea what was under the wrap.

"Skip? Do you know what time it is?"

"Four oh three." I breathed in her soft, sweet scent.

Angie glanced at her watch. "This thing always was a little slow. What do you want at this ungodly hour?"

"James."

I was in no mood for polite conversation. I knew the time. I knew what I wanted. I depended on Angie to get it done.

She walked back into her trailer and a full sixty seconds later my roommate staggered to the door.

"Skip, what the hell—"

"Same thing I was going to say, James." I stood in the doorway, not having been invited inside. "What the hell, James?"

"I'm missing something here, compadre."

"Yes, you are. Come with me."

James stood there, his face hanging out. I figured he'd go back and at least get dressed, but he walked outside with just his boxers on and a pair of sandals.

"Want to get dressed first?"

"No. Because once you tell me what this is about, I'm going back to bed—with Angie."

I grabbed him by the arm and steered him toward our trailer.

"This had better be really good, amigo. Because right now, I am seriously pissed. I may not show it, because I'm tired and hung over, but I am pissed."

"And I don't care."

He could tell I was mad. There was no more conversation. When we entered the Airstream, Emily did a double take. I don't know that she'd ever seen James in his underwear, and it did take her aback.

"I'm here for a very short time, Em. I'm sorry to shock you, but I'd like to get back to bed, and soon. If I'd taken the time to dress—" he spread his arms out as if the hassle of the dressing process would overwhelm him, "I would have added a couple minutes to my time."

She looked confused.

"And by the way," James appraised Em, "nice T-shirt. Very nice."

She walked back into the bedroom, coming out seconds later in a pair of jeans.

"Skip, please show me whatever it is you want me to see. Then get out of my way and let me go back to Angie."

James sat down as I opened the screen, waited until the computer awakened, then pulled up the zoom photo of the big-screen TV.

"What are we watching?"

"Video from the pen."

"The pen?"

"The one I was going to have to pay for if we didn't get it back."

"Oh, yeah. The ballpoint pen. With the new truck, you getting smacked around, Angie getting frisky, I completely forgot about the pen."

"Yeah. Maybe the above reasons are why we should stay out of the private investigator business."

James said nothing.

"So, my friend, are you ready to see what I've found?"

James studied the screen intently. I zoomed in as close as I could.

"I have no idea what I'm looking at here."

"This is a reflection from Moe's big-screen TV. The pen camera that's in Moe's pocket is focused on his blank screen."

"So we're inside Moe's American Eagle?"

"We are. And there are three players in the room. Here—"

"Appears to be the dog."

"Here." I touched the computer screen.

"All right, I would guess that's Moe. It's hard to tell. Too fuzzy."

"And here. Who is this, James?"

"Amigo, the tone of your voice is almost accusatory."

"Who is it?"

He studied the picture, frozen on the laptop. I'd brought it in as tight as possible. Finally he leaned back and looked at me, a bemused grin on his face.

"That's Charlie, from the Dragon Tail. Is this your big revelation?"

I leaned in and looked.

Em leaned in and looked.

Sure enough. Moe's guest was Charlie, from the Dragon Tail. Bo's partner.

CHAPTER TWENTY-NINE

We were hunched over the table, four thirty in the morning, hearing for the fourth time what Moe said to Charlie: "You were right. They're looking at you as a, let's say, a person of interest. I think they suspect you and your partner. And I'm warning you, you'd better be able to cover your ass. Understand?"

Then the second part of the conversation: "You and what's-his-name, people are starting to talk about the two of you. Maybe we just need to distance ourselves right now. Take a break."

"It's still not much to go on."

"James, it's all we've got to go on."

"What does it mean?"

"Moe sounds like he's warning Charlie. Warning him that someone suspects him of something. Probably of sabotaging the rides." I just had a strong feeling. That had to be what they were talking about.

"And I still think Winston is our man." James was adamant.

"And I think you're wrong. Why couldn't it be Charlie and Bo? They have access. They know how to manipulate the machinery."

"I'm not sure they're that bright, amigo."

"Skip, that makes no sense." Em spoke up, now curled up on the couch.

"Why?"

"Because Moe is intent on finding the people involved. The people trying to take down his show."

"And?"

"And? Why would he warn Charlie that he and Bo were suspects? If he wants to find the bad guys, he's not going to warn them."

"We've talked about Bo and Charlie, but have we ever seriously considered them as suspects? Have we?" I didn't remember Bo and Charlie being talked about as possible players. But again, in their current positions, they would have access to the rides. A good point to consider.

"Yeah." He seemed deep in thought. "We had a conversation. Nothing serious, but I seem to remember we said they should be considered persons of interest." James tapped his fingers on the table. "I know we had that conversation."

James had always figured Pugh as the primary suspect. I didn't believe it.

"In fact, I think it was your idea, amigo."

And then it hit me. "*You* said that." There was no conversation. Just James spouting off. "You said that Bo and Charlie were persons of interest."

"Whatever." He shrugged his shoulders. "It came up." He kept tapping fingers. "But maybe Moe *isn't* intent on finding the people sabotaging the Show." James sitting there on the kitchen chair in nothing but his boxers.

"Why would you say that? He hired you and Skip to find the culprits." Em was in his face.

"When we talked to Ken Clemens, he claimed that Moe didn't want any investigation."

"What? He hired you for heaven's sake."

"He's right, Em." I nodded. "I didn't tell you, but Ken Clemens dates Judy Schiller and Clemens claims the sisters insisted on an investigation. They *made* Moe hire an investigation company. He says Moe was adamantly opposed to the idea."

Em stood, walking to the door and opening it, letting the early morning breeze blow through our stale trailer. Turning to the two of us she said, "I don't get it. Moe Bradley hires you as private investigators, but he's opposed to the investigation. Makes no sense."

"Ken said the sisters own controlling interest in the Show. And they get what they want. They wanted an investigation; they got us." I stood up and put my hands on her shoulders, massaging her neck.

"So," Em relaxed as I squeezed her tight muscles, "he didn't want to hire you, but they forced the issue."

"They didn't necessarily want *us*. Clemens made it clear that the sisters thought we were bozos. He seemed to recognize that we were uniquely unqualified for the job." I hated to admit it. "But they wanted an investigation. And we were close at hand." I squeezed her shoulders again.

"If you two want to get cozy, I'll just head on back to Angie's."

"Hold on, James." I let go of Em and looked him in the eyes. "Tell me again, who is Angie?"

"Come on, Skip."

"Where is she from, what does she do for the Show?" All the players were suddenly important.

"I'm not sure. This is the exploratory stage, pardner. We've only known each other for a couple of days."

Em walked around and stared him in the eyes. "That's when all this stuff usually comes out, James. In case you haven't dated before. The first couple of dates usually consist of talking about your backgrounds."

He smiled. "In this case, and I have dated before, something else has been more pressing. We've been preoccupied."

"Oh, give me a break."

"Okay," he said, "I know she went to Bluffton College. Someplace in Ohio. They are known as the Bluffton Beavers. I know that she was in finance. She worked for some bank."

James's private banker.

"And she was married. Clark is her married name. Other than that, you're right. I don't know much."

"And she just volunteered to lend you the money for your truck? After you've known her for what? Two days? Is she crazy?" Em shook her head.

"I think it was a good investment." James stood up. "She thinks it's a good investment. She asked me a lot of questions, Skip. It's not like she just handed me the money." He licked his lips. "You know, I don't need to sit here and be insulted and questioned like I am a criminal. Don't need it."

"James, I'm sorry." I was. It was his life, but right now our possible career hung in the balance. "I just think we should know what her interest in this is. Shouldn't everyone involved with the Show be considered a possible suspect?"

"Oh, you give *me* a break. Angie Clark? A suspect?"

He walked to the open door and started down the two steps.

"James, why can't you just get a little more background on her?"

He turned and looked at me. "This is personal, Skip. Personal. I would appreciate it if you would just drop it, okay?"

"Okay. I won't bring it up again. But, James, we've got tomorrow," I glanced at my watch, "actually we've got today to solve the crime. Or Ken Clemens says they're going to pull the plug."

"I understand. I really do. I want this business to work, Skip. I'll be back by nine and we'll get this thing figured out."

"Eight, buddy."

"Eight?"

"Moe wants a meeting."

"Oh, jeez."

"A meeting at eight."

"At eight? What are we going to tell him?"

"That you're convinced the saboteur is Winston Pugh, but you have absolutely no proof."

"I'll think of something."

"You always do."

"Meet you here at the Airstream in—" he looked at his watch. "I don't believe it. In three hours."

"We'll be waiting, roomie."

"Our love to Angie," Em shot at him as he headed across the lot.

She walked back in and smiled at me.

"None of this makes any sense, does it?" I asked.

"Nothing the two of you do ever makes any sense." Em walked back to the bedroom, stripping off the blue jeans.

I followed her, snuggling when we got into bed.

"You know, Skip, I've never seen James in his underwear before."

"Pretty scary, huh?"

"Actually, he's got a pretty good body."

CHAPTER THIRTY

It was seven a.m. when I heard the alarm go off. I tried to roll over and ran into my bedmate.

"Em, where's the alarm?"

She rolled over, rubbing her eyes. "You don't have one."

"What's that sound?"

She struggled to sit up, and looked around. "Here." She grabbed the tiny receiver from the miniature nightstand.

"What's going on?"

"Someone is calling Pugh."

"Come on, Em. It's personal. You said no personal—"

Holding her finger to her lips she pressed a button. There were voices, but I couldn't make them out. She kept her finger at her lips, her eyes showing surprise. She nodded her head a couple of times and finally put the receiver back on the stand.

"So what was it?"

"Somebody called for Winston."

"Obviously."

"They wanted Winston to know that he is your prime suspect."

"What?"

"The voice said that the two private investigators were narrowing their list of suspects and that Pugh was the number one guy."

"You're kidding me." I thought I was still asleep and dreaming. What she was telling me was impossible.

"No."

"Who was it?"

"He never identified himself. I assume they knew who it was, but it sounded like Mr. Big to me."

"Moe? We haven't even had our meeting with him." I shook my head to get rid of the cobwebs. This was not good news. It meant that our employer was spilling the beans ahead of us. "This is impossible. Have you told—?" I realized that Em would never tell, and I realized she didn't know anyone in the Show.

"Word travels," she said.

"We've only talked to ourselves." I was out of bed, struggling to get my jeans on. There wasn't going to be any more sleep. "Why would he—?"

"I just know what he said."

"But, we're on *his* side. Moe Bradley is the reason we got the job, Em. You know that. I mean—"

She nodded. "You told me last night that Moe Bradley never wanted an investigation. He only hired you and James for that job because he was being pressured by his two sisters."

Together, almost like a rehearsed act, we said, "Schiller and Crouse."

"That's true, Em, but I can't believe he's warning people about us. First off, Charlie and Bo, then Winston. Our employer is telling our suspects to go for cover. That's just too strange."

"You said it. James said it. The man didn't want an investigation. So maybe he's torpedoing this one."

I thought about that for a moment. Moe felt that an investigation was useless. Apparently his opinion was that *bad things happen*. It was a natural cycle. And yet, he told us he was certain someone was out to get him. Maybe his enthusiasm for the private investigator work was just to make sure we said yes. And I had to factor in the fact that at that time, Moe Bradley apparently was trying to appease his sisters. The team of—ah, you already know who they are.

Make a note to self. Make a note to James. Moe cannot be trusted. Too bad. I thought he was the one steady rock in this entire place. God knows we could use a steady rock.

"One more thing, Skip. You need to know that Winston was busy. Apparently he doesn't ever answer his phone."

"He was busy?"

"He wasn't the one who answered the phone. I got the impression he was either on the toilet or out feeding the animals."

"Oh. Let's go with the animals."

"Linda answered and took the message. She said he was indisposed. And if it was Moe, he told her not to make any mention of this except to Pugh."

"Oh, crap. She's not happy with us anyway. Now if she thinks that we're after her boyfriend—"

Em held up the receiver. "We are, Skip."

"Yeah, there's that."

I found the cheap instant coffee that James had used before in the cupboard. As adverse as I was to tasting that dishwater flavor again, I mixed the required amount with water in the pan and heated it up.

"James needs to know. Before your meeting."

I was tired of Em being right all the time.

"Are you going to go tell him?" She gave me a disapproving look.

"Yeah. I'll go down there. Right now, so just settle down. I'm sure Angie will be glad to see me again." She'd shuffle to the door in that pink bathrobe.

"Well, she's going to get a good sense of what James is all about."

"If she can deal with that."

"I deal with you." She smiled.

"You've got a good sense of what I'm all about."

"You don't understand, Skip. I'm a part of what you're all about. Angie Clark has yet to reach that status with James."

There was something very reassuring about that. She admitted to being a part of me. That's pretty heavy.

I pulled on my Green Day T-shirt. "Watch the coffee, or whatever that stuff is. I'm off to see James. The one with the good body."

"Jealousy does not wear well on you, boyfriend."

She'd picked up on that immediately.

"I'll be back."

"Schwarzenegger said that, and then he actually *came* back, Skip. Look at California now."

Nodding, I walked out of the trailer and hiked over to Angie's place. James was going to flip when he heard this story.

CHAPTER THIRTY-ONE

"How is that possible?"

"I asked myself the same question. But Moe knows we suspect, or rather *you* suspect Pugh."

"There couldn't be a mistake?"

"Em was pretty sure."

James stared out over the desolate show ground, sipping some really good coffee from a china mug. We sat in the lawn chairs outside Angie's trailer, watching the mist in the distance and the dawn light coloring the blue sky with a light shade of pink on the horizon.

I took a swig of Angie's home brew, thinking about Em drinking that swill in the Airstream.

"And, Moe is telling Charlie that we think he and Bo are persons of interest. Do we bring this up at our meeting? Do we tell him that we know he's trying to sabotage us?" I figured we would have to tell him that we knew.

"What's the motive? Is Moe trying to save money? Is that it? If we do find out that Pugh or Charlie or Bo is trying to sabotage the Show, he owes us more money. Maybe he doesn't want to pay that money."

"James, think about it. To a guy like Moe Bradley a couple of thousand dollars isn't even a drop in the bucket."

"Then why is he trying to do us in?"

I'd thought about that. "He never wanted an investigation in the first place." Ken Clemens had been adamant about that. It was the sisters who insisted on an investigation. The only reason we had been hired was for expediency.

"Skip, plain and simple, Moe wants to mess this investigation up. He doesn't want us to find anything. He wants us to admit that there's no proof that there was any foul play. We're both on the same page, right?"

I nodded. We were both silent for a moment.

"James, the question is, how did Moe know? How did he know what we were thinking?"

He shook his head. "We have Pugh's phone bugged, right?"

"We do now. Em was able to break into the system. Every cell phone call Pugh gets, we can hear. She intercepted the phone call to Pugh this morning. That's why you and I are here."

"So what's the chance that Moe is breaking into our system? The Airstream is his trailer. He owns it." James was dead-on. And I countered.

"And, Angie Clark's trailer is his. He owns it as well."

"So he could bug these trailers."

"Makes sense," I said.

"So," James took another swallow of his creamed coffee, "that's the answer. Moe is bugging our trailers."

I really hadn't considered that. The guy who was paying us, was bugging our private lives to find out what we knew. There was no other answer. James was right.

"The question is, do we let him know that *we* know?"

"No."

"No?" I was planning on the confrontation. Had a speech already written in my head as to what I would say.

"Let's go on with the investigation."

"James—" I was halfway to a scream, "today is the last day we have. If we don't turn in proof that the culprit is Pugh or Charlie and Bo, we are fired." And I for one could not afford to lose the money that had been offered.

James took a deep breath, rolled his eyes, and held his coffee cup out to me. "Pard, pally, amigo, let me lead, okay? I'll take the horns here. I don't want Moe to know what we know."

"He's the one who's paying us."

"True, but we still hold the winning card. We know he's bugging us. He doesn't know that we're aware."

That made sense. We had the upper hand.

"Skip, we're going to go to that meeting, and we're going to play innocent. We're going to pretend that we don't know anything."

"And James, right now there are two groups of people who may be guilty."

"Yeah?"

"Somebody out there is a killer. And either one of them might want to kill us."

He thought about that for a moment.

"Nah. We don't know enough for them to want to kill us."

"They don't know that."

"Let's proceed."

"James, as much as I need the money, as much as you need the money, we'd be better off walking out of here right now and chalking it up to experience."

"We're professional P.I.s, Skip. I'm not going to let Ken Clemens prove us wrong."

The song says *You've got to know when to hold 'em, know when to fold 'em.* And we didn't have that figured out yet.

CHAPTER THIRTY-TWO

I stepped outside the trailer, walked twenty feet away, and called Jody on my cheap cell phone. It was obvious I'd gotten him out of bed. Surprisingly he didn't sound too upset, maybe because he knew he was making a sale early Sunday morning. Our mentor was still in bed, and here I was, up trying to solve a case. I wondered if maybe James and I had the wrong end of the business.

"Someone is bugging one of our trailers."

"You're not talking near the trailer?"

"No."

"Smart. There's really no problem, Skip. Here's what you do." He cleared his throat and I figured he'd probably been up late drinking and having a party. Unlike his protégés, who had been up analyzing computer screens.

"I've got a little handheld box. You walk around the inside and outside of your trailer. Every time that box detects a bug, a red light comes on. If someone is miking your trailer, you'll know exactly where the bug is. Pretty cool, huh?"

"Then what?"

"You just remove the bug."

"That simple?"

"That simple."

"The only problem is, we need it like now."

"*Now* now?"

"Yeah."

He hesitated. "Tell you what. I can drop it off to you in maybe fifty minutes."

"That would be great. It's the Bayview Mall, but there's no bay."

"No bay?"

"Nope. And not really a mall. Just a string of cheap shops."

He took a second. "No bay, no mall. Kind of like the garden spot of Carol City, eh?"

I smiled. "Exactly." There wasn't one of those, either.

"Let me get my coffee and I'm on my way."

Glancing in the kitchen window I realized the coffee *I'd* made had disappeared. It was no longer sitting in a pan on the stove.

"Uh, Jody. How much is it?"

"It?"

"The box with the red light."

"Price?"

"Yeah." He had a way of dodging the subject.

"I'd have to check, Skip. Don't know for sure."

"Have you run the total on those other things I took?"

"No, but I'll get to it."

I was especially wondering about the pen with dog slobber on it.

"I'd kind of like to know what I'm spending here, you know?"

"Hey, Skip. If you need something, you need it. Can't put a price on safety, my friend."

I could picture Jody's final bill. Hundreds of dollars, maybe over a thousand. Being the trusting soul I was, I had thought he'd look out for us, but deep down inside I knew that probably wasn't the case.

"We're in the Airstream trailer."

"Got it. I'll just set my GPS. And Skip, see if James has that money he owes me."

"I'll be sure and check, Jody."

As long as Jody Stacy was running an unknown tab on me, I figured we'd string out payment on his seventy some dollars.

Em stepped outside, walked down the steps, put her arms around my waist. "Who was that?"

"Jody."

"Oh?"

"He's going to drop off a little black box that tracks bugging devices."

"So you can check out the trailers?"

"Yeah."

"God, Skip. Sometimes I feel like I'm in a Nancy Drew novel."

"Somehow Bradley is getting inside information." It was a Hardy Boys mystery, but I didn't want to correct her.

"It makes sense. He's probably using the same type of equipment that you are."

We were about to find out.

"Did you really want some of that stuff you had on the stove? The stuff you asked me to watch?" Her voice was sweet and sounded like sugar.

"No. Angie made some really good coffee and we had a cup at her place."

She pulled her arms from me. "Oh? Angie served you? Well good. I'm glad you had a nice cup of coffee. I didn't have any coffee. I took the crap you made and threw it down the toilet. I think it ate right through the porcelain."

I had a feeling she wasn't happy. I'd left her out of the meeting, and on top of that I'd had a decent cup of coffee. She had nothing. I owed her, and as soon as we made our money from this case, assuming we ever made any money at all, I'd treat her. I didn't know exactly how I'd treat her, but I'd treat her.

Pulling on a collared shirt with my jeans, I found James halfway to Moe Bradley's trailer. He'd thrown on a worn, wrinkled Transformers T-shirt and cutoffs. After all, this was a business meeting.

There was no conversation. I was going to leave this strictly in James's corner.

Moe opened the door before we got to the landing.

"Boys, come on in." He spread his arms as if glad to see us, and motioned us into the spacious trailer.

"Moe, we've got a suspect." James waded right in.

"Have a mimosa boys." He handed us glasses of orange juice and champagne, guiding us to the leather sofa.

"Did you hear me?"

I wasn't sure Moe even cared.

"Okay, you've got a suspect. And you realize that suspecting someone is not solving my problem?"

James took a sip of his drink and said, "Then let me rephrase the statement. We know who the guilty party is."

"You do?"

"But before I tell you who it is, I should alert you that someone is working from the inside."

As he sat down, Moe said, "What do you mean? Inside?"

"Someone from inside the Show is telegraphing possible suspects."

"You've lost me, James."

I couldn't believe James was leaking our information. He'd spilled the beans. We'd agreed to keep that a secret.

"Someone from the Show is calling people who work for you, Moe, and telling them that we are private investigators."

"No."

"Yes. And also giving a heads-up to these people. Telling them that Skip and I," he nodded toward me, "are considering them as the possible saboteurs."

Moe leaned forward and took a gulp of his mimosa. "So who do you think it might be? This insider? Did someone tell you this? Tell me. Come on."

I hadn't seen this side of the man. Usually calm and cool, Moe was flustered. He was obviously worried that his cover had been blown.

"Who? Who told you there was an insider? I want to know."

It occurred to me that he hadn't been interested in who our suspect was. James had opened up the conversation by telling him that we knew who the guilty party was. All Moe cared about was who was leaking the information to the suspects. And he already knew the answer. Very strange.

"Don't have a clue." I saw James glance in the blank big screen and run his fingers through his hair. "We picked up this information from a third party who was reluctant to tell us how they found out."

"Skip? You don't know who this person is?"

"You know, Moe, James is calling the shots on this one. I'm just along, sort of—"

"For the ride." James finished the sentence. "It's the best I can tell you now. But we do know who is sabotaging the rides, Moe."

It was obvious the man already knew who the suspects were. He tried to rally some interest but wasn't very convincing.

"Yeah?" A big scowl on Moe's face. He wasn't sure that we hadn't found him out. "Well, that's what I'm paying for. Although there's been no problem so far. No one has tried to sabotage any of our rides this trip. So who is this suspect?"

Moe moved right along. He didn't have to know who we thought was calling people in the show. He already knew. It was him. And we had it on video, we had it on audio.

James glanced at me, hesitating for a moment. He took a sip of his drink, then shook his head. "Too early."

"What?"

"It's too early to announce who it is."

Moe took a sip as well. He studied James for a moment, then stood up.

"Mr. Lessor, I'm the one who is paying you for information. You tell me right now who you think it might be. I don't understand this little cat-and-mouse game you're playing, but if you know who is behind this—"

"We're pretty sure."

"Tell me, James. Or you're fired. Right now."

And again, Moe already knew who we thought it might be. He'd called Pugh and told him. He'd sat Charlie down, on this very couch and told him.

And I didn't want James to do it. I didn't want him to open up to this distinguished, gray-haired man. I wanted him to clam up. Or maybe just pull a name out of the hat and totally surprise—

"Ken Clemens."

All three of us were silent. Moe sat back down. We all took a sip of our mimosas and listened to the sounds of morning slipping through the open windows in the showman's American Eagle. A whisper of fresh breeze, carrying the sound of a mockingbird. The faint sound of a radio coming from one of the trailers down the way and muffled conversation as carnies walked by outside, talking about the dawning of the last day.

Finally, Moe spoke. "How do you even know who Ken Clemens is?"

"Moe, we're professional private investigators. We've been working on this since you first hired us."

He was confused. Hell, I was confused. Moe had called Linda and told her that we suspected her boyfriend, Winston Pugh. He'd talked to Charlie right where I was sitting, on the leather sofa. He'd told Charlie that we thought he and Bo were "persons of interest." And then, when he'd confronted us—

"Ken dates my sister."

"I know." James sat there with his arms folded. "We know."

"He's your suspect? He's it? Ken Clemens?"

"He's the only one we've ever seriously suspected."

So Moe Bradley had erroneous information. He'd been led to believe that we had other suspects. And when I found the plants, the bugs in our trailer, James would have to explain that, well, yes, we'd suspected Pugh, Charlie, and Bo. But for now, Moe sat there with his eyes closed. Trying to make some sense out of this.

And I tried to make some sense out of it. What the hell was James trying to prove?

"We've still got until nine tonight, when the Show closes. Right?" James looked him in the eyes.

"You're going to prove to me that Ken is the guy who's trying to destroy the show?" Moe shook his head. "Ken Clemens is the one who sabotaged the rides? Who is responsible for one, maybe two deaths?"

"Give us until the show closes, Moe." James stood up and motioned to me.

"If you weren't so serious, I'd laugh. Out loud. Ken Clemens is a lot of things, but he's not a killer."

The same had been said of Winston Pugh. By me.

I could read the confusion on Moe's face. He had no idea where we were going with this.

Neither did I.

"Okay. Till nine."

"Thanks, boss."

"But James, you've got to get me evidence by nine. Understood?"

"Of course."

"Because if you don't," Moe stood up, moved to the door and opened it, looking out on the dusty, dirty show arena, "you're fired."

"I understand. You'll find another investigator, right?"

"And another marketing director. You will be history, my friend. You're going to blow a pretty good job, possibly a career. Either you prove to me that Ken Clemens is guilty or you're gone. Please, take that not as a threat, but a promise."

CHAPTER THIRTY-THREE

"You constantly surprise me."

"Hell, Skip, I constantly surprise myself." He was taking big strides, pumped up after the meeting, and I was struggling to keep up.

"Ken Clemens?"

"I could have mentioned one of his sisters, but that would have been stretching it."

"Why Clemens?" Breathing hard.

"Because as far as we know, he hasn't called Clemens and given him a heads-up. Moe Bradley is trying to bury us, and I figured throwing him off would help our case."

"You didn't just throw *him* off. I had no idea where you were going with that."

"Sorry, bro. You played it well. The bit about 'I'm just along for the ride.' He bought that."

"James, where the hell do we go from here?"

He stopped, looked at me, and in dramatic fashion said, "Amigo, we've still got one weapon."

"Yeah?"

"Yeah. You've got a program that infiltrates someone's computer, remember?"

I did. And my assumption was that we were going to tap into Pugh's laptop. We were going to see what kind of prescriptions his pig had to take. What kind of feed the goat needed on a daily basis, besides those pressed brown pellets. And if James and Em were right, we were going to find evidence that Pugh was the one who was sabotaging the rides at the Show.

"We send a Trojan horse," I said, "a message that the other person has to reply to. That's the way Jody explained it."

Carnies walked by us, smoking cigarettes, sipping on coffee in cardboard cups, and shaking the morning fog from their heads. I pictured their night before, drinking themselves into a stupor and passing out only hours after closing down the show. Not unlike the way James and I spent our evenings. The thought frightened me.

"Once they respond to the message, we can see everything there is in their computer."

James started walking, picking up the pace. "How cool is this. On one hand, we tap into a cell phone. On the other, we tap into a computer. There's no longer any privacy, Skip. George Orwell was several decades off, but it's come to pass. Big Brother is watching. And we, pardner, are Big Brother."

"You're not talking about bugging Winston Pugh, are you?"

"You catch on quickly, grasshopper."

"Yeah. But James."

"Think about it amigo. We'll be able to explore Moe's computer all we want to. Pretty cool, eh?"

"Apparently Moe is bugging us as well. So it's Big Brother versus Big Brother."

That shut him up. He was silent until we reached the Airstream.

I opened the door and there sat slick Jody. On the small couch. Very close to Em.

"Hey, Skip. James."

Em slid to the left, away from the spy guy. Just a couple of inches, but it was obvious she knew I wasn't happy.

"What happened to your face?" Jody asked.

I reached up and touched my jaw. The skin was still raw and it felt like there may be a slight swelling. "Somebody actually hit me."

He reached over and patted Em's hand. "Was he getting a little fresh?"

Neither of us commented.

"Brought the little black box. Want to see it in action?"

I actually did. I also wanted to see Jody in action, as in running out the door, getting in his car, and driving down the dusty road toward Delray Beach.

"Little black box?" James was confused.

"Hold on, boys." Jody pulled a disc the size of a silver dollar from his pocket, flipped a small switch and set it on the kitchen table. "That sets up interference in the trailer. If you're being bugged, that little disc disrupts any signal. Now, you can talk all you want."

I have to admit I was impressed. The guy thinks of everything.

"I called Jody, James. Asked him if we could debug our trailer. He suggested a black box that flashes a red light when it detects a bug."

Jody picked up the black box sitting next to him and offered it to James.

James flashed me a smile. "Smart thinking, pard. So this thing will pick up any bugging device, right?" James took it from Jody's hand and studied it.

"You flip this switch and just scan the room. Here, let me

show you." Jody took the box back, stood up, and moved the black detector over the couch. Nothing. He walked around the small kitchenette, moving the box high and low.

"A bug would be here, in the living area," James said. "I mean, this is where we talk. Got to be here."

Jody shook his head. There was nothing.

We followed him down the very short hallway and into the bathroom. He stopped for a second as he passed the box under the small medicine chest, then over the toilet and into the cramped shower. If we were bugged, it had to be someplace close.

Nothing.

Walking back into my miniscule bedroom, he ran the box over and under the bed and around the window. Nothing.

We three musketeers stood in the doorway, watching with baited breath.

"Well, so far you're clean." Jody smiled.

"You're sure the batteries are good?" I was sure that we were being bugged.

"Skip," Em gave me that look, "I think Jody's been doing this long enough to know if the batteries are working."

Feeling chastised, I didn't respond.

Jody slowly ran the box over the dresser and that's when it happened. The red light flashed and we all saw it. I think four of us gasped together, although I'm not sure Jody gasped. As Em has pointed out, he was the real professional of the group. Pros don't gasp.

"It's here, folks. The red light never lies." There was a self-satisfied smirk on his face as he hovered over the wooden chest of drawers.

One sweep to the left and the light went off. A sweep to the right and it was back on. Jody opened the top drawer and there were several of my T-shirts and a pair of boxer shorts inside. He glanced back at me.

"Do you want to come over and check the drawer?"

Obviously he didn't want to rummage through my underwear drawer.

Walking into the room, I wasn't quite sure what the bug would look like. Maybe just a tiny microphone. Or a listening device taped to the bottom of a drawer. I pulled out two shirts and the shorts.

"Do you see anything?"

And there it was. Lying in the corner. There was no question what it was and what it could do.

"Sure enough, there *is* a bug."

I pulled our gray audio/video pen from the drawer and tossed it on the bed.

There was a moment of silence, then James said, "And it got into that drawer because?"

"I put it there, James. We were done with it so—"

"Isn't that the pen I sold you?" Jody picked it up, possibly examining it for dog tooth marks.

"Yeah."

"So there really is no bug in here? Nothing someone else would have planted? Just this pen?" Jody gave me a disgusted look and switched off his black box.

"So, Jody, if we don't find a bug, how do we explain someone knowing our every move?"

Tapping the black box with his index finger, he smiled. "Oh, I think we'll find a bug. It's the easiest way for someone to know exactly what you're doing."

Everything had a tech solution. GPS units, hidden cameras, disguised microphones. That was Jody Stacy's world.

"Let's check outside."

"Outside?"

"Yeah. We're going to debug the outside of the trailer."

"Why would someone plant a bug on the outside of the trailer?"

"I saw lawn chairs out there."

"And?"

"Do you and James have conversations while you're sitting outside?"

We were both silent. Obviously we'd thought we were safe outside. And this was why Jody Stacy was a professional and we were floundering with a case we couldn't solve.

CHAPTER THIRTY-FOUR

I led the bumbling spies outside where Jody, the master spy, swept the outside of our trailer. We watched the red light indicator, waiting for the signal that he'd found the hidden bug. Over the front, around the door frame. Windows, the front, the back, even a pass under the trailer. Finally Jody passed the box over the two lawn chairs. Nothing. Nothing at all.

"Well, we can always try the other trailer. Where is it? The one where James is staying?"

Traipsing across the lot, we walked up the steps to Angie's trailer. James opened the door and yelled but no one was home.

"Come on in." James waved us through the entrance.

Jody made his way through the living area, more slowly this time. He wanted to impress us, show off not only the box, but his skills as a P.I. I could sense it. And I'm sure he wanted to show off his prowess to Em.

We were silent, as if the sound of our voices might set off the red light. Six pairs of eyes trained on the black box in Jody's hand.

Nothing.

The kitchen area, the bedroom where jeans, shorts, T-shirts, boxer shorts, a bra, and other clothing were strewn everywhere, the miniscule closet. Nothing, nothing, and nothing.

He took a deep breath. I could sense the disappointment in his voice. "Well the last place to try would be outside."

We stood to one side as the modern-day James Bond walked the perimeter. He walked back to us with a frown on his face.

"Guys, I can say with a great deal of certainty that neither of these trailers has been bugged."

"Nothing at all?"

"Nada." I could see the disappointment on his face.

The three of us looked at each other. The three of us who were just this side of amateur status.

"Maybe they removed the bugs?" I was looking for the obvious.

"Very possible." Jody nodded. "Once they got the information they needed, they found a way inside and they took the device away."

"But," James interjected, "Moe has never been in this trailer. I'd lay odds on it. He hasn't set foot in here since the show opened."

"We don't know that for sure." James hadn't been here the entire time.

"Well I'm pretty sure he's never been inside the Airstream. Skip, you and Em have been there most of the time, and when you haven't been, I was there."

I caught movement on the show grounds and glanced over at the Ferris wheel, now making lazy circles in the sky. The carnies were warming up the rides for the last big day.

Glancing at my ten-dollar watch, I saw it was a quarter of ten. Fifteen minutes before the show opened.

"Jody, since you're here, can you give us a hand on another project?" As much as I wanted him gone, he knew better than anyone how to handle the EMT.

"What's that?"

"We've got a message we'd like to send to a friend. An e-mail message we want to send to his computer. We're hoping for an answer back."

I saw recognition dawn on his face. He smiled. "Oh, I love this one. Be more than happy to help you set it up. You won't believe how slick the EMT is."

Twenty minutes later we could hear the music, blasting from the show speakers. Two or three classic rock songs fighting each other for dominance.

"All loaded in." Jody sat back, beaming. "Anything special you want to say?"

"Do we even have his address?" I didn't even know where Moe Bradley lived, much less what his e-mail address was.

"I do, amigo. Right here." James passed a matchbook over to Jody. "I wrote it on the inside."

"Does he have to know where the message is coming from?" I didn't want Moe seeing that the message came from me. And again, this was my company's computer. All I needed was to lose my job. This wasn't the best market to be shopping for new employment.

"This is Skip's computer. Can't have any trace of that with the message we're sending." James was looking out for me.

"We could set up a phony address." Jody was rubbing his hands together. "This guy, Moe, he probably reads the trades, right?" He was really getting into this.

"Trades?" James raised his eyebrows.

"Magazines about rides. About shows, gross profits. Come on, James. I get mags about spy equipment, surveillance techniques. This guy must subscribe to magazines regarding his business. Carnival trades." Jody was the professional. We were just along for the ride.

"Your point is?" James needed clarification.

Jody punched in some words, turned the screen toward us and smiled. There in bold letters we saw **The Carnival Crusade, a magazine about making your business the best it can be.**

"Here's our magazine, guys. Now, we offer Mr. Moe a discount on his subscription."

"Discount?"

Jody turned the screen toward himself and muttered, "Yeah. What the hell would he want with discounts." He typed in several words then turned the screen toward us again.

Free six-month subscription

"Wow." James was impressed. "How could he turn this down?"

"I don't think he will."

"So where do we go from here?"

"You simply ask him to respond."

"And?" Em was skeptical.

"That's it."

"It's as simple as that?" She stared at him.

"I told you it was cool. The EMT. You're going to find out everything about this guy." Jody grinned. He'd impressed Em, and my guess was that was his intention all along.

CHAPTER THIRTY-FIVE

So we waited. And waited.

Walking outside the Airstream, I watched the Dragon Tail whip through the air and plummet toward the ground, stopping at the last second and gently landing in the dirt. My stomach did a flip as I remembered the ride. Just yesterday.

It was an impossible task. How were we supposed to find the bad guys in two and one half days? The whole thing was smoke and mirrors, a magic trick that Moe had set up to appease Virginia Crouse and Judy Schiller. The evil sisters.

I'd mulled it all over, and pretty much decided that Moe didn't want to admit there were problems, because problems drove people away. And without people, the Show wasn't worth much. Without value, Moe and the Show would go broke. So it just made sense. Moe was ignoring the problem and hoping it would just go away. The only reason he'd hired us and given us a compelling reason to take the job, was to keep his sisters happy and to stop anyone with real credentials from investigating the Show.

I was quite pleased with myself, the fact that I'd come to this conclusion. And pissed off at the same time. It meant that he had no intention of paying us any more than the bare minimum he'd promised.

Still, someone had killed Kevin Cross. That was a real murder. So it stood to reason that there was a killer in our midst. As if James and I would ever have a real chance of proving who it was.

"Skip." Em was leaning out the door. "Come here a minute."

They were gathered around the table.

"Check it out, compadre." James was pointing at the screen.

And there it was. Moe Bradley's home page, in all its glory, plastered across the screen of my computer.

"We're inside his computer, Skip." Jody sat back with a big grin on his face. Showing off again. But he'd actually done it. The last trick was now out of the bag, the last weapon had been used and we had nothing left.

Half an hour later we'd only explored about twenty files, scanned some e-mail, and found the Show schedule. So far there were no surprises. There were hundreds of files listed, and all seemed easily accessible.

Jody pushed back from the table and folded his hands. "You get this sometimes when a guy has a lot of stuff stored. It just takes time. Nice thing is, this Moe is organized. Very methodical. Everything is where it should be. I've been in some systems where the guy has stuff everywhere. Spread out like a giant quilt. You can spend hours and not find anything."

"But we don't even know what we're looking for."

"That's true, Skip, but you'll find it. It's here."

I found that to be a very strange statement.

"Trust me, man. Something will jump out if this guy has anything to hide."

As he opened the next file there was a knock at the door. "James?"

"Shit." James jumped up from his chair. "Jody, quick, shut it down. Close it up. It's Angie."

Jody closed the screen as James opened the door.

"Hey, it's a party and I wasn't invited." She stood on our landing, her blonde hair in ringlets. She was dressed in a simple blue and white checkered top and jeans that might have been just a little too tight. And wearing that soft scent.

"No," James shook his head. "No party. No. We're just having a conversation. Just old high school classmates." James introduced Angie to Jody.

"And Jody, what do you do?" She stepped into the room. "You're not involved in the carnival business are you?"

"No, no." He glanced at me. "I'm, uh, in the audio/visual business."

"Producer? Do you make movies?"

He laughed. "No, nothing as glamorous as that. I sell equipment. Cameras, sound systems. But," he gave her that dazzling smile, "if I was making movies, you would be someone I'd cast."

"And how many times have you used that line?"

James put his arm around Angie's waist. "Actually, I was talking to Jody about maybe making a short video for the Show. Sort of a marketing tool. We could send it out to prospective county fairs and other sites."

He was winging it as only James can do.

"I was just checking on the cost of an inexpensive camera." He squeezed her and steered her toward the door.

"Hold on, sailor." Angie pulled free. "Moe is looking for you two. Says he wants you to be on the grounds, seeing the Show firsthand for the last day. He was pretty insistent that you be out there."

Moe wanted us in plain view? So we couldn't do any sleuthing? Or maybe it was a legitimate request.

"Any place special?"

"He mentioned the Dragon Tail. Apparently there's a problem with the landing mechanism and we've got a technician working on it. He just wanted you to see the inner workings of the machinery."

"No more rides?" I didn't want to sound too disappointed.

Angie beamed a smile at me. "No, Skip. I don't think you have to ride it again. Although, I'd love to have you take me for a spin."

She and James headed out and I turned to the table, realizing I was about to leave macho Jody and Em together. Alone.

"You two will be all right?"

Em rolled her eyes.

Jody gave me a sly smile, reached out, and patted Em's hand. "We'll be just fine, Skip."

"You know, I can come back and go over that computer site as soon as—"

"Skip, go." Em pointed toward the door.

I went. I wasn't happy about it, but I went.

CHAPTER THIRTY-SIX

Bo and Charlie were standing by the housing unit where the bottom half of a bent over technician was sticking out. His ass and legs were outside the metal casing, the rest of him was buried in the gears and motor that drove the Tail. And just like the stereotypical repairman, his pants were down below the crack of his ass. I quickly averted my eyes.

Charlie's half-burned cigarette dangled from his fingers as he watched James and me approach.

"It appears maybe you guys gummed up the works yesterday. Amateurs shouldn't be runnin' the equipment."

"Screw you, Charlie." James glared at him.

A muffled voice came from inside the metal house. "This happens from time to time."

"Still think it was something you did." Charlie frowned and took a drag off his smoke.

About twenty would-be riders lined up by the gate, but no one was taking their money. If I'd seen a repairman working on the ride, I think I'd have second thoughts about riding it. Of course, I had second thoughts anyway.

James looked at me and asked, "What is it we're supposed to learn from this experience?"

I shrugged. "James, this is your baby. I have no idea what we're doing here. None. I decided about an hour ago that this is the dumbest thing I've ever done. If I had it to do over again, I wouldn't. This is by far the dumbest thing I've ever gotten myself involved with."

"And you've done some pretty dumb things, pard." I could always count on James to give me support.

Bo walked over, standing close enough that I could smell his sour breath. "Got a bruised jaw there, guy."

I studied him for a moment, finally dropping my gaze to his right hand. His knuckles appeared to be raw and bruised as well. It didn't surprise me.

"Listen, you turd. I heard you've been mouthing off about Charlie and me. If you think you're gonna pin any of those accidents on me," he motioned to Charlie, "or my partner, you're dumber than you appear. And you appear to be pretty dumb."

I'd just told James how dumb I was. And now Bo was in my face. This was a case of dumb and dumber.

The technician pulled the upper portion of his torso out of the housing unit and, looking away from us, pulled on his blue cap. Yanking a handkerchief from his pocket, he wiped perspiration from his forehead.

"Okay. It was a sticking valve. I lubed it, reset it, and the ride should run smooth from this point on."

Charlie and Bo walked away, both of them flipping us the middle finger as they strode back to the control panel. The tech slammed shut the door to the metal housing unit and tugged his cap down low over his eyes. Without looking at us, he walked away, head down.

"What an ass." James shook his head, his eyes trained on Charlie. "So what do you think, compadre?"

"What do I think?"

"Hey, he noticed your bruise. And I think you noticed his." James pushed back the hair from his eyes. "I'm under the impression that Bo's the one who broke into the Airstream. Agree?"

"It appears."

"He might have taken the bug." James stared after him. "Hell, he might have been the one who planted a bug. I think these guys were feeding Moe all the information. Moe got the bug, downloaded it, and knew who we suspected."

I hadn't considered that. Bo would have been the perfect plant.

"He's the one who busted you in the chops?"

I pictured Bo's red bruised knuckles. "I don't think there's much question about it, James."

"Damn. If I pop him, I'll lose the job. But I'm tempted."

"Don't, James. The guys are pond scum, just not as bright. Leave them alone."

"Think they're the ones who jammed up the rides?"

I would have loved for Bo and Charlie to be the bad guys. That would have made my day.

"I don't think they've got the brain power to pull it off."

In the distance I saw Em running toward us in her jean shorts and yellow halter top. Bo and Charlie watched her as well, with leers on their faces.

She got close and started shouting. "Skip, you've got to come quick." Her breath was coming in short spurts. "James. You come too. There's something you've got to see." She spun around and started jogging toward the trailer. Over her shoulder she shouted, "We've got a problem."

I looked around. Moe was nowhere to be seen, and we'd done what he'd asked. We watched some uniformed technician fumble around in the guts of the Dragon Tail. Why, I hadn't a clue.

But as a bonus, we'd figured out who broke into our trailer. And now, according to Em, we had a problem. My God, that's all we had were problems. And more problems on top of those.

Both of us jogged toward the Airstream, gasping by the time we got halfway back. I swallowed mouthfuls of Florida show dust as I finally slowed down, ending up just walking fast the last one hundred steps. James was behind me as I entered the trailer.

"Boys, I told you this thing would spill the beans."

Jody was grinning, cock-of-the-walk style.

"Look at this. Just look at this." He spun the computer screen around.

I leaned in to read the fine print. It was an e-mail.

James joined me and together we read the printed screen.

Dad, James said that he and Skip were leaning toward Winston Pugh as the guilty party. They thought that Charlie and Bo were "persons of interest," but they felt Winston had the best motive. I'll keep you informed.

A.

I read it a second time. Someone had played back a bug? So there was a real spy planting a bug in one of the trailers. This *A* seemed to know exactly what we'd said. A? I glanced at James and his face was white. And then it hit me.

"I am so sorry, guys."

"Hey, James, you had no—" What was I going to do? Rub it in? Granted, his indiscretion could not only jeopardize our investigation but jeopardize our lives, but still—

"Skip, you told me to do some background on her. I just never thought that—what an ass I am."

"Hey, you had no—"

"Yes, you are." Em was firm. "You are an ass. You leave your friends hanging out there, James. You always believe that only

213

you have the right answer." She threw her hands in the air. "Well this time, you were wrong. We begged you to do more homework on this girl, but you had all the answers." Spitting out the words as she spoke, "Remember how you told us, 'No. This is personal. Angie couldn't be a suspect?' You're never wrong are you, James? And you're taking everyone else down while you're trying to defend yourself."

"I'm an ass, Em."

"Never wrong."

"Hey, I was wrong this time. Okay?"

"No doubt about it. However, we found the information we needed. Angie Clark is Moe's daughter. And she's been feeding Moe all the information you've been gathering."

CHAPTER THIRTY-SEVEN

Steam was still rolling out of Em's ears. I put my hand on her shoulder, trying to calm her down, but she was pissed. I think part of the problem was that a girl was at the heart of the problem. A girl James was seeing.

"I told her a couple of things. I mean I didn't really tell her much, but—"

"Enough to totally screw up this investigation." Jody piled it on, and it wasn't even his case.

"I admit it." I'd never seen James as contrite. "I told her that we suspected Winston Pugh."

"No great revelation, James." Em kept nailing him.

"I may have told her that Bo and Charlie were persons—"

"Of interest?" Em finished his sentence.

James took a deep breath. "But she doesn't know."

"Know what?"

"That we know."

I wasn't quite sure where he was going. I knew James would eventually defend himself, but I was trying to decipher his defense. "That we know what?" I asked.

He took a deep breath. "Angie doesn't know that we've figured out that she's feeding information to Moe."

"So?" Em wasn't willing to quit.

"So I can feed her anything and she'll take it to Moe."

"Maybe."

"Well, let's think about what we might tell her."

He was squirming, trying to put a positive face on his screw up.

Jody, the pro, nodded. "Not a bad idea. Let's revisit that one a little later."

"So, what are you going to tell her?" Em wasn't done chastising my roommate. "Can you be trusted to quit feeding her every thought you have? Everything you know? James, you are a screw up. Truly, a screw up."

We were all quiet for a moment. James's silence simply meant he had no defense. There was nothing he could say.

"We still don't know everything that's on Moe's computer. Maybe we should do a little more exploration," I said. I'd been out watching some repair guy fixing the Tail while Jody and Em had found the e-mail. Maybe I was feeling left out.

"Good idea, Skip."

Jody flipped on the screen and studied it for a moment.

"Let's go back to the files. There's a file called tech report. Don't know what it contains, but it's a good spot to start." His fingers flew over the keys and he intently watched the screen.

"Nothing here."

Again his fingers typed away, fifty times faster than I could do it, and finally he stopped, giving us a grim smile.

"Interesting. He's got schematics of three of the rides. All the specs and a diagram of the inner working of each ride."

"Which rides?" I needed to know.

"The Ferris wheel, The Sidewinder, and—"

Em, James and I all shouted out together. "The Dragon Tail."

"You all get a gold star."

"But he *should* have all that information stored somewhere, right?" Em asked. "The manager of a show needs to know that stuff. I'd expect him to have the information at his fingertips. I mean, no big deal."

"He should," Jody agreed. "However, each one of the rides has arrows pointing to what are described here as 'vulnerable points' on the ride. Handlebars, carts, and certain gears..." he studied the diagrams. "Here's an example: a detailed description of how four bolts hold the Tail cars to the steel bar sections."

"So what?" I didn't see a problem with that.

"I don't know what, but there's an arrow to each of the bolts. They attach the roof of the cars to these steel sections. If something happened to those bolts—"

"Oh, come on." Em threw her hands up.

"All right, here's something on the valves that operate the Dragon Tail."

"Valves?"

"Valves." Jody was nose to screen, following the drawings.

"The tech today was talking about a sticking valve," I said.

"Moe has written a note in here. He says, quote, "valves that stick can cause a ride to malfunction.""

"Again," Em said, "he's aware of potential problems and he wants to point out those problems."

"Fair enough." Jody smiled at her and I wished they'd quit flirting with each other.

"Show Skip and James the other e-mail." Em leaned over and touched his shoulder, as if trying to get his attention.

"Oh, yeah."

Jody switched modes and punched in some keys. "Here." He flipped the screen back to James and me.

A,

Your aunts are bound and determined that they will win this war. I've made two offers and they've refused both of them. The longer this goes on, the less this Show is worth. They've always had a special place in their heart for you. Why not suggest to them that they sell now? Tell them I'm a jerk, a nonrelenting business freak who will never stop trying to win control. Inform them that, as their niece, you think it's in their best interest to divest. I mean, come on. Your aunt Judy and aunt Virginia are in their 100s!

Maybe I exaggerate (lol), but they could use the money in their waning years. And, of course, I would like to own the Show outright. You and me. Work with me, baby girl.

Love,

Your dad

I read the letter twice. He'd made the same point that I'd considered. The more accidents and murders, the less the show was worth. No one wanted the show to lose money. Moe, the sisters, Angie, the carnies, even Ken Clemens, and now James and me all made their living at the show.

"Jody, you're the pro here. The only detective with real experience."

Nobody disputed my statement.

"Tell us what you would do right now. Because, and I think I speak for the entire group," I looked around and no one stopped me, "we are lost. Totally lost. I don't think we have a clue how to solve this case."

Jody worked the computer keys, nose buried in the screen. Thirty seconds passed as a fly buzzed by, dive bombing me twice. No one said anything. Finally he looked up and smiled.

"I'm sorry. You guys were waiting for my response, right?"
We nodded.

"I went back to the tech report file. There's something very strange about listing only three rides and highlighting their vulnerability. Why not have all of the rides listed? I mean, you have over fifteen rides out there, right?"

"Maybe these were the most susceptible rides." I was playing devil's advocate.

"Maybe. But why have arrows in the schematic, pointing the way to danger?"

I knew where this was leading. However, Em had made a good point. It was perfectly natural for Mo to have this information on his computer.

"Jody, this is going nowhere." James spoke up.

"Trust me, it's going somewhere, James. Read this little statement at the bottom of the Dragon Tail passage."

Flipping the computer around so that we could see the screen, we all leaned in and read.

Sticking valves are usually caused by resinous deposits left by improper lube or fuel. A thick grease or oil will often cause the valve to stick. Dirt, sawdust, and other debris that can get into an engine can add to the problem. To free the valve, use a solvent, usually a kerosene based solution.

Jody smiled. "You see?"

"See what? It's a paragraph on how to fix a stuck valve. We saw a repair guy fixing a valve on the DT. It's not a big deal."

Jody took a deep breath. "Let me give you a little lesson in P.I. one oh one."

James rolled his eyes.

"You're supposed to be looking for things that don't quite fit.

This file on Moe Bradley's computer doesn't quite fit. Only three rides? I would guess that every ride on the grounds out there has valves. And taken another way, this paragraph on how to *fix* a stuck valve."

"Yeah?"

"It also explains how to *make* the valve *stick*."

"Oh, jeez, you could do that with almost anything. You're just twisting the thing around and—"

"When it has to do with your case, you've got to take a long hard look at it. You twist it, you turn it until you see all the angles. This paragraph contains information on how to make a valve stick." He pointed at the screen. "And I'm sticking with that."

Everyone was quiet.

"Skip, you asked me, as a professional, what I would do."

"I did."

"I'd take this very seriously. The day isn't over, gang, and I think these three rides may very well be targeted."

"But Moe?" Em studied Jody. "Why is he sabotaging his own business?"

"I'm working on that. But I feel very confident that it's Moe. He's put out the word on James and Skip knowing that with everyone coming down on you guys, paranoia strikes and you're not looking where you should."

"Explain." I wasn't sure why that should hinder our progress. Hell, there was no progress.

"You're in a defense mode."

"We're in a clueless mode."

"No, you're defensive. Someone told the air rifle guy, Kevin what's his name, that you two were investigators. Remember?"

Of course I remembered.

"Then you got crap from the two guys who run the tail. They knew right away you were P.I.s. And they're going to watch you like a hawk. Winston Pugh and his girlfriend, they know you're after them. Someone warned you in the Fun House. Think about it, guys. Everyone here is aware you're private investigators. Someone is giving the entire entourage dangerous information about you. You guys are quickly becoming impotent."

Jody gave Em a mischievous grin and I had to agree. We were impotent.

"So again I ask," it was almost noon and our day was rapidly evaporating, "what do we do, Jody?"

"This isn't my case, boys."

James nodded. "No, it's not."

Jody shrugged his shoulders.

"James—" We couldn't afford to lose Jody at this stage of the game.

"All right, all right, if it was your case, what would you do?" James was tired of playing with him.

"Am I being paid as a professional consultant here?"

I couldn't believe it. Now we were dividing the pie even further. And there never was much of a pie to divide.

"How much?"

"I'll figure it up and let you know."

"Give me a price." I was going to add this up in my head.

"Skip, I'll get you a bill when I'm back at my office." Jody was firm. He wasn't committing on the price.

At this rate, we were going to owe Jody a whole lot more than we were making. Assuming we made anything.

"Fine. What's our next step?"

"Your next step, James. You're going to give Angie Clark some erroneous information."

"What am I going to tell her?"

"Tell her that you think the Sidewinder and the Ferris wheel are about to be sabotaged."

"And I really don't think this at all?" James had no idea what to think.

"No. Because the problem is going to be at the Dragon Tail."

"And you know this because?"

"Somebody has tampered with the valves, James. Come on, pay attention. You watched it happen."

"Skip and I watched someone fix a valve. *Fix* it, Jody. *Fix* it." My partner's irritation was coming through. There was an edge to his voice, and when someone questioned James's reasoning, watch out.

Jody just shook his head. "You haven't paid any attention. Twist this thing around, look at it from every angle, expect the unexpected."

I decided to defuse the conflict, "So what we thought we saw—"

"Didn't happen. You were sent down there by Moe Bradley to watch someone fix a valve. Because Bradley told you that was going to happen, that's what you *thought* you saw. Someone fixing a valve."

And I remembered what he'd told me about the video pen. Everything is as it appears, except that it's not.

"So you and Skip are going to monitor the Dragon Tail and the two guys who run it. Em is going to visit Winston Pugh and his girlfriend and keep tabs on them, just in case."

I still wasn't sure where this was all going.

"Just in case what?"

"Just in case I may be wrong."

"You mean that there's that possibility? You, Jody Stacy, could be wrong?" James did not disguise his sarcasm.

"Another rule for your crash course in P.I. one oh one, James." Jody said flatly. "Cover all bases."

CHAPTER THIRTY-EIGHT

"This is it, James." I kicked a stone and felt it sting my big toe. "Damn. I am not going to do this again. I'm not going to let you drag me into any more of your crazy business ventures." I kicked another stone and watched it skip across the dirt brown field. "The next caper, you're on your own."

James paced beside me, keeping his eyes straight ahead. "You say that now? When we're this close to solving the case? This close to getting a pretty good paycheck?"

Throwing my hands up, I shouted. "We're how close? You think it's Winston, Jody thinks it's Moe, and Angie's been playing you for a sucker. On top of that, Jody is now in charge, we owe him for all that equipment, and we're not even sure how much money we're going to make. Where does that leave us, James? Huh? Tell me. Where the hell does that leave us?"

"Dude, settle down." He gave me a stern look. "Just keep it together. We've got," he glanced at his watch, "nine hours. First let me go in and talk to Angie."

"You're going to tell her about the Sidewinder and the Ferris wheel?"

"I am. Can't hurt anything."

I left him at the trailer and started toward the Tail.

"Skip."

I turned and he stood with one foot on the step.

"You okay?"

I thought about it for a second. "Yeah, I'm fine."

James gave me a wide smile.

"You'll never be fine, and neither will I."

With that he waved and walked into Angie's trailer. I knew where the line came from. The Will Smith movie, *Hitch*. But he was right. I would never be fine, and neither would James.

Passing a carnie's trailer to the left, I saw a quick motion out of the corner of my eye. Someone ducking behind the aluminum structure, hiding from me. My instinct was to run, but I slowed down, waiting to see if anyone appeared. Nothing. I could swear I'd seen something.

I chalked it up to nerves and kept on walking.

"Mr. Moore."

The voice rough, a loud whisper. Turning, I saw Ken Clemens, snow white hair, dress pants, collared shirt, and sport coat, even in this Florida heat and humidity. He stood by the edge of the trailer I'd just passed.

"Meet me in ten minutes at Harry's Hideaway." A coarse, raspy voice.

He moved behind the trailer and didn't reappear.

Conflicted, I looked down at the Tail, realizing that even if I monitored the ride I couldn't stop anything from happening. If there was going to be a malfunction, there was absolutely nothing I could do to stop it.

It was a quarter past twelve, Harry's Hideaway bar would be open, and on a weekend, aren't you socially allowed to start drinking after the noon hour? I think so.

I thought about telling James, but decided against it. Let

him deal with Charlie and Bo. I'd learn what I could from the personable Mr. Clemens. Maybe he had the case solved.

I never crossed paths with Clemens in the short walk to Harry's Hideaway. While I hiked to the strip mall I remembered the bartender's warning to the older gentleman. "You're not welcome in this establishment again." Imagine, someone calling Harry's an establishment.

Winding my way through the rides and concessions, I glanced at Winny Pugh's Petting Zoo. What kind of thin excuse was Em going to use to keep an eye on Winston and Linda? And what if they were the guilty culprits? What kind of danger was she in? I didn't want to even consider that.

The door to Harry's was wide open, and a beer-infused cloud of cigarette smoke rolled out of the entranceway. I waited a moment for my eyes to adjust. Clemens was sitting at a table across the room, and two other seats were occupied by his two female companions. I didn't need to see them close up. It was obvious the two females were Judy Schiller and Virginia Crouse.

Where was James when I needed him?

As I walked to the table, Clemens rose and introduced the ladies. "Mr. Moore, this is Mrs. Schiller and this is Mrs. Crouse. Your employers." The ladies sat there with what appeared to be glasses of white wine in front of them. It surprised me that Harry's even carried wine, much less white wine.

Nodding to them, I sat down.

"Where is your business partner?"

Which one? Jody? James? Em?

"He's on assignment. As you know, he's the marketing director for the show and—"

"We've been through this before, Mr. Moore. Let's not be tedious."

Tedious was the last thing I wanted to be.

"The last time we met, Mr. Lessor told me that you had a suspect in the killing of Ellen Bernstein."

I was drawing a blank. "Ellen who?"

Turning to Mrs. Schiller, Clemens said, "You see? He hasn't done any homework. The two of them are useless."

"Mr. Clemens, who is this Ellen?"

"The lady who was killed on the Cat's Pajamas ride."

Oh, yeah. I was going to do a little research on that accident, but I hadn't gotten around to it. Things had been just a little hectic recently.

"Well, do you have a suspect?"

"Yeah, we've got a suspect."

"You wouldn't tell me who it was. I believe your friend said it was too early to divulge the name."

That was James's excuse. The real reason being he had no suspect at all at that time.

"Do you know who Ellen Bernstein was?"

"No, sir. I don't." I noticed I hadn't been offered a drink. And I was just about ready for one.

With that disgusted erudite attitude, he told me who Ellen Bernstein was.

"Ms. Bernstein was a federal investigator."

"Federal?"

"The U.S. Occupational Safety and Health Administration was looking into one of our minor accidents. Ms. Bernstein was the assigned investigator."

"Wow."

"It's something you would know if you'd done your homework."

"And she was the one who fell from the ride?"

"She did."

The silent ladies nodded.

"Why didn't her death trigger a larger investigation?"

I wanted to wipe that smirk off his face.

"It did. You would know that if you were doing your job."

James could have the entire detective agency. At this moment all I wanted to do was get as far away from this fiasco as possible. Except that I'd stuck James with the Dragon Tail, and Em was stuck watching the dwarf and his girlfriend. And so it was my job to take Clemens's abuse and find out why this summit meeting had been called.

"For two weeks, every ride was inspected. Every employee was inspected. And as hard as it is to believe, the government found that there were plausible reasons for each accident. The verdict was that there was no foul play."

I put my hands on the table, palms down. "Then why are you forcing a private investigation? I mean, if the federal government is satisfied that these are purely accidents, then why can't you let it go?"

Judy Schiller put her hand on Clemens's arm. "Ken, let me."

He started to speak, then shut up and watched her.

"For the past year, our brother has been offering to buy our shares of the business." For a frail woman, her voice was strong and confident.

I nodded. Clemens had already told us that.

"The accidents that have plagued the show started almost at the same time he tendered his offers."

"It could be a coincidence."

Virginia Crouse spoke up.

"It could be a coincidence. It could be." Very sarcastic. "But every time we had an accident, every time that one of the rides malfunctioned, something happened that triggered our suspicion." She pushed her glass of wine from in front of her and frowned. "Something that gave him away, Mr. Moore. Something that proved to us that our brother was involved."

"You can't really believe that Moe is involved. What happened? People were injured for God's sake, a woman was killed. And the federal government found no fault with the show." I wish I'd done a little bit of investigating. "What else could possibly happen that would make you suspicious?"

Judy Schiller leaned toward me. Her eyes were on fire, and she grabbed my hand and squeezed it till my fingers ached. "Every time there was one of these so-called accidents, Mr. Moore, Moe's next offer was substantially lower than the one before."

CHAPTER THIRTY-NINE

I sipped my beer at the bar. My hosts had moved on, without so much as an offer of one small beverage. Screw 'em. I had to get my head on straight, and the ice-cold Yuengling helped.

I'm new to the real world of business. I majored in business, but what I learned appeared to be quite different when applied to today's companies. I thought that everyone profited when you made a lot of money. Conversely, I thought that everyone sucked wind when you fell on hard times. Why would someone deliberately try to lose money?

So it turns out people will drive down the value of the company when they are trying to leverage the buyout.

James and I dreamed of having a company worth millions of dollars. Millions.

What Clemens, Schiller, and Crouse were proposing was that Moe Bradley dreamed of having a company worth almost nothing. Then, being the white knight in shining armor, he would swoop in, offer to buy the property for pennies on the dollar, and save the day.

At the same time, he was probably prepared to rename the

business, rebuild the value, and in a very short period of time it would be worth much more than what he'd paid. What a guy.

What a dangerous guy. Whether he'd planned to kill the government agent or not, it made no difference. Once he'd killed someone, it was easy to kill again. I wondered if he personally shot Kevin Cross or had it done professionally. Shot him while he was on the john. Nasty stuff.

And if he suspected James and me of suspecting him, well, I didn't want to think what he might have planned for that eventuality.

That's what Schiller and Crouse proposed. They figured that brother Moe was the guilty party.

But that still left Bo and Charlie, the questionable ride operators. And that still left Winston and his girlfriend, Linda. And where the heck did that leave Angie Bradley/Clark? The banker?

I gulped my beer and ordered another. James and I drank too much. But at least I had company.

I drank it in five minutes, put my money on the bar, and walked out. By now I was sure that James was wondering where his partner was. I was sure that Em was either finding it impossible to deal with Winston and Linda or she'd gone back to the trailer. And if she'd gone back to the trailer, was Jody still there? Now that pissed me off.

A gust of wind kicked up dust from the show ground as I walked down to the Tail. I wondered if James was hanging at the outskirts or if he'd gone into the fenced area and was wiping up customers' urine-covered seats.

From a distance I could see the Tail, stretching out up in the sky. The appendage snapped to the left, hung there for a moment, then snapped to the right. Viewing the ride from this distance was almost more frightening than riding it. If something happened to that ride, people could be scattered all over the landscape.

And there, parked by the fence, was James's newest possession, his sacred white box truck. It was the first I'd seen it in the daylight, and I wondered what had possessed him to drive the very short distance to the Tail.

As I walked closer, I saw the aluminum ladder, stretched across the top. The vehicle looked like a poor man's construction truck, a look that I'm sure James was going for.

When I finally arrived, the ride was loading again. Three people stood in line. Searching the immediate area, I saw no sign of James. Just like him to desert his post. But to leave the precious truck?

"Skip Moore."

I spun around and Moe was standing behind me, his steel gray eyes looking into mine and his arms crossed over his sculpted chest.

"Looking for your friend?" He almost yelled to be heard above the blasting music.

"As a matter of fact—"

Moe made a sweeping motion with his arm. "He's on the Tail."

"What?" We must have been right in the path of a bass speaker. I felt my head vibrating.

He spoke louder. "He's on the Tail. Back there."

I jerked around, trying to find the car that carried James. The tail was surprisingly empty. I saw one car with an elderly couple sitting patiently.

"Oh, trust me, he's there. I personally escorted him to his seat." He kept pointing. "And, Skip, I thought Angie told you to be down here this morning. Your partner is here. You weren't."

"We were here. Both of us, but something came up."

"Son, you're working for me. If you want the job, then nothing comes up. Your friend is back there, on the Tail."

"Impossible. He's scared to death of the Tail."

"Are you calling me a liar? I told you, I seated him myself."

Very strange. "Moe, James hated this ride. He hates any ride."

"Well, why don't you go out there and see for yourself. Maybe you can coax him off the ride."

Frantically I kept looking.

"Come on, I'll take you out to his car." He was shouting, but no one could hear.

And then I saw James. Halfway back in the line of cars that made up the Tail. He was slumped in the seat, all by himself and there were only two more couples to be seated.

"Moe, he doesn't look—"

"Healthy? I think he's probably just resting, Skip."

"What happened to him?" I glanced back at the tall gentleman with those commanding features and the steely gaze.

"Nothing. I suggested that he get on the ride one more time to check it out." His voice told me he was lying. "Come with me. Let's see if he's okay."

He grabbed my arm, pushed past the last couple in line and moving quickly, hustled down to James's car.

"James." Moe yelled his name. There was no response.

"James." I yelled his name. No response.

"What? Is he drugged?"

"Very perceptive, young man. You're sharp, I'll give you that. But maybe not sharp enough. Imagine you coming back at this very second. Not the brightest thing you've ever done, but it's perfect timing, Skip. Perfect."

As I glanced up at Moe, I saw the needle in his hand.

"You weren't supposed to see this, but—"

"What the—" I stepped back, the metal fence stopping my escape. He took two steps toward me and I pressed into the fence, feeling the cheap metal dig into my back. There was nowhere to go.

"You won't feel a thing."

"You're going to—" I lashed out, connecting with a bone-shaking kick hard on the shin. Bradley's eyes widened as his hand flew open and he dropped the needle.

Sliding to the right I took two steps and he caught me across the throat with his arm. I thought I'd swallowed my Adam's apple. I tried to groan, but no sound would come out, and I fought to catch my breath.

Picking up the needle, he made a jab at me and I spun. The needle punched open air and he regrouped.

"Look, punk, you're joining your friend," Moe reached out and grabbed my shoulder with the strength of a vice.

I winced, looking around for some help. No one was paying any attention. Only four cars were full, and Bo and Charlie were laughing and smoking cigarettes in the control booth.

"Trust me, this is painless." Moe shot for my arm as I jerked. He missed and tightened his grip.

The music blared "Don't stop believin'" as Steve Perry belted out the lyrics, and I screamed at the two dimwits by the buttons. I screamed, but not loud enough. They were lost in their own world.

"Take it like a man." I sensed the irritation in his voice, the frustration that he wasn't getting his way.

Once again I watched the needle in his right hand. I wasn't going to be slumped over in the seat next to James, because it appeared that this ride to hell wasn't coming back. Once it started, it appeared there was only one conclusion.

Moe's eyes shone and he raised his needle arm once more. I threw my elbow back and up, catching the big man under his chin. So close I could hear his teeth slam together even over the loud music. As his head snapped back, I jerked away from his loosening grip, spinning again and catching his chest with my open palm. Moe staggered back and I ran.

Running as fast as I could I headed for the open ground. I heard loud puffing and looked behind me as the shimmering Tail rose slowly in the air, steam pouring from the mouth of the beast, and I ground to a halt, spinning around and searching the area. No Moe. Anywhere.

Standing twenty feet from the Tail was the small zookeeper, hands shoved deep into his overalls. Winston Pugh was watching the Tail, and as the long line of cars rose from the ground, I saw James, eyes closed, leaning over the handlebar, oblivious to the world below.

CHAPTER FORTY

If Jody was right, if the valve was going to stick, it was going to happen on this ride. I moved quickly to the control panel. Charlie stood there, giving me a dirty look.

"What the hell were you and Moe arguing about?"

"Arguing? He was trying to kill me."

Charlie smirked and turned his attention to the ride. "If Moe wanted you dead, you'd be dead."

The Tail snapped to the left and even from the ground I could see James's body flop like a limp rag.

"Charlie, stop the ride."

"You don't just stop the ride after the first twist up there." Paying no attention to me, he watched the Tail.

"Look, somebody put some grease or something on one of the valves. This machine is going to gum up and the whole ride is going to—"

The Tail snapped to the right.

"I'm not gonna stop the ride." He shouted over the music.

There was no sign of Bo as I stepped closer to Charlie. "Look, Charlie—"

The James look-alike glared at me, the only real barrier between the ride and me. "Get away."

All I had to do was get close to the yellow button. Arm's length. The ride would stop, the Tail would sink slowly back to the ground, and this nightmare would be over.

He swung for my jaw and I jumped back.

"Don't screw with my ride."

"The ride is going to freeze up. I'm not making this up. You're going to have a serious problem, dude. Stop it."

"Bo should have knocked a little more sense into your head." He swung wildly again and I deflected the blow with my arm.

The Tail thrashed, then plummeted to the ground, slowing down at the last second. As it gently glided to earth I thought about the split second I could get James out of the car. It was too late already.

"Kid." The voice fought over the music of Journey, and from the corner of my eye I saw Pugh, trudging toward us in his floppy rubber boots.

"Get the hell away from here." Charlie stood in front of the machine, arms spread as if daring me to come closer. "I'll kill you. So help me God."

Screams came from the ride as the tail started back up again, rising from the ground in its green and gold glory. I prayed James was still out cold.

"Charlie, the valve—"

"They fixed the valve this morning. Weren't you paying attention?" Charlie screamed, staring at me wildly as I moved from side to side, trying to find my way in to push that yellow button.

I jabbed and he covered, jabbed a second time and heard a thud in the gears. Looking up at the Tail, hovering at forty feet, I saw it shake, then freeze. Another clunk and I looked back at Charlie. A look of surprise and fear frozen on his face.

"Do you keep a solvent? Come on, man, you've got to have something. Something to spray on the valves." I remembered Moe's tutorial on unsticking a valve. It was on his highjacked computer screen. Spray a kerosene solvent on the valve.

A crunching sound and the Tail quivered. Only two of us knew the ride was in serious trouble.

The red and white can set beside the control station was emblazoned with the word Kero-Spray in bright bold letters. I threw open the metal door on the housing unit and leaned inside. Piston-like tubes of steel were lined up on the right, and I sprayed. A lethal shot of Kero-Spray, just hoping upon prayer that things would straighten themselves out. I sprayed again. And one more time for good measure.

As the fumes hit my brain, I backed out, stumbling in my woozy state. Feeling something grabbing my wrist, I tried to shake it off, but someone twisted my arm behind my back and pushed me away. Bo, Charlie—somebody pushing me to the ground.

"Kid. I'm trying to get your attention. Are you listening?" Pugh stood above me, sweat dripping off his shiny forehead. He spit tobacco not two inches from my face and stared at me. It was at that very second that the ride exploded with a roar of raw thunder and the housing unit ripped apart as a giant ball of fire erupted from the metal box.

CHAPTER FORTY-ONE

As I lay there on the ground, shards of hot metal cascaded on me like a swarm of bees, their stingers jabbing my tender skin. Pushing myself up, I started to run, watching behind me as the ball of fire contracted and seemed to die as quickly as it started.

Feeling the pain of the stinging burns, I brushed at my arms and face, stopping in a short distance to catch my breath. I had to stop this slovenly life. Too much drinking. Too little exercise.

"Holy shit."

I spun around and there was Winston Pugh, watching the Tail in the sky. The Tail, frozen, not moving at all as the handful of riders screamed at the top of their lungs. All the riders except for one. James was still passed out, leaning over the rail, as if he'd just upchucked and was too weak to sit up.

"What the hell were you doing?" I glared at the short little man.

"Kid, I had a message for you. You were so tied up with Moe and Charlie I couldn't get your attention."

"What message?"

Together we watched the black smoke pouring from the

mechanical structure. The ride was rigid, frozen in time. High up above the landscape of Carol City and stiff as a board.

"Emily was visiting us when she got a phone call."

"And?"

"Some guy told her that he needed to see her right away. Something about Moe having an offer."

The first thing that hit me? Em hadn't been with Macho Jody. She'd been with Winston and Linda. Great news.

I glanced back at James and I was consumed with the thoughts of how to save him. Screw the other people up there. James was and still is my best friend. I needed to get him down.

"And something about not applying the solvent while the ride is in motion."

"What?"

"Boy, I didn't memorize what she told me. It was something about a solvent. She said you'd understand."

Don't apply while the ride is in motion? All I knew was that I had to get James out of there. Before the entire ride came crashing down.

"Where is she?"

"I think she went back to your trailer. She seemed to want to talk to some guy named—and this is very weird, Judy?"

"Jody. It's a guy."

"Oh, my God." Charlie was screaming and pointing. The Tail remained frozen at a forty-five-degree angle in the bright blue Carol City sky, but one of the cars was hanging low, gently swinging as if only one or two bolts held it in place.

"That car is gonna fall. Swear to God."

The hanging car groaned as it dropped another inch, the metal stressed from the weight.

And leaning over the rail, oblivious to it all, was my roommate, James.

CHAPTER FORTY-TWO

"Charlie." I grabbed him by the arm, breaking his hypnotic stare. "Will the yellow button or the red button bring them down?"

He stared at the console for several seconds.

"Come on, man. This depends on you."

Charlie pushed the yellow button and immediately jumped back as sparks shot from the control box.

"Holy crap."

"Those bolts aren't going to hold."

He shook his head. "I don't think so."

James was sitting up. A good thing. But he looked dazed and confused.

"Charlie, how strong is the Tail?"

"Strong?" He couldn't take his eyes off the Tail, eighty feet above the ground.

"Is it pretty rigid in this situation?" I was shouting to be heard above the roar of the music. Turning, I saw a swell of people running toward the DT.

"It's made of sections."

"What do you mean?" I shouted.

"Like, sections of steel. The Tail has to twist and turn. It twists and turns in sections. Jesus, guy, we've got to get that Tail down."

Ignoring his panic, I pressed him. "But now it's stationary up there. Is it stiff in this situation?"

"Is it stiff? What the hell are you talking about? Hell, how do I know? It's never *been* in this situation." He kept his gaze steady on the Tail.

I sprinted toward James's truck, opened the unlocked driver's door and stepped on the running board. Reaching up on the roof, my hands grabbed the ladder. I pulled on the rail, easing myself up, straining every muscle in my arms, my hands clawing to hold on. Finally I sprawled on top of the truck and I looked up at the Tail. The Tail car groaned again and swayed. Below me were about thirty people—carnies, paying customers, and gawking business owners from the Bayview Mall. I didn't see Jody or Em.

Directly below me stood Pugh, gazing up with a question in his eyes.

"Winston. If I can get this ladder free, can you take it when I hand it down?"

I had to take a chance on someone. Charlie I still didn't trust. Bo was nowhere to be seen, so I picked James's number-one suspect.

"I'll do it," he shouted back up.

The ladder was tethered to four hooks, and with a simple jerk of the ties I freed it. Quickly pushing it off the top, I lowered it down to Pugh. He grabbed the end, and pulled on it, and within seconds the ladder was on the ground.

I grabbed the side of the roof and let myself go, my feet hitting the running board. If I'd just jumped, with my luck I would have broken my neck.

Grabbing the ladder I struggled to drag it to the Tail.

"What exactly are you gonna do, young fella?" Pugh trailed

behind me, and when I turned he was looking up at the Tail, then looking up at me. The poor guy looked up no matter what he was looking at.

"That ladder ain't high enough to reach that car. Not by a long shot."

The riders were screaming from fright, and James sat at the top, still trying to comprehend what had happened.

And now I could hear Foreigner, singing "*Countin' every minute . . . I'll make every minute count . . .*"

"Boy, what the hell are you gonna do?"

"Hold the ladder, Winston."

He grabbed the legs and I eased the thirty-some-foot ladder up against the base of the ride. God, I prayed this would work. It had to. I looked up and saw the car moving ever so slowly.

"James," I yelled. "Don't move. Whatever you do, don't move."

I climbed the ladder one foot after another as fast as I could, and halfway up knew it was a big mistake. The farther I went, the more queasy I felt. Once I looked down and felt my stomach about to turn. My heart was beating double time and my hands were cold and clammy in the South Florida heat and humidity. Sweat ran from my forehead into my eyes and I couldn't take either hand off the sides of the ladder to wipe it away. My death grip on the ladder was a lock.

At the top, I looked up. Considering the angle of the ladder and the angle of the Tail, I hadn't climbed nearly as high as I'd hoped. I was up to the second car and thank goodness it was empty.

I stepped off the ladder and grabbed the rectangular gold colored section of bar that supported two of the cars on the Tail. The tops of all the cars were securely bolted to this bar. Well, the tops of almost all the cars were securely bolted to a section of bar. James's car did not seem to be securely bolted at all.

Stepping on the roof of the car I wrapped my arms around

the bar and reached one hand up, pulling myself very carefully. Now I had nowhere to go but up. My stomach was in knots, sending flutters to the heart and all I could think of was falling thirty, forty, or fifty feet to my death. What the hell had I been thinking?

Now I was midway between cars. Another empty green car was two pulls ahead and I reached and pulled. Reached and pulled.

At this point I thought about dropping into the vacant Tail car and letting a professional emergency team get us all down. And then I heard the groan and I stepped lightly on the top of the next Tail car and pulled myself up, up, and up along the bar to the third car.

"Get us down! Now." The young lady was screaming at me as her nerdy boyfriend sat pressed against the side of the car, shaking nervously.

I stepped on the roof of their car for a second to steady myself, pushed off and squeezed my legs and arms around the bar. I was on a new section and it seemed to be holding. There was a slight tremor and the bar moved just a bit. I stopped for a second, my shoulders aching from the struggle to hold onto the cold, hard steel bar. I kept telling myself that I was too far along to stop. I pulled again. And again.

Another empty car, then a full one. Four people looked up at me, this crazy acrobat crawling on a tightrope. There was pleading in their eyes and I kept moving. Two more empties, and a new section. A tremor and the bar shook. I was petrified. I considered freezing in place. Again I wondered what I had been thinking. There was absolutely no way I was ever going to get myself down, much less get James to the ground. Finally I saw his car. Two pulls and then what? I could see two massive bolts that appeared to be severed, and the two remaining bolts that held the car to the bar were strained, tugged from the roof with visible steel showing. The sparkling green car listed at a strange angle and seemed to be ready to drop at any moment.

If I stepped into the car, the weight would probably send it plummeting to the earth. Probably should have considered that from the beginning.

"Skip."

James's voice was weak, and it was obvious he saw me coming. I pulled and advanced on the bar. Trying my best not to look down, I did. And there, seventy some feet below was Em. And Jody. And about fifty people, all looking up at me. What the hell was I doing? My stomach flipped and I almost lost my grip.

Drained of energy, I tried to pull myself one more time. My tendons screamed, my muscles ached, and my hands were rubbed raw, every joint in my body calling for relief. I felt the moisture on my palms, either sweat or blood, I couldn't tell.

Finally, I was over his car. I couldn't put my foot down. I couldn't lower myself into the car. Any movement could mean his death.

"James, dude, how strong do you feel?"

"Strong?" The voice was weak.

"Listen, James. I'm going to be very brave and lower one hand down from this bar. Do you understand?"

"And we're what? Going to shake?"

I almost left him there and crawled back down.

"No, dumbass. I want you to grab it. Grab my hand and I'll pull, and as soon as you're up about three feet, you should be able to grab this bar. Are you strong enough to do that?"

"I don't know, Skip."

An honest answer. And we were going to have to go with that. If I dropped him, if he fell back into the car, chances are the bolts would pop and it would plummet to the earth and he'd probably be dead. I couldn't live with the idea I'd done nothing. And I couldn't live with the idea that I'd helped cause his death.

I figured that if he dropped, I'd let go and drop too. Probably fall on Em, and take her out as well.

But seriously, facing death is a very scary proposition. I'd done it before, but I'd never, ever been this frightened. My stomach was in knots, my heart was hammering in my ears, and every instinct in my being told me to hold tight and never move again.

"If you can reach this bar, hold on and move back about ten feet, we'll be poised right over an empty Tail car. Do you understand?"

"What?" He had no clue.

"James. Listen. Process this, please. You're going to grab my arm. I'm going to pull you up here and we're going to work our way back about ten feet to the next Tail car. Then we're going to drop into that car.

I had to make him understand.

"Then what?"

"We drop into that car and wait for the fire department. Know what I mean?"

"What's wrong with this car?" He was confused.

And it hit me that he had no idea the peril he was in. He had no idea what danger we were both in.

"James, your car has at least two bolts that are broken. If you move much at all, or if I dropped into the car, chances are—"

"Whoa! Dude. You're here to save me?"

I couldn't help but smile. He was starting to get the bigger picture.

"Well, I kind of figured you'd do it for me."

"Skip—"

"James, you'd better summon up every bit of strength you've got."

"I'll do it, amigo."

I looked down at him, still foggy, trying to focus on me.

"Give me a second, man."

The car groaned and swayed in the breeze. My bar section moved with it and I squeezed my arms even tighter around the cold gold steel. I could not let go. I'd wrapped my legs too, and the last thing I wanted to do was drop one hand down to James. But I did. And I felt myself start to slip. Whoa.

"Hold on, James." I pulled my hand back and hugged the steel bar. Taking a deep breath, I dropped my hand again.

"What do I do?"

"Grab my arm, James." I yelled at him, the sweat soaking my upper body. I was losing my patience as well as my balance.

He grabbed my hand.

"My arm. Pay attention."

One hand on my arm, and my section of bar shook.

"Both hands. Hold on tight, James."

He grabbed my arm, and I pulled anyway. If it worked, it worked. If it didn't— Immediately I knew it wasn't going to work. James's weight was going to pull me off the bar and if I let him go now, he'd drop back into the car and it might break loose in free fall.

Totally screwed. Totally. Jesus and Mary. I was never a religious person but I prayed. Like no one has ever prayed before.

Rolling to my left and squeezing with my legs and left arm, I tugged as hard as I could with my right arm.

James was slipping, losing his grip from the sweat of my hand.

"Come on man, hold on."

"I can't hold on, pard."

If he couldn't hold on to me, he'd never hold onto the steel bar.

I glanced down. Only for a brief second. Em was looking up, her mouth wide open.

CHAPTER FORTY-THREE

Prayer, persistence, stamina, strength. Maybe they all come into play when you ask for divine intervention. My thighs were chafed and the muscles in my legs cramped as I rolled, pulling him up. His grip slid and I pulled harder, hoping to get him to the hard steel of the bar.

Maybe seeing Em down below played a factor. The thought of never seeing her again banged inside my skull as I pulled with more might than I thought was in me. Breathing hard and wishing to God I'd taken better care of myself, I yanked one more time. My arm felt like it was going to separate from my shoulder.

James came up, gulping in air and without instructions from me he let go with his right hand and grasped the metal bar. I laughed out loud. He was coming out of his Moe-induced coma.

"Can you hold on by yourself?"

"Don't know, amigo. Almost all my life I've needed you. Not sure I can do this on my own."

With that statement I was certain that my roommate was still under the influence of drugs.

Inching back, I tugged him. His one arm wrapped over the

bar, one hand still clutching my arm in a death grip, James came with me.

"James. Hang onto the bar tight, man. Then throw your other arm up. Get both of them over the bar."

He glanced toward the ground.

"Oh, shit, Skip. That's a long way down. Look at you. You're up on the beam, you're on top with your legs and arms. I'm hanging here, pard. Legs down, ready to fall at any moment."

Yeah. I was high and dry. Thank goodness I wasn't in any peril.

"Damn it, James, do it. You've only got to work yourself down about eight more feet."

"Skip."

One more glance at the crowd below. The burned-out metal housing unit on the ground and the gears from the Dragon Tail. He let go of my arm and threw his other hand up and over the bar.

"Skip, I love you man. If I drop, tell Em I'm sorry."

"Move. Just inch yourself down. Follow me."

I'd thrown my arm back over the beam and as strange as it felt, I started backing up.

James hung down, jerking his arms along the bar, centimeters at a time.

And the bar shook.

"What was that, pard?" He froze, looking up at me with raw fear in his eyes.

"Move, James. Don't stop." Me being the old pro.

He moved.

"Skip, if I drop—"

"Shut up."

We moved, another foot, then two. Hanging in the sky like some carnie freak show. It was just too ironic.

"Amigo, I'm serious. Bury me in the truck and don't pay that bitch Angie one cent back on that loan."

"Move."

"Skip—"

"Would you shut up and save your strength?"

We moved another foot, then another. He was shaking and I could see his hands slipping, losing their grip on the bar.

"Skip, this isn't going to work, man."

"It will." I heard a siren in the distance and wondered just how long it had been. Maybe an hour, maybe two?

"I've got five hundred bucks in the inside pocket of my sport coat."

"Five hundred bucks?"

"Can you buy me a funeral for that?"

One more foot and he was wheezing. His hands were clawing at the metal and there was nothing I could do.

"Come on pal, one more foot."

His legs kicked out and he forced himself toward the empty car. Inches at a time.

"James—"

"What pard?" I could hear the weakness in his voice. He'd all but given up and I looked down and saw the weariness in his eyes.

"I'm taking that five hundred bucks."

"Yeah?"

"Come on, move."

He inched along, almost by remote control.

"You know what I'm going to do with that?"

Silence.

"Move, James." He moved. I slid back and saw the empty green car below me.

"I'm going to pay myself back, dude, for all the beer you've made me buy over the years."

I moved. He moved. I dropped my feet and hit the roof of the car.

Oh my God, did it feel good to be on something firm. Even if it was seventy feet above the ground and swinging beneath me.

"Come on, James."

He inched down and his feet hit the roof.

Unbelievable. I let out ten sighs of relief.

"Son," he looked at me, still grasping the metal bar tightly, "you don't want to drink beer."

"No?" I let myself down over the edge, into the seat and reached out to him. He dropped one hand and reached down. I steadied him as he swung down and lowered himself into the car.

"No. That's for daddies and kids with fake IDs."

"Homer Simpson?"

"You got it, dude."

We both heard the groan, felt the Tail shake and shimmy as the car at the end dropped from the bar.

CHAPTER FORTY-FOUR

The hook and ladder truck showed up about four minutes later. By then James and I were shaking in our seat and the fireman had to almost pry us from the hard plastic. Someone told me it was an aftershock. The adrenaline that had been pumping all that time had stopped, and the shock to our systems was severe.

As they lowered us to the ground I saw the aftermath of the fallen Tail car. It was like someone had dropped a pumpkin to the ground from a twenty-story building. Splat.

We stepped from the bucket and there to greet us was detective Bob Stanton. His shirt dotted with perspiration, his thin hair plastered to his head, and his jacket hung over his shoulder.

"Just what the hell did you boys get yourselves into?"

I glanced around and there were dozens of people gawking. There really isn't a lot going on in Carol City so I suppose I should have been happy, providing the amusement for this entertainment-starved community. But I wasn't. I wasn't happy at all.

"Moe Bradley tried to drug me, and he did succeed in drugging James."

"Drug you. Just how did he accomplish that?" He turned to my roommate.

"A needle. I have no idea what was in the syringe." James pointed to his right bicep.

Stanton pointed to a uniformed officer. "Get a blood sample from this man, immediately."

"Bradley sabotaged this ride."

Stanton glanced over at the wreckage that was the Dragon Tail. The bombed-out crater of the former housing unit, the remains of James's Tail car smashed on the landscape, and the Tail itself, high in the sky. Riderless. Made of six sections of gold-colored metal that probably had our fingerprints embedded in each section.

"I've got more questions," he looked me in the eyes, "but you probably want to go get cleaned up."

I glanced at myself, arms and hands raw and streaked with grease. My clothes covered in black grease and torn beyond repair.

"Skip—"

I turned and there was Em.

She ran toward me and hugged me, apparently not worrying that she was going to get some of that grease on herself.

"What the hell were you thinking?"

"What?"

"My God, Skip. Dumbest thing you have ever done. Dumbest."

James was being led away by a uniformed officer to a rescue unit, its red light flashing on the roof. They'd probably find the drug that Moe injected, and maybe find some of last night's beer.

Em was saying this was the dumbest? There were some things she didn't even know about, however, she may have been right. I responded, "Hey, James would have done the—"

"No. He wouldn't have." She shut me off with the curt statement and a harsh glare. "There is no question about that. He would never have done that for you. Don't ever let me hear you say that again."

I didn't say anything else.

"Let's get you back to the trailer. Or maybe you should be going with James to the hospital."

I shook my head. The crowd, the commotion, the music still blaring over the speakers, it was all a little overwhelming. I saw Linda Reilly, several rows back, and grabbed Em by the arm as I approached her.

"Hey, Linda. Where's—" And I saw him, standing behind her and closer to the ground. "Winston, thanks for your help."

"Hey, kid," he walked from her shadow. "That was a very brave thing you did."

I reached down to take his hand, but he kept it by his side. Just as well. My raw hand, my sore forearm, and aching shoulder would not respond well to handshaking.

"Also, it was very, very stupid what you did."

"So," I pulled my hand back, "for whatever reason, it appears that Moe is guilty of sabotaging the rides and probably killing Kevin Cross."

Linda, silent until now, nodded. "I told you, Winston, it must be Moe. And he wanted to shift the blame to you. Trying to make these boys believe you were the killer."

"Looks that way." Pugh scratched the white hairs on his bare chest.

"Who would have thought?"

"Not you." He stood back and gazed up at me. "Definitely not you."

"No, we never—"

"You never thought it was Moe, because you were accusing me." Pugh stomped his foot. "You and your drugged-up partner were telling people that I was responsible."

"Hey, if it means anything, I always believed in—"

"Don't even try to explain it." The dwarf grabbed his girl-friend's hand and pulled her away. "Linda told me. She got a phone call telling her you thought I was the killer. Number-one suspect. Well I'm gonna remember that."

I could hear the distant barking of their sheepdog from hell as the two of them headed in the direction of the zoo.

Em walked up shaking her pretty head. "I would have sworn it was Winston. He's paranoid about losing this job and he just seems like the likely candidate to try to discredit the rides," I said.

She grabbed my arm and held on tight. "Skip."

"Yeah." We walked toward the Airstream.

"Jody and I—" she hesitated.

"What? Jody and I are having an affair? Are going to elope?"

She squeezed my arm. "Jody and I found some interesting stuff on Moe's computer." She kicked me in the shin without missing a step and kept holding on. "First of all, there was a line regarding the sticking valves that he didn't read to you. It was down a paragraph. You can't use kerosene solvent when—"

"The ride is in motion." I stopped and looked at her. "I found that out the hard way."

"The brief comments I heard after the explosion, were that if you hadn't blown up the motor, James's car would have shaken loose while he was still in it. I would bet that the bolts in that car had been cut. And from what I can figure out, you were supposed to be in the Tail car too. Right?"

"If Moe had his way."

"They'd be picking up pieces of you guys for days. Scraping the ground with—"

"Em, enough with the graphic description."

We walked, and I suddenly realized that the show had shut down. The Ferris wheel was motionless, the Sidewinder, the Fun

House, and food vendors were quiet, eerily quiet. The roller coaster sat still and the strangest sensation of all was silence. No rock and roll or big hair music. My throat was sore, but I wasn't yelling anymore.

"And we found a letter."

"Yeah?"

"Some big holding company was willing to buy up the Moe Shows for a whole lot of money."

"Why?" I couldn't imagine someone wanting to own a carnival.

"Limit the competition. They were making offers to about a dozen carnivals. The fewer rivals, the more money they could charge."

"So why didn't he sell?"

"Moe?"

We'd reached the Airstream and I just wanted a hot shower and a beer.

"It appears in the correspondence that the longer Moe held out, the more money this company offered."

"So he was holding out to get rich."

"Remember," she stepped up on the landing, "Moe didn't own that much stock in the company. The only way he could really clean up was if he moved out the ghost sisters."

"Ghost sisters?" I'd only been gone, glancing at my watch, for about twenty-five minutes. And now there were new players in the game?

We walked into the trailer and I opened the refrigerator. No beer.

"Jody calls them the ghost sisters. You just see them from a distance and they appear and disappear from view."

"I saw them up close. I talked to them. Schiller and Crouse. They are far from ghosts."

"Oh?"

"Yeah. So this letter, you think he was trying to get a bigger share of the pie?"

"The whole pie, James. There was a lot of money at stake. He had to get his sisters out of the business. And he thought the accidents would scare them into selling their shares."

"At a fraction of what they were worth." It made sense. This was like going to business school only the stakes were a lot higher. It was better for Moe Bradley to bring down the value of the Show. The lower the value, the less he would offer the ghost sisters. If they walked away from the Show, Moe could have it all.

"There were millions of dollars involved, Skip. This other company really wanted the Moe Shows."

She leaned into me and started unbuttoning my shirt.

"Em?"

"Skip. It's important that you know everything we found."

"You think?"

She kept unbuttoning the shirt. After pulling it off my shoulders, she started unbuckling the belt on my jeans.

"Em?"

"I thought you were going to fall. I had no question about it. You and James were going to drop to your deaths and I was so sick, I can't even tell you. I mean, my stomach was rolling, Skip. By all rights you both should have fallen. My God, it was the hardest thing I've ever watched. I've seen you in the hospital when you were on life support, but—"

She pulled the belt from its loops.

"Hey—"

"Get a shower. Take some aspirin. We need to celebrate your victory today."

Who the hell was I to argue.

Em turned and walked to the door of the trailer. "I'm going

outside. I'll be back in twenty minutes to see if you're a little cleaner. I hate to say it, Skip, but I hate a dirty lover."

I wondered how James was doing. I thought about the idiotic stunt I'd pulled, the danger I'd put myself in, and wondered what was wrong with me. Seriously. There was something, maybe a screw loose. But hey, I'd saved my best friend's life, and I was going to get laid, so maybe it wasn't that bad.

CHAPTER FORTY-FIVE

The trailer shook from the pounding on the door.

"Your husband?"

Em punched me on the arm. I gently eased out of bed, pulled on a wrinkled pair of semiclean jeans and removed a T-shirt with a pocket from the dresser, and there in the drawer was that damned pen. Pulling the shirt over my head, I dropped the pen into my pocket and stepped into the living area.

"Kid."

I jerked the door open. Looking down I saw Pugh.

"What, another dead body?"

"Is Linda here?"

I looked around. As strange as things had been, you never knew.

"I'm pretty sure she's not here."

He pointed back to the tiny bedroom.

"Winston, give me a break. I'm not taking your paramour back to my trailer."

He bit his upper lip. "She's gone."

"Where?" I wasn't quite sure what this had to do with me.

"I wish I knew." He scratched the hair on his chest, pushing his hand down into the flap on his overalls.

"Winston, I have no idea where she is."

The little man stared up at me, a puzzled look on his face. "Why?"

"Why what?"

"Why did you accuse me of being responsible for those accidents?"

"I didn't."

"Linda said—"

"Linda got that information from Moe."

He stood there on the landing, giving me a sideways glance. "So?"

I gazed out over the Show ground and saw Bob Stanton walking toward us, long strides and a determined look on his face.

"So, did it ever occur to you that Moe Bradley was trying to cover his ass?"

"Where is Linda?"

"Winston, I don't know."

"And why would you think I was the bad guy here?"

"Because," the voice behind me said, "you were afraid that the Moe Show was going to fire you. That they were going to add more rides and wouldn't need your zoo."

He looked up at Em. I turned and she was dressed in one of my T-shirts and a pair of baggy shorts. Still sexy, no matter what she put on.

"That didn't mean I'd risk killing someone."

"But you had a very good reason to defend yourself." Em stepped up to the entranceway.

"You really think that I would rig a ride to kill someone?"

"Not now. I don't think you'd do that."

"Who could think such a thing?" Pugh turned and stepped down. "Was I really that—"

"That what?"

He turned to us. "Did I really come off like that?"

"Yes." We both said it at the same time.

"Mr. Pugh." Stanton stood at the bottom of our steps. "I have a search warrant for your trailer. Would you come with me, sir?"

"A what?"

"Search warrant. I have officers at your establishment, sir, and they have a warrant to search your premise."

The dwarf turned and gave me a pleading look. "Young man, please, find Linda. I can't do this without her."

It was becoming increasingly clear that Winston Pugh couldn't do anything without Linda.

They walked off together, Pugh's oversized boots flopping on his feet, and Stanton's shirt sticking to his back from the late afternoon heat.

"Search warrant?" Em stared after them. "What are they looking for?"

"Computer? Cell phone?"

"Maybe proof that Moe is the one who rigged the rides."

My cell phone went off, with Bruce Springsteen's "Born in the USA." Glancing at the screen, I saw James's name.

"Hey, you all right?"

"Skip. You saved my life, man."

"I've saved you so many times already that—"

"Yeah, yeah. Listen. They found Propofol in my blood."

"Propo what?"

"You remember that stuff that some doctor was giving to Michael Jackson when he died. Stuff that put him to sleep?"

I did. Sort of.

"Anyway, I'm okay."

"You're never okay."

"Pard, listen. Two of the officers were talking. They confiscated Moe's computer."

"Then they've got the same information we've got."

"Exactly. And they read some letters between Moe and Linda. Stuff that talks about Winston."

"Stuff like what?"

"Linda is assuring Moe that Pugh is not causing any problems. Apparently, even before Moe called Linda and told her that Pugh was our main suspect, Moe got word that Pugh was mouthing off to everyone. Pugh was accusing Moe and the sisters of trying to get rid of him."

"So Moe was communicating with Linda?"

"Yeah. Moe wrote Linda a letter about Pugh. He told her that the little guy's mouth was making him look like someone with an axe to grind. Used those very words."

"Axe to grind. Yeah. If Pugh was mouthing off like that to everyone else, then I could see where people thought he might be sabotaging the rides."

"Anyway, I'll be back on the grounds in an hour. Hold down the fort, amigo."

"James—"

"Yeah?"

"Do they have Moe Bradley?"

"His computer. They've got that."

"What about him? The guy who shot you up with Propo whatever?"

"I don't think they have him."

"James, they just got a search warrant for Pugh's trailer."

"Turns out Moe is the bad guy here, Skip. That's the fact."

Em came up behind me and put her arms around my waist. "Let me talk to him."

I put the phone down where she could talk and listen.

"James, you'd better bring a case of beer back for your friend. It's the least you could do for him."

I could hear him saying, "Yeah, yeah."

"And, James, does it sound to you like Moe was trying to cast blame on Pugh? To divert it from himself?"

"And cast blame on Bo and Charlie. Remember the video from our pen?" I could hear his voice on the tinny speaker.

All of a sudden it was *our* pen. I couldn't believe he'd help pay for the thing.

"Pally, Em, got to go. I'll see you in a short." And he was gone.

We were quiet for a moment, trying to absorb what was happening. My muscles still throbbed, and I was developing a splitting headache. I was hoping that James would hurry with that case of beer.

CHAPTER FORTY-SIX

We took a walk down to the Tail, stopping by Angie's trailer on the way. No one was home. No surprise there. My guess was that daddy and daughter had hightailed it to higher ground, leaving the team of Schiller and Crouse, along with Ken Clemens, to clean up the mess. And actually it was probably much better for us. I mean, Judy Schiller and Virginia Crouse were much more likely to pay us than Moe Bradley was. Especially since no one had a clue where he was. I know I was looking out for myself, but hey, I could really use the money.

Walking by James's truck, the acrid smell of burned rubber and oil still hung in the air, and the Tail spiked the sky like the show's middle finger. Parked along the road were the two flatbed trucks that had carried the Dragon Tail to the Bayview Mall. Where there was no bay, and technically, not even a mall. If those trucks were to haul it back, the Tail would be in pieces.

"Look up there." Em pointed.

It wasn't easy.

"By all rights you shouldn't be here." Em gazed at the phallic symbol in the sky. "You shouldn't even be alive."

"But I am. And so is James."

"Skip, do you think Bo and Charlie were involved?"

I hadn't given them a whole lot of thought. "Charlie, no. He was dumbfounded when the ride malfunctioned. Refused to believe it, but he hung in there. He tried to help me and bring the ride down. When he pushed the yellow button, the entire control box could have blown up in front of him."

"Bo?"

I remembered the pen video where Moe told Charlie that he and Bo had better be able to cover their asses.

"You know, Em, I don't often listen to Jody's philosophy. But in this case, you've got to remember what he said about working a case. 'Everything is as it seems. Except it's not.' You've got to take facts and information and turn it every way possible. So, maybe when Moe told Charlie that he and Bo had better get some distance—cover their asses, maybe he was just warning them that people were going to talk. Maybe it wasn't at all what it sounded like."

"He was throwing the blame, Skip. The more he got other people to believe that they were suspects, the more innocent *he* seemed."

We wandered through the grounds, the food booths locked tight. Late afternoon and not a person in sight. Tomorrow morning was tear down and I planned on waking up in the comfort of my own bed. If James still had a show job, he could participate in tear down. I'd done enough to support the cause.

But my guess was that James wouldn't have the job. The ghost sisters were not amused. Anyone associated with the ride debacle would probably be let go.

As for me, it was time to get back to work. I couldn't afford to lose my job.

"Do you think that he deliberately killed the investigator?" She held my hand loosely and it felt so natural.

"Moe?"

"Who else?"

"I believe he probably was responsible for killing Ellen Bernstein. If he didn't deliberately kill her, it was one heck of a coincidence. I mean here was a lady who could have shut the entire operation down."

She nodded. "After the first accident, the sisters refused to sell, right?"

"Exactly."

"So Moe had to keep making the accidents worse." Em paused, letting out a deep breath. "You know, Skip, I think he probably got in too deep too fast. Once he'd injured someone, it just didn't seem that bad to kill someone. Once he'd killed someone to get these millions of dollars, it didn't seem impossible to kill someone else. You know what I mean?"

I did. "And he was afraid this lady, Ellen Bernstein was going to discover who was tampering with the rides."

"And," she squeezed my hand, "he was afraid you two already had it figured out. And my guess is he knew you didn't really suspect Ken Clemens, and when James told Moe that you knew there was inside information being handed out, he figured it was only a matter of time before you came after him."

"You're right. Moe hired us because he thought we were too stupid to figure it out."

"If it hadn't been for Jody's spy equipment you never would have figured it out."

I didn't know if that made us dumb or smart.

"You know, if we'd looked a little deeper, if we'd done some research, some homework, we might have found the information about all those accidents. Could have saved us some serious problems. We probably should have looked into the accidents, but this agency is young. You'll learn."

"Yeah." I hated it when she was right.

And my biggest concern was that we would never learn. Never.

CHAPTER FORTY-SEVEN

We strolled by the Fun House. And the rifle booth where I'd met Kevin Cross. Both were shuttered, and the Ferris wheel rounded out the skyline, casting a late evening shadow on the ground.

"Skip."

I looked at her. She had tears in her eyes.

"I'm just thinking. You mean a lot to me. I must have thought a thousand times while you were up there that I would be lost without you."

"So you're saying—"

"Thanks for not falling off that ride."

I laughed. "Yeah. You're welcome."

We headed back to the trailer.

"Are you staying tonight?" She stood on the landing.

"No. I've got a handful of things in there, and I'm clearing them out. We found the bad guy. Don't know where he is, but we found him and my job is done."

"Well," she smiled, "I should probably call Jody and tell him the place is ours for the night then."

I didn't find it that funny.

"You're welcome to stay at my place." She tried to make amends.

"As tempting as that is, I'm tired, sore, and I should show up at work tomorrow morning. I'm going to pass, but it's not because of you. Got it?"

"I've got it."

Em opened the door and stepped in. I followed closely.

"James." She sounded happy to see him.

I took a shallow breath and detected the soft smell of frangipani. "Hey, dude." I smiled. "Are you a little less drugged?"

My roommate sat on the couch, staring at us, the fear of God in his eyes.

"Are you okay?" I walked to the sink, pulling a plastic cup from the cupboard, filling it with water.

He didn't answer.

"Hey, James, did you bring beer? It'd be better than this crap water."

He stared into my eyes, twitching ever so slightly.

"Beer? Where is it?"

Opening the tiny refrigerator I saw there was no beer.

"You son of a bitch. I'm going to take the five hundred dollars you offered me and—"

"Don't move. Not one inch."

My eyes darted to the bedroom doorway and there was Linda Reilly, a pistol leveled at my head. I didn't move. Not one inch.

CHAPTER FORTY-EIGHT

"Sit down."

"But you said don't move an—"

Em elbowed me. "Sit, Skip, sit." Like a lapdog I followed her command.

"James," Linda nodded in his direction. "You've got that ugly white truck down by the DT, right?"

He nodded, still not saying a word.

"Go get it."

James stumbled off the couch, apparently eager to do her bidding. Or eager to get the hell out of this Airstream trailer.

"Not a word to anyone, do you understand?"

He shook his head.

"Your friends' lives depend on it."

James moved to the door.

"Oh, and James, if you aren't back here in three minutes—three minutes, I may just shoot everyone in this room." She looked scared. Someone scared with a gun—not a good combination.

Finally James spoke. "I'll make it three minutes or less."

"Good." Linda pushed back the hair from her face with her free hand. "I don't think I have to demonstrate to you folks that I can and will shoot this gun."

James was out the door and running.

"You've shot someone before?" Em stared at her.

"The police are searching my trailer right now for this." She touched the barrel with her finger. "Of course, it's not there."

"Oh, my God." I saw the lights come on and Em's eyes got wide. "You shot Kevin Cross."

She moved to the trailer window and looked out, tapping the barrel of the gun on the wall of the trailer.

"Why?" I decided get to the bottom of this.

This lady who fried frogs, kicked goats, guzzled tequila, shoveled crap from Winston's zoo, and waved a pistol around like a hired assassin, had tears in her eyes. Wiping at them with the back of her gun hand, she turned to me, holding the pistol back down at her side.

"Because Kevin Cross threatened to go to the authorities and tell them who was responsible for the accidents."

It made absolutely no sense at all.

"Cross threatened to go to the authorities? How did he know?" I realized we weren't going to be killed, at least for the moment. So I wanted to keep her distracted. And, I wanted some answers. "How did he know who had tampered with the rides?"

She was silent. Looking out the window, waiting for James to show up with the box truck.

"Moe Bradley? You were defending Bradley?" Em kept probing. "Linda, why?"

"No, you don't understand."

I heard the rumble and realized that if we ever got out of this alive, James was going to have to replace the muffler along with the turn signal.

•　•　•

Linda ushered us into the truck. Four of us jammed into the cab with James driving.

"Pull out of here and take a right. I'll give you directions as we get closer."

As James started the truck, the muffler coughing, I realized this was the maiden voyage of the new spymobile. It might be the last voyage, but it was the first as well. Em sat beside me, clutching my arm and not saying a word.

"Just keep driving. Maybe three miles. You turn left on Pine Sap Road."

"Linda," I was trying to put it all together, "why were you defending Moe?"

She blinked back tears. "I wasn't."

"You killed Kevin Cross. All because he threatened to expose Moe Bradley?"

"No. No. It wasn't like that."

"Then what was it like?"

James kept driving, the muffler rattling beneath us.

"Winston was distraught."

I don't think I'd ever heard anyone use the word distraught, but there it was, on the table.

"He was certain that the zoo was going to be closed down. It's his life. It's the only thing that matters to him—except, except maybe for—"

And I knew where she was going. Linda mattered to him, but she was embarrassed to admit it.

"When Kevin called for Winston, Kevin threatened to blackmail him."

"I thought Kevin was his friend." I was getting more and more confused.

"Kevin was out to take care of Kevin. Carnies look out for themselves first." She stared at me with those deep green eyes. "He said he had proof."

"What kind of proof?"

"The night before the lady, Ellen Bernstein, was killed on the ride, Winston had been the security guard. Moe pays some paltry sum for employees to wander the grounds at night and make sure no one steals anything. Winston was on duty that night."

"And?" James entered into the conversation.

"And Kevin claims he saw a flashlight down at the Cat's Pajamas ride."

"That's it?"

"He'd talked to Winston about his situation. Winston would tell anyone who wanted to listen that he thought everyone was out to get him. Disney, Moe—" She took a moment and composed herself. "Kevin knew that Winston was scared to death about losing his job. And Kevin claimed there was a light down at the Cat's Pajamas for at least forty minutes. He figured that Winston was rigging the ride, and was responsible for the lady's death."

We were all quiet for a moment. James and Em would have agreed. They thought that Winston Pugh had the best reason of anyone to sabotage the rides.

"You're lying." I suppose it's iffy to tell a person with a weapon that they're lying. But I did. "Kevin never called Winston, did he?" It took me a while, but I was slowly figuring this out.

"He did. He most certainly did." She was agitated, her voice rising in volume.

"But he never talked to Winston. Am I right?"

She stared straight ahead, the pistol in her lap.

"Winston can't even answer a cell phone. He has no idea how a computer works. I'm not sure he can even read that letter from Walt Disney Corporation that he carries in his pocket. You take care of all that for him, don't you?"

She continued to stare ahead.

"Oh, my God." Em was having another revelation. "You took the call. And when Kevin threatened to blow the whistle on Winston, you set Kevin up. You told him that Winston would be down to talk to him, but you showed up instead."

"He was a terrible person." She sniffed and tears ran down her cheeks.

"But you thought he was right." James kept his eyes on the road and talked loudly over the roar of the faulty muffler. "Linda, you thought that Winston was trying to destroy the show. You thought he was responsible for the accidents and the death, didn't you?"

Now she was crying, wracked with sobs, and I considered leaning over Em and grabbing the gun from her lap. Grabbing the pistol from a lady who had shot a man, head-on, as he was sitting on the toilet, relieving himself? I thought twice about it.

"I did. He was obsessed. I knew, at least I thought I knew, that Winston had fixed the ride so there would be a major accident."

"And you were trying to protect him?" Em got all soft and mushy.

"The man needs protecting. Desperately."

"So you threatened us."

James looked at me. "When did she threaten us?"

"She threatened you, then threw you out of the Fun House."

He looked back at Linda and she nodded, blinking back the tears.

"And now?"

"It wasn't Winston. I made a terrible mistake. Until today, I thought—"

"It was Moe, right?"

"Moe. And a helper."

I was pretty sure who the helper was. "Linda, where was

Winston the night someone rigged the ride? Did he ever tell you?"

She nodded, and wiped at her eyes, the pistol still firmly clutched in her hand.

"Moe had given him an early birthday present."

"Birthday present?"

"A bottle of tequila. Winston took it on his security rounds and was passed out at the Fun House about two hours later." Linda took a deep, ragged breath. "In the meantime, Moe or his partner was down at the Cat's Pajamas. I made a terrible, terrible mistake."

She really had. But I wasn't that concerned about her prior mistake. What concerned me was that she might be ready to make another mistake. And that was one mistake that none of us could afford.

CHAPTER FORTY-NINE

"Turn left."

James swung onto Pine Sap Road, and I realized we probably would need shocks. On top of the muffler and turn signal. The truck swayed back and forth like a carnival ride.

"Two miles down this road and you'll see a stone drive off to your right." She sniffed and controlled the tears.

And James kept on driving, keeping the speed steady, and two miles passed in a few minutes.

"Right."

He turned right, and I thought about the movie *Swift Night into Hell*. Ben Salaman, the driver, wrecks the car, killing his kidnapper passenger. I couldn't remember if James had seen that movie. Obviously not.

We drove for half a mile down a narrow road bordered by brush and pine trees. Finally the landscape opened up and there were several buildings on the left. A large parking lot accommodated several flatbed trucks, and there was a faded, hand-painted sign above the long garage that said Moe Shows. We'd found the headquarters.

I wanted to allay her fears, her frustrations. Not so much because I felt sorry for her, but because I still thought there was a chance she would kill us. She'd already shown herself to be a cold-blooded killer, and I somehow felt responsible for Em's life. And, I suppose, since I'd put my own life at risk to save him, I felt responsible for James's life.

Linda motioned us out of the truck, her gun waving in the air. No one said a word. What appeared to be a graveyard of rides and attractions stood off to the right. Broken-down concession booths and trailers leaned at strange angles with stuffing pouring out of their sides. Rusted steel grid works and faded signs and posters were piled on each other and cast shadows on the ground like large chunks of confetti.

The air was eerily silent, and we all stood there, not sure what the next step would be.

"Maybe he's already been here," Linda said.

"Moe?"

"Moe." She walked to the end of the main building and disappeared around the side.

"Now would be a perfect time to make like a tree and leave." James held the keys in his hand.

"We can't go now." Em was talking crazy talk. I disagreed. We not only could go now, we should.

"Guys, this lady is hurting, big time."

"She's a killer, Em." I was sure she'd made that connection.

Linda walked around the other side of the building. "He's not here. Not yet. But he will be."

"How do you know?"

"He has a safe here, with a lot of money. He's going to need every cent of that money after what happened today."

"So what do we do?" Maybe it was some sort of a female thing, Em wanting to be supportive. The lady had a gun, for God's sake.

"Move the van. Behind the building."

James stepped up into the truck, bristling at the spymobile being called a van. I could tell it upset him. He started it up and rattled around the building. I wondered if he'd find a road back there and just keep on going.

A minute later he walked out and joined our group.

"He'll be here. Soon," Linda said flatly.

"And?" I was waiting for instructions.

"And we'll be inside to give him a surprise greeting."

Fifteen minutes later we heard a car coming up the gravel drive. My guess was a black Cadillac Escalade. The vehicle pulled up out front, and peeking through a crack in the heavy wooden door I saw Moe Bradley step out. Pulling in behind him was a rusted-out Ford something, and Bo got out of that. Moe and Bo. What a team. So maybe Charlie had just been along—for the ride.

"Skip," Linda motioned to me. "Call 911 and tell them that you've got a killer here."

"Linda," in a whisper, "those two are going to be inside this building in a second. Why didn't we call the cops about fifteen—"

"Call them. Now."

And I did.

Footsteps on the gravel and muffled conversation told us they were almost to the door.

"Shit."

"Got a problem, Moe?"

"Somebody shot the padlock off the door."

Linda had blown it to hell.

"Nothin' worth stealing other than what's in the safe. They can't shoot the safe open can they?"

"No."

Everything was quiet. The four of us stood off to the side,

pressed against the wall behind a beat-up Dragon Tail spare car. I felt perspiration running down my face, the second time I'd put myself in danger today.

Squeaking and squealing, the door slowly opened. Bo stuck his head through the doorway, then walked on in.

"Nobody here." He turned as Moe moved in. "This safe you've got—"

The roar of the gunshot startled me, and I couldn't catch my breath. Gazing around the curtain I watched Bo pitch to the floor.

As the repercussion faded, three of us looked at Linda. She stood with the pistol by her side, as surprised and stunned as we were.

CHAPTER FIFTY

Striding to the heavy metal safe that sat against the far wall by a cheap wooden desk, Moe kneeled down and started dialing numbers.

Linda held up her hand as if to silence us. She softly walked from behind the curtain and approached the show's spokesperson.

"Hey, Moe."

Spinning around in a crouch, he started to stand, putting out his hand and catching himself on the top of the safe.

"What the hell?"

"Where are you going to go?"

He stood there, stunned and puzzled at the same time. The three of us moved out into the room, but I don't think he was even aware of us. I stepped closer and he never noticed.

"There's number two." She waved her hand at the motionless body of Bo. "And you tried to kill Skip and James today, but that didn't go so well, did it?"

"You're a crazy lady. You and that psycho midget."

"Dwarf." She leveled the gun at his head. "My dwarf."

"Whatever. What do you want? Money?"

"How much?" Linda was playing with him.

"There's about five hundred thousand in here. I'll give you one hundred."

"Thousand?"

"Why not?"

She turned and looked at the body on the floor, thick red blood pooling on the tile.

"My guess is you asked Bo how much *he* wanted, too. I see where that got him. You're not the best business partner to have, are you?"

And then he noticed us.

Pointing his finger to a spot behind her he said, "What? Did you bring the entire show?"

And for just a split second she turned. Her head spun around, and I yelled.

"No."

And as she spun back, he'd already pulled the gun from his belt. The pistol exploded. Not once, not twice, but three times. Linda Reilly crumpled to the floor, blood pouring from her wounds.

Moe stepped back, admiring his work as I hit him. Never having played football in school, I'd like to think that this was one of the cleanest tackles ever. I connected just below the hips and he went down fast, cracking his head on the floor. His gun went skidding across the room, and I saw Em pick it up. James stood there with a look of astonishment on his face.

I felt weak, tired, drained, and I remember lying there on the floor, too exhausted to stand. The entire event was all recorded for evidence and posterity on the video pen in my T-shirt pocket. I prayed to God that I'd turned it on.

And for the second time in twenty-four hours, I heard sirens and realized this hero thing was just a little above my pay grade.

CHAPTER FIFTY-ONE

I let Em sit on the stained cloth sofa. The one with the ugly green pillow. It was still the most comfortable seat in the apartment. I perched myself on a folding chair, sitting backward, and James stood by the window, sipping on a Yuengling that he'd actually bought. In fact, he'd bought a case.

"And Angie's going to continue working for the ghost sisters?" Em couldn't believe it.

"She didn't do anything criminal." James stared out the window as if looking for someone or something. "And, she's blood."

"James," I was with Em, "Angie tried to sabotage us."

"Dude, she was looking out for her dad. I dig that. I don't have a father, and you have no idea where yours is. Respect it, amigo."

"Has anyone talked to Winston?"

"I did." Em spoke up.

"You talked to him? What did you say—better yet, what did he say?"

Em took a swallow of her beer and smiled. "He's bonding more and more with his dog, Garcia."

"The hound from hell."

"Now, Skip. Winston is devastated. He loved Linda and depended on her for everything. But I think he'll be all right. He's really good with the animals, and Virginia and Judy have agreed to keep him on and get him someone to help with the office duties." Em gave me a soulful look. "Oh, and that perfume you mentioned? When you thought Angie had been at Kevin Cross's trailer? It turns out Linda and Angie both wear Frangipani from Key West Aloe perfumes."

Who would have thought.

"Does anyone know if they're going to sell the shows?" James asked the bottom line question.

"I had a brief talk with Ken Clemens, all of five minutes, and we agreed that we would never agree about much of anything." I hoped to never run into him again. "However, he did tell me that the sisters were going to become a little more hands-on and try to run the shows themselves. So the answer is no. They're not going to sell. At least at this point. And, they're no longer calling it Moe Shows."

"Mmm," James said. "I wonder why?"

"From now on, they will be called The Schiller and Crouse Extravaganza."

"And Charlie?" Em hadn't heard the latest.

"Bob Stanton is determined to prove him guilty. He was Bo's confidant, and Stanton is convinced that Charlie is as guilty as sin. But, like Angie, he can't find anything that will stick." I finished my first bottle. One down, and I was sure, several more to go.

"You know, someone who's still with the show tried to kill us." I was so happy to be away from that group of freaks.

"What are you talking about?" James took a swallow. "Moe tried to kill us."

"Somebody rigged the ride, James. Somebody who posed as a technician gummed up the mechanism."

"While you two guys watched." Em nodded.

"Yeah. And we thought he was fixing the ride."

"Who?" James was watching my eyes. Maybe I knew something he didn't.

"It wasn't Charlie. Wasn't Bo. Couldn't have been Moe."

"Then who?"

"I have no idea, but I'll bet he's still with the Show."

Em twisted the idea. "Maybe whoever was working on the ride thought they were fixing it. What if Moe gave them something that actually gummed up the works and the repair guy didn't have a clue? I mean those people don't seem too bright."

James got that look on his face. "No, no. I think Skip's right. The guy who worked on the Tail tried to kill us. Which means there's still someone working for the Show who is serious trouble."

"James, don't even go there."

"Skip, we can call the ghost sisters, make our case, hire on, and find this guy."

"Yeah. That's what I want to do. Go back to the Show."

"Just a thought, amigo. Just a thought."

And it's almost always James's thoughts that get us into trouble.

"I hate to ask this with Skip in the room," Em gave me a condescending smile, " But what do we hear from Jody?"

My fists clenched, I gave her my update.

"We just got his bill."

"And?"

"Even if the sisters pay us, and they're arguing that fact, we'll be in the hole."

"One good thing comes out of it," James sucked on his beer. "Angie is giving us the truck."

"James." We both said it at once.

"We don't need the damned truck."

"Dude, she's giving it to us. It's free. I've finally got some wheels."

And he was right. It was found money. "We can sell the damned truck and pay Jody for all the spy stuff."

"Funny, Skip. Funny."

"You know, James, this spy thing is costing us a lot of time and money."

"Amigo, we're going to strike it rich. This is a great business we're in, and you've got to give it some time. We're not going to give up here, pally."

And I remembered that we almost weren't in this business. We almost weren't alive. James could pick up and pretend nothing had ever happened. I wasn't made like that.

"The heart dies a slow death, shedding each hope like leaves. Until one day there are none. No hopes. Nothing remains."

"What?" James gave me the strangest look.

"What?" Em was baffled.

"*Memories of a Geisha*, 2007."

"Oh yeah?" James walked to the refrigerator and grabbed another of his beers. "Well take this. 'When you wish upon a star . . .' *Pinocchio*, 1940."

Em picked up the ugly green pillow on our sofa and threw it at him.

CPSIA information can be obtained
at www.ICGtesting.com
Printed in the USA
JSHW021251210622
27225JS00002B/129